THE RIG

Richard Douglas

The Rig

Futura Publications Limited

A Futura Book

First published in Great Britain in 1975
by Futura Publications Limited
Copyright © Futura Publications Limited 1975
The excerpt from 'The Great Gatsby' is
quoted by permission of Bodley Head.

ISBN 0 8600 71898
Printed in Great Britain by
Hazell Watson & Viney Ltd
Aylesbury, Bucks

Futura Publications Limited
49 Poland Street
London W1A 2LG

DAY ONE: MONDAY

'Don't you know there's a war on?'

Phoney War Slogan. Winter 1940.

1

Five hundred metres away, the *Aeroflot* TU 104 from Beirut hit the snowy runway with its usual ugly thump. The screech of protesting rubber and straining metal could even be heard inside the Frankfurt tower.

'*Scheisspopov!*' the burly blond ATC standing up at the tower window cursed aloud. 'Fly their shitty planes like cowboys, they do.'

His colleagues in the humming, overheated tower, paid no attention to him or to the Russian jet. The February snow was hitting the windows like streams of white flak, and they had their hands full with their own flights. Shrugging grumpily, the blond Air Traffic Controller focused his binoculars on the sleek Soviet jet with the great red star on its tail, as it rolled closer to the hardstand and the little cluster of waiting yellow tenders.

The Popov pilot wasn't helping much either. He was throttling back with much more power than was necessary, throwing up a blinding cloud of snow so that it was damnably difficult to follow the plane's progress. The German ATC adjusted his glasses angrily, cursing under his breath as he did so. He didn't like the Ivans. In 1943, the year of his birth. they had killed his old man with the First SS *Leibstandarte Adolf Hitler* at Kursk. He had never even seen his father. Besides his head hurt like hell after the night's Carnival celebration and his mouth felt like the third class waiting room at Frankfurt's Main Station, despite the two *Unterbergs* he had downed just before he had come on shift half an hour before.

Suddenly he caught his breath sharply. A dark object cut into the bright circle of glass. An olive-drab saloon! He couldn't make out the type. But it was now roaring across the snow-bound field towards the TU 104 from the direction of the nearby American Air Force field.

'Shit in the wind,' he yelled in alarm, 'what's that?'

'What's what, Manfred?' Wehner, the shift chief, called out.

'Over there – *ein Scheissauto!*'

Wehner swung up his glasses just as a sudden vicious gust of wind howled in from the east. The snow flurried against the tower's window in a solid white wall. Helplessly Wehner fiddled with his binoculars and tried in vain to penetrate the howling white gloom. To no avail. Then as abruptly as it had come, the wind vanished and Wehner could see out once more. But there was nothing there save the wintery landscape and the *Aeroflot* jetliner drawing up near the waiting tenders, the howl of its engines dying dramatically to a whisper.

Wehner lowered his glasses and turned to the blond ATC, 'I can't see anything, Manfred.'

The younger man stared incredulously out of the window at the plane, already beginning to be shrouded by the falling snow. 'But there *was* a shitty car out there, Herr Wehner,' he said weakly. He touched an aching temple with a hand that trembled slightly. 'I'm sure of it. A big old-fashioned sledge – it could have been an Ami model of about ten or twelve years ago.'

Wehner looked at the ATC in silence. Around them the other shirtsleeved controllers bent over their green-glowing instruments discreetly.

'I'm sure I saw it,' the ATC repeated, but with less conviction. Down below the fur-coated, hawk-faced new masters of the Western World were beginning to descend now, ignoring the stewardesses' farewells.

Wehner gave the ATC a bleak smile. 'Too much Carnival last night, Manfred,' he said. 'That's probably it. By the end of the shift I sometimes see things out there too. Little garden dwarfs with pink heads.' He came closer to the puzzled ATC. 'And lay off the sauce,

10

will you,' he hissed into his ear. 'I can smell the booze on your crappy breath from here!'

'But Herr Wehner—'

The supervisor stopped his protest with an angry wave of his hand. 'Come on, Manfred, let's get on with it, let's get on the stick! The shift's just started and it's going to be a long snowy sow of a day, I can feel it in my crappy old bones.'

Manfred stared out at the jetliner and the driving snow; then shook his head, as if he had already begun to doubt the evidence of his own eyes.

But Manfred Herz had not been mistaken. Someone else saw the old-fashioned, olive-drab car, as it left the airport and began to edge its way on to the fly-over outside Frankfurt's International Airport, heading for the south-bound *autobahn*.

Most of the weary GIs of the 6th Infantry Regiment in the Frankfurt shuttle bus had closed their eyes and fallen into an exhausted sleep as soon as it had drawn away from the *Hauptbahnhof* on the thirty minute haul to the airport. The training exercise at Grafenwoehr in near Arctic temperatures had been tough. Joe – Washington's side-kick, now muffled in his muddy parka and snoring contentedly at his side – had sighed, slumping into his seat, 'brother, am I bushed!' and dropped off at once.

But Washington, a member of the regiment's Intelligence section, could not sleep. He was thinking lasciviously of Gerda, the blonde short-order cook in the PX snack bar, with whom he would be sleeping in West Berlin that night, and that delightful prospect allowed him no rest. 'Built like a brick shithouse!' his side-kick Joe had commented often enough about her in admiration, and it was true. Even the broads in the *Playboy*'s centre-fold didn't have knockers like Gerda's. Thus it was that while the rest of the company snored all around him in wide-mouthed weariness, including the head shirt

11

Collins who had won four Silver Stars in Nam, the teen-age Intelligence specialist spotted the snow-covered Moskavitch with its Soviet Military Mission tags.

For a moment the tags didn't register, although the day-room walls back in their Berlin barracks were plastered with pictures of them, next to the blue and white posters captioned 'This is my code-of-conduct as an American Soldier!' By the time it did, the big Soviet sedan that looked like a 1960 Buick, had disappeared into the stream of German traffic following the big *autobahn* EINFAHRT sign.

By then Spec Four Benny Washington Lee, hurriedly dismissing Gerda's ample white breasts from his mind, knew he hadn't been mistaken. It was a 'broken arrow' all right!

Hastily he got to his feet and stumbled his way through the line of snoring young infantrymen and the pools of water forming at their feet from the melting snow in the heat of the bus. 'Sarge,' he said urgently, shaking the First Sergeant's big shoulder. 'Wake up, willya?'

Collins, the head shirt, woke up at once like all the guys who had seen combat in Nam did. 'What is it Lee?' he said thickly through scummed lips.

'Broken arrow, Sarge,' the young Spec Four answered eagerly. 'I spotted one of their vehicles – a Moskavitch, I think – heading into the southbound autobahn!'

'You sure, Lee?' Collins asked, his windburnt Irish face suspicious.

'Yeah, Sarge. The tag was just the same as the ones they've got on the walls of the day-room back in the casern.* Couldn't mistake it. It's broken arrow all right. Are you going to report it?'

Master Sergeant Collins was completely awake now. 'No sweat GI. Sure, Lee, we'll goddam report it as soon as this bomb of a bus gets into Main.' He grinned. 'Hot

*GI slang for barracks, borrowed from the German word *Kaserne*.

12

shit, Lee! A broken arrow, eh! They might give you a medal – or something.'

'Broken arrow – you reporting a broken arrow?' the suspicious policeman's voice asked at the other end of the phone in the RTO's office.

'Of course, I am,' Spec Four Lee answered determinedly.

'*Sir*,' the MP lieutenant snapped.

'Sorry – *sir*,' Lee said. 'It was a Moskavitch, heading south-bound on the autobahn to Mannheim. The auto couldn't have been going more than ten miles an hour with the snow and the traffic and everything, so I got a good look at it – *sir*.'

The young soldier could almost hear the MP officer thinking at the other end. Outside the RTO's office, he could see the rest shouldering their duffles and picking up their AWOL bags, ready to board the plane for Tempelhof.

Collins leaning at the RTO counter looked at his watch impatiently and nudged Lee in the ribs. 'What's the poop?' he asked. 'What did he say?'

Before Lee could answer, the policeman asked: 'Listen Lee, can I talk to your head shirt?'

'Yessir. One moment – *sir*.' He handed the phone to Collins.

'Master Sergeant Collins, Second Battalion, Sixth Infantry, sir,' barked the head shirt. 'Can I help you, sir?'

'Lieutenant Carter here. Listen Sergeant, are your Joes sober?'

Master Sergeant Collins contained himself. In Nam, his Irish temper had won him his stars; now the war was over, it could get him a pretty swift BCD.* As his buddies of the Top Four Grades Club in Berlin were wont to observe: 'War is hell, but peacetime can kill yer.'

'Yessir, they're all perfectly sober. We're straight in

*Bad Conduct Discharge.

13

from Grafenwoehr and we haven't tasted as much as a 3.5 beer for a week, not to mention a Kraut flip-cap.'

Lieutenant Carter absorbed the information for a moment. 'Funny, then, Sergeant, because there isn't a Russ mission vehicle within one hundred kicks of here. The Commies at Seventh Army HQ, Heidelberg, are confined to base – heavy snow warning. And the British First Corps at Bielefeld report all Russ mission vehicles accounted for. How do you explain that, eh?' He laughed shortly. 'Do you think some Kraut has stolen one of their autos! Who the hell would want one of those goddam crummy Moskavitchs they drive?'

'I don't know, sir,' Collins said, fighting his rising temper. 'All I know is that Specialist Four Lee reported a broken arrow.'

'Then Specialist Four had better have his eyes tested. There are *no* Russ Military Mission vehicles on the road that we've not accounted for.' The MP lieutenant lowered his voice. *'Benny Washington* Lee,' he emphasized the Spec Four's given names significantly. 'A black?'

'Yessir,' Collins rapped.

At the other end, the MP lieutenant, in charge of the broken arrow reporting centre, laughed triumphantly, as if Collins' answer had explained everything. 'Well, there you are, Sarge,' he said easily, relief in his voice. 'That explains everything, doesn't it? You know what those goddam spades are like, Sarge. They'd do anything to get their names in the *Stripes** or a chance to goof-off for a while. Typical spade trick, if you ask me.'

Master Sergeant Joseph Patrick Collins, whose life had been saved in Nam by the coal-black staff sergeant whose widow he had married one year later in Alabama, fought his Irish temper and lost.

'Listen Lieutenant,' he said thickly, 'you can take your goddam broken arrow and – stuff it right up your big white prejudiced ass!'

'Sergeant,' the MP gasped.

Stars and Stripes, US military newspaper in West Germany.

Collins did not wait for him to go on. He smashed down the phone and grabbed the black Spec Four by the arm. 'Come on Washington,' he said, 'let's get the hell out of here and back to Berlin.'

'But what did he say, Sarge?' the young soldier protested, as Collins hustled him out of the RTO's office into the stream of heavily laden GIs heading towards the Tempelhof plane exit.

Collins struggled to compose himself. After all he had four black bastards to look after himself now and jobs did not grow on trees for thirty-eight-year-old infantry sergeants, even if they did have four Silver Stars and two Purple Hearts.

'He said,' he answered carefully, 'that he would look into the matter – thoroughly. Now for Chrissake, let's get on that plane.' Understandably neither of the two soldiers saw the fat German standing watching the RTO's office, only half attempting to hide his face with yesterday's *Bildzeitung*.

The little Czech was confident that everything had gone off well at the airport. As he steered the Moskavitch through the driving snow, he kept saying in his heavily accented English, 'I am sure they have not seen us. Very sure. The snow, you understand?'

The Palestinian had nodded. But he could not quite conceal his contempt. Husak was badly scared. Ever since Frankfurt he had smoked *Eve* after *Eve*, the German woman's cigarette, grabbing the wheel with both hands anxiously as soon as he had lit them, his eyes wrinkled up with smoke, fighting the driving snow on the autobahn. His sigh of relief was audible when the rendezvous loomed up out of the white fog – the Aral filling station.

The Moskavitch followed the blue and white signs, swinging by the pumps with the freezing attendants in their thin uniforms, complete with black bow-ties, on to the self-service cafeteria beyond. Husak stopped, but he

15

did not turn the engine off. Obviously he was still not taking any chances, despite his confidence in the success of the transfer. Stiffly he looked over his shoulder to check whether there was anyone on his back. There wasn't. The Palestinian followed the direction of his gaze as he checked the steam-filled cafeteria. It was empty save for a truck driver munching greedily on a *Bockwurst*, and a scruffy *Gastarbeiter*, staring confusedly at the coin-changing machine, a five mark piece held in his dirty hand, his lips moving slowly as he tried to read the instructions in German.

'Okay,' he said, 'nobody, eh!' He turned and smiled thinly at the Palestinian.

The Palestinian nodded, but still he did not say anything. For a moment Husak stared at the man from Beirut. After all he was a major in the Czech service and in spite of what their comrades from Moscow thought of Prague, he was a man of importance; he could afford to stare.

What he saw did not displease him. The Palestinian was tall, lean and tough-looking in a quiet contained way. Not a man who would force an issue, he thought, but one who would carry it to the bitter end if he had to. But the Palestinian's eyes bothered him. Since Husak had joined the Czech service after the Frolik defection in '70 when half the operatives had been forced to go, he had become something an expert in eyes: the soft eyes of the weaklings, who broke as soon as they took them down to the cellars of the Third Special Department of the FDIS in the Loretanska Street; the bulging unwinking eyes of the nuts who would kill with the same psychopathic lack of concern with which they would swat an irritating fly; the cold watchful eyes of the professional soldiers, who would break only when their icy military logic told them that there was no other reasonable course open to them.

But the Palestinian's eyes were different from any other he remembered seeing in these last four years.

16

They were frank and dark – after all he was an Arab of sorts – and stared back at him across the front seat in open candour. Yet somehow they remained emotionless and blank, revealing nothing. Husak shivered. Like all products of the system to which he belonged, he did not like the unpredictable. Such things could not be controlled. Such things were dangerous.

He lit yet another *Eve* and said with calculated insult, blowing a thin stream of blue smoke in the Palestinian's face: 'I am sorry – would you like one?'

The other man shook his head and waited. Husak let him wait another couple of draws, then he got down to business.

'Here is the passport,' he said. 'British. Genuine, complete with residence permit till September 1976.'

The Palestinian flicked open page two. 'Doctor J. Rahim, born Rawalpindi, 18 December 1943,' he read aloud in his excellent English. 'Place of residence – Federal Republic of Germany. 'He checked the photograph of himself on the next page. It was an expert job of insertion. Swiftly he leafed through the passport, while Husak watched him silently. Page fifteen was filled with the bold black stamp of the German residence permit *'Aufenthaltserlaubnis fuer die Bundesrepublik Deutschland einschl. des Landes Berlin'*. He checked the signing authority *'Landratsamt Bernkastel-Wittlich, Auslaenderbehoerde'*. It looked okay. He made one final check, turning to the front page. It was decorated with the dull-pink two pound stamp of the British Diplomatic Service and the legend 'British Embassy Consular Section – Luxembourg.'

His handsome face creased in a frown. 'Luxembourg,' he said. 'Small office they've got there. It would be easy to check?'

'Our local resident – *Russian* resident,' Husak emphasised the word carefully and significantly, 'felt a passport issued in Luxembourg would fit better into the picture. You are a naturalised British citizen working and living

17

in the Eifel region of the Federal Republic. It would be quite natural for you to obtain a new passport just across the border in Luxembourg rather than go all the way to Frankfurt or Dusseldorf to get one. Okay?'

The Palestinian nodded but privately he decided the passport would only be of use in Germany; he would get rid of it before he arrived there.

Husak stubbed out the *Eve* only half smoked and pulled out the thick wad of notes from his pocket. Ever since he had penetrated the American Air Base across from Frankfurt International Airport under the cover of the snow storm and with the aid of the fake green American military number plates, he had been worried that the *Verfassungsschutz** might have picked up his trail. The Fritzes from Cologne weren't smart, but they were damnably thick on the ground. He wanted to get rid of the Palestinian and be on his way before they turned up, flashing their 'dog licences' and asking awkward questions. Heydrich's Gestapo had put his father inside Auschwitz in forty-one and he had an almost pathological fear of the German police, although R, the Russian resident in West Germany, always maintained with a chuckle, that 'we've got the Fritzes in our little pocket, Husak'.

'Here's two thousand marks in fifties,' he said hurriedly. 'Eurocheques. You've got five thousand marks in your account in the Deutsche Bank, Wittlich. Remember you can draw a maximum of three hundred marks per cheque.'

The Palestinian grunted. He had been briefed well on such things a long time ago, but Husak did not need to know that.

'Savings book.' He tapped the little red book. 'You're saving two thousand marks a year from your salary. You opened the account as soon as you started working in Germany in seventy-two. And here, a few assorted letters,

*Bundesverfassungsschutz, literally Federal Office for the Protection of the Constitution. West German Counter-Intelligence.

18

including one from your girl friend in Cologne. Very pornographic – with picture.' For the first time since Husak had picked the Palestinian up, the Czech permitted himself a little smile of relief. He was nearly at the end of his part in the mission now. 'Now, this is the plan from here. Across the autobahn there,' he indicated the filling station on the other side of road and thus did not see the quick flick of the Palestinian's hand which sent the packet of Eve to the floor, 'behind the cafeteria in the trucking area, you'll find the Hungarian, that is if he's on time. He's driving a meat truck – German built Fruehauf. White-painted with "Hungaria" in red on the sides.'

'And the approach?'

'You offer him a cigarette. He says – what kind? You say *Eve*. He says – castrated, hell no, give me the real cancer sticks.'

'Good. And how far does he take me?'

'Koblenz. From there you take the train to Trier. Your rendezvous is Trier this night – *evening*, I mean,' he corrected himself quickly. 'Four thirty, Karl Marx House. Any taxi-driver will take you there. Second floor.'

'The contact?'

'Roughly forty. Long hair, horn-rim spectacles, carrying the *Trierer Volksfreund* under his right arm, *rolled*. He speaks English, but you will ask in German. You speak, don't you?'

'Yes.'

'Good, well you ask "*Sind die Dokumente echt?*" The contact will answer "*Nein, die Scheiss-Iwans haben die in '45 geklaut*".* *You understand?*'

The Palestinian repeated the words. 'All right, what about the cigarettes? I've got none. I don't smoke.'

'Of course – the *Eve*,' Husak said hurriedly. 'Where are they?'

The Palestinian indicated the wet rubber mat. 'You must have dropped them – there.'

*Are the documents genuine? . . . No the shit-Iwans pinched them in '45.

19

Husak bent down to pick up the white and green packet. It was the last thing he was ever to do. The Palestinian struck him a back-handed blow across the side of the carotid artery, choking off the sudden scream. Husak caught a last glimpse of the diamond-shaped pattern of the mat. Then the Palestinian grunted and gave him a forehanded chop with the edge of his palm, bringing it down hard on the back of his shaven neck. Husak slumped dead to the wet floor. The Palestinian ripped his nails across the Czech's face. The blood welled up in five thin red lines. He bent down and tore the dead man's flies open. The penis welled out with the rest and the Palestinian noted automatically that Husak was circumsized. He pulled the homosexual photographs out of his pocket and spread them on the back seat. The Beirut resident had given them to him. 'Genuine West German stuff,' he had told the Palestinian, pleased with the expertise of his service. 'We bought them from an ad in the *Nachrichten.** The Fritzes are very corrupt. You'd better watch your arse when you're there.'

The Palestinian gave a last look around the car. It would fool the German police for twenty-four hours at least; that was what the Russians believed anyway. The Chief thought differently. After all he had worked for the *Abwehr*† in the last couple of years of the war and he should know. Everything seemed okay. As an afterthought he opened his case and poured the rest of his Brut after-shave over the dead Czech. The smell of perfume was overpowering. His nose wrinkled up in disgust. Hastily he opened the door and gasped with relief as the cold snowy air poured in. '*Shalom Aleikhem,*'‡ he said contemptuously to the dead Czech and slipped out.

Seconds later he was running swiftly across the snow-bound autobahn.

---

*The reference is probably to the *St Pauli Nachrichten*, a Hamburg semi-pornographic publication.
†Wartime German Secret Service.
‡Peace unto you, Land of Israel.

2

'*Great Crap on the Christmas Tree!*' Voelker Krause yelled and hit the brakes as the thin man suddenly appeared out of the driving snow and pelted across the autobahn towards the filling station. In spite of the snow, the Mercedes coupé answered immediately. For a moment he sensed a slight, but very frightening slithering. Then the tyres bit and he sighed with relief. Behind him an Ami truck with a trailer jack-knifed. In his rearview mirror, he saw a *Kaufhof* van smack into the trailer's side. A second later another truck, desperately trying to brake, careened off the centre rail and crashed head-on into the yellow van, Voelker Krause shook his head and thanked God for spikes. Behind him vehicle after vehicle started to pile up in helpless confusion.

He put his foot down gingerly on the accelerator. The sleek coupé started to pick up speed. He drove off cursing the stupid fool who had run across the lane and caused the pile-up. His hands were shaking now and his heart had begun to beat wildly; his face was suddenly burning hot. But he knew he could not stop. Trees, the pilot, was waiting for him with the Cessna at Frankfurt and he had to get to London before the afternoon board meeting. Both the *Welt* and the *Sueddeutsche* had reported the London situation in alarmist headlines in their morning editions. Even the staid, old-fashioned *Frankfurter Allgemeine* had been unusually outspoken in its headlines: '*Britoil in ernster Geldschwierigkeiten. Was macht "Englands Stolz" nun?*'*

What indeed? Voelker Krause asked himself, fighting his trembling hands as he turned off towards Frankfurt Airfield. After three years of trying, what particular

*Britoil in serious financial troubles. What is 'England's Pride' going to do now?

rabbit would Colonel Hammonds, Britoil's chairman, attempt to pull out of the hat this time? Hadn't he exhausted his supply of white rabbits after three years of failure? Wouldn't Hardman, the American spokesman of the Houston interests, finally elbow him out of the chair? It was an open secret in Frankfurt as well as in the City and Wall Street that Hardman had been gunning for the Colonel ever since *England's Pride* – what an absurd name – had failed to produce last year. What would the Colonel have to offer the board, apart from his usual appeal to the 'Dunkirk spirit' and the 'general good of the old country'? As Krause pulled the gleaming white coupé off the approach road and headed for the waiting company Cessna, its engine already roaring, he smiled to himself. The British Colonel, who headed Britoil, was really something of a fool – a nice one though. Perhaps as his wife Clarissa always maintained he should have died in that old war which seemed to dominate his thinking so completely.

'There she is, sir,' Trees bellowed over the noise of the motor. 'Portside – *England's Pride*!'

The snow have given way to a thin bitter rain over the North Sea and Krause spotted the rig without too much difficulty. He sniffed and flashed a look at the crew-cut pilot who was grinning as he always did when he mentioned the Britoil rig's name.

'Dammit Trees,' he exclaimed angrily, 'why do you always have to look like that when you say it?'

Trees's grin vanished. Krause took offence easily and this private pilot thing was a cushy number after flying the shitty Starfighter for the *Bundeswehr*; most of the jocks who had trained with him in Texas ten years before were dead or disabled by now. 'It's just the name, sir,' he said hastily. 'Translate it into German, sir, and you must admit that it sounds a bit off. *England's Pride* – not much of that left these days, you must admit.'

But Voelker Krause was admitting nothing. He

didn't have to. Instead he said coldly: 'Send today's signal before some nut down there starts shooting at us. 'You know what they're like?' He thrust Britoil's list of code-words for the current week under Trees's nose. The pilot nodded his understanding and picked up the signal lamp while Krause focused his binoculars on the rig.

20,000 tons of steel rose four hundred feet above the swaying green sea. Red warning lights flickered across its top deck stacked with the steel drilling pipe – 40,000 feet of it, laid out in thirty foot lengths. Below the derrick floor, the rig's centre of activity sparkled with high-power arc-lights, illuminating the rotary table which turned the string of the drill-pipe with the bit at the bottom that at this moment was drilling deep into the seabed, 600 feet below, and on another 9,000 feet.

As the Cessna banked and came in closer, Krause could see the men working on the scaffolding below the derrick. He guessed they were fitting the fourteen-foot-high casing of the BOP package, a routine task they did every day. But they were moving slowly, almost casually, as if their shift were already over.

'You can see that their tour is almost finished,' Trees said using the English word, drawing it out like the roustabouts did so that it sounded like 'tower'. 'They're already thinking about those Hull whores – how many teeth they're going to fill this time.'

'Wish you would stop that damn *Bundeswehr* coarseness, Trees,' Krause snapped irritably. 'You're not a jet-jockey now, you know.'

'Sorry, sir.'

Krause focused his glasses on the tiny figures below. The men in their white hard hats and black donkey jackets were moving like old age pensioners. He lowered the binoculars and flashed a glance at the date on his expensive gold watch. The sixth. Today the men below would end their tour and the forty odd roustabouts, floormen, derrickmen and the rest, who would change over, returning to Bridlington to be relieved by a new tour.

'Who's in charge of the new tour, Trees?' he asked as the ex-Bundeswehr pilot finished his wide circle of the gigantic Britoil rig.

Trees consulted the clipboard in front of him. He chuckled. 'The big Ami bastard— Big Tex, sir,' he said. 'You know him?'

For once Voelker Krause was not offended by Trees's crudeness. 'Yes, I know him.' Big Tex was one of the most experienced 'pushers'* in the business. If anyone could finally get the rig to produce anything but a disappointing series of dry holes, it would be the big leathery-faced American, who was in fact from Oklahoma, and was as coarse and as rough as the crude oil for which his home state was famous.

Voelker Krause settled back more comfortably in his seat for the rest of the flight to London. Behind him the great rig slipped away into the gloom: a symbol of the feebleness of man, dwarfed by the enormous cruel green expanse of the sea; yet at the same time a symbol of the strength of human will and determination.

Big Tex picked up the phone as soon as it rang. 'Watson,' he growled.

'One moment, sir,' the girl at the London HQ of Britoil said in a carefully cultured voice. 'I'll put you through to the Colonel immediately sir.'

'Thank you,' he said moodily and stared at the flat expanse of the North Sea. There was nothing to be seen except a couple of local fishing boats filled with mugs from inland who fondly believed they could catch anything but a cold off the Head. Outside in the corridor of the hotel the elderly cleaner, whose grey dirty hair seemed to be permanently encased in ancient metal

*Roughly – foreman.

curlers, was running her vacuum up and down the carpet as if she were trying to wear a hole in it.

'Tex – is that you Tex?' It was the Colonel's clipped military voice.

Hurriedly the big American shook himself out of his reverie. 'Yes sir, it is me.'

'Morning, I trust you are well?'

'You trust wrong, Colonel. I'm about ready to turn up my toes and give up. We're in trouble once-a-goddam-again.'

'What's it this time?'

'I'm ten men short of the new tour – or at least I was thirty minutes ago. I've got one of my guys looking for fresh bodies downtown. Once they get their dirty paws on their dough, they're off like a shot to hit the high spots – or what you English call the high spots. Then when you come to look for the bastards again at the end of the downtime, you find they've gone, vanished, got the pox, got married, signed on with somebody else.' He let the sentence trail away. The Colonel had problems enough; he did not want to overdo it.

'So it's more money, is it?' the Englishman at the other end of the line sighed wearily. 'We could up the roughnecks' pay by another tenner and the roustabouts – er – let's say another fifteen quid. But that's about it. Tex, I don't have to tell you the fix we're in, do I?'

'You don't, Colonel. I know. But it ain't just that – not the dough. 'The American rubbed his big calloused fist across his face, as if he were finding it difficult to express his next thought. 'It's not just this tour – it's everything these last few months. I've had three different nipple-chasers* working for me here in Brid since Christmas – and still I've not been getting my gear on time. On my last tour it was the rod-packing for the circulating pumps. The time before that it was

---

*Men who are responsible for delivering supplies to the rigs.

the pump liners. Every time they send the boat out something seems to be missing. Then there's something wrong with the men. A year ago these dumb bunnies of Yorkshire fishermen were standing three abreast in line to get a job on *England's Pride*. Now they walk around the rig, as if they're gonna goddam rupture themselves when you ask them to pick up a wrench. Now this morning, I'm missing ten of the crummy bastards.' He hesitated, then added 'You know what, Colonel, I think we've got a lemon on board.'

'A lemon?' the Colonel asked.

Through the big picture window of his seafront hotel, the American oilman could see the white-painted company Cessna, based at Frankfurt Field, turning south on the last leg of its journey to London for the afternoon board meeting. He let the plane's noise die away before he explained what he meant. 'Yessir, Colonel, somebody on board the Pride is trying to give us the purple shaft, and has been trying to slip us it for the last couple of goddam months. It's my guess, sir, that we've got an ape-shit of a union man on board.'

'Oh Christ,' the Englishman groaned at last. 'That too!' For the first time since he had known the Colonel, Big Tex detected a note of despair in his voice. After three long years of disappointment after disappointment, Colonel Harry Hammonds, DSO, MC (and bar) was just about at the end of his tether.

3

For the Colonel the whole business had started on the morning of June 22nd 1971. He had entered the palatial offices of the US oil giant for which he had worked for the last previous ten years after a sleepless night with his mind still not made up. For an hour he had toyed with his mail. Then he had dismissed his secretary and gone through the whole bloody business one more time.

He knew from the magnetic survey of the early sixties, sparked off by the Groningen discoveries of vast pockets of natural gas on the Dutch side of the North Sea, that there was a thick layer of oil-bearing sedimentary rock on the British side. But the magnetic survey measurements were not accurate enough and detailed to such a degree that they could pinpoint the underground humps in the rock which would be any driller's target. If he went ahead with his plan then, he would risk his job, his savings, perhaps his young wife Clarissa. He had no illusions about his second wife's ability to live without the luxuries that his position as senior executive bought her. At midday, he had placed his bowler firmly on his neatly trimmed greying hair, slung his umbrella over his arm, despite the bright sunshine outside, tugged at his East Yorks tie – the only sign of his nervousness – and had said to his secretary: 'Going out for a bit. Hold all calls till two thirty, will you?'

For over an hour and a half he had walked the streets of the city aimlessly, still fighting the problem until finally he had made up his mind. At five minutes to two he had bought some cheap notepaper and a packet of envelopes at a street corner shop and scribbled his bid on a piece of the paper, enclosing it in one of the envelopes, which was a devil to stick. Five minutes later at two o'clock precisely he had walked out of the sun and deposited his bid at number 1247 Thames House South, Millbank. Thirty minutes later he had been back at his desk at the company skyscraper, as if nothing had happened.

A month passed. July had given way to a burning August. Then things had started to happen. Oilmen from the Gulf, Houston, Venezuela, North Africa – men the Colonel had worked with fifteen or more years before at fields stretching from Java to Mexico – began to arrive in London; the hotels and company offices were full of their bronzed faces and now heavier figures disguised in expensive Brooks Brothers' suits. On the 19th, the President, Dave Ehrlichmann, arrived and the Colonel knew that it was going big. It was, much more than he had ever anticipated. For as he trooped into the dingy little cinema in the basement of the Thames side offices of the Department of Trade and Industry on that wet afternoon of the 21st August, where the auction of the blocks was to be held, he spotted the wrinkled ancient face of the richest man in the world, already seated in the centre row. If Paul Getty was present, there was going to be big money involved.

A few minutes after two, Angus Beckett, the Under Secretary, entered from the rear of the cinema, exchanged a few words with his officials and then took up his position at the microphone on the table in front. He cleared his throat and opened the proceedings by apologising for holding the auction at such an 'unearthly hour'. There was a slight murmur from his audience. The Colonel, for his part, wondered why the early afternoon should be regarded as an 'unearthly hour'. But already Beckett was explaining how the auction was going to be run. The bids would be flashed on the two screens flanking him while he opened the tender envelopes, 'one by one maintaining tension to the end'. Cheerfully he added, 'It is not our intention to present losers' cheques for payment. Winners will be given two days' notice before their cheques are cashed.'

At ten minutes past two, Beckett opened the first envelope. Europe's first cash sale of oil concessions had begun, or as the cheap dailies were to express it the next morning: 'THE GREAT NORTH SEA OIL RUSH IS ON!'

At first, the auction moved along quietly. An American consortium from Houston offered half a million for a block. Several others of a similar kind followed. Then in a matter-of-fact voice Beckett read out an Esso-Shell bid. £21,050,001 for a single 100 square mile block located seventy miles off the Shetlands. For a moment there was a stunned silence among the oilmen as they grasped the full implication of the bid. 'Twenty-one million, fifty thousand.' Beckett repeated the offer unemotionally, and suddenly the Colonel felt again the feeling he had experienced on the morning of June 6th 1944 as he had led his company of Yorkshiremen down the ramp of the landing craft into the Boche fire. A new, exhilarating but also frightening phase of his life had begun.

Sixty minutes later the auction was over and he found himself in possession of one hundred square miles of the North Sea, sixty miles east of the Yorkshire coast at a cost of three thousand pounds. Next morning, precisely at nine o'clock, Dave Ehrlichmann fired him: the same Dave who had given him his first job in the autumn of 1945 when he had wandered into Esso's head office, dressed in his new demob suit looking for 'something in oil'; the same Dave who had given him the name by which he was known throughout the industry when he had discovered that the cleancut twenty-six-year-old in his ill-fitting blue pin-stripe was an ex-infantry half colonel with three medals for bravery, who had commanded a battalion from the Rhine to the Baltic.

'Christ on a crutch, Colonel,' he had exploded, half in rage, half in wonder, 'what the hell has gotten into you. This isn't your league. This game of craps is being played with multi-million dollar dice!'

But all the Colonel would say was: 'Dave, that oil out there belongs to the people of this country – I'm going to see they are going to get it.'

Dave Ehrlichmann had looked at him as if he had suddenly gone crazy and he had still looked like that as the Colonel, slim, trim and erect despite his age, had left his office for the last time.

Ehrlichmann had not been alone in feeling that the Colonel had gone crazy, but the trade's opinion changed when he floated his first company Britoil, with the slogan to be seen everywhere in the winter of 1971 – 'Put a penny in Britain's future! Get your share of Britain's oil!'

The 'Britpennies', as the *Daily Express* called them after the Beaverbrook press – predictably enough – took up the idea, came pouring in in their millions to buy a share in the 'all-British' oil exploration company. Even Clarissa was convinced finally that he had not gone mad – at least not completely. She was even flattered when he asked her to name the company's first – and, as it turned out, only – rig, though she did feel the name was 'completely square and out of tune with the times!' But she read the speech he had written personally (heavy with stodgy phrases such as 'this symbol of our crusade to gain the North Sea oil for Britain' and 'a kind of new dawn for a new, powerful Britain') well enough, despite the Force Eight gale blowing off Middlesborough.

Two months later *England's Pride* had spudded in during the long awaited 'weather window'. It's ten giant self-elevating legs had been lowered to the sea-bed nearly one hundred feet below and then, at the command of the tug's computers, the rig had literally hoisted itself to its feet and out of the water. For one nerve-pounding moment it had loomed out of the water

30

at a 45° angle and the Colonel found himself holding his breath the same way he had on the Rhine when the assault Buffaloes had been halfway across and the first tremendous crack of an 88mm indicated the Germans were beginning their ranging-in. Then he had breathed a fervent prayer that the first wave would get across before the enemy had completed the process. They had. Now with one last great heave, the gigantic rig freed itself of the sea's green embrace and stood upright at last.

A day later drilling started and had continued day after day, week after week, month after month, year after year as the diamond studded drill bit deeper and deeper into the sedimentary rock on the sea-bed. One thousand feet – two thousand – three thousand feet. By the winter of 1973 they had been drilling at eight thousand after six 'dry holes', making only two feet an hour through the tremendously hard rock instead of one hundred feet an hour as they had the earlier days. Every two hours the bit had to be changed and that meant that the whole eight thousand feet of pipe had to be brought up and unscrewed until the bit could be changed and then the whole length re-assembled again – a ten-hour, back-breaking job in the freezing misery of a winter North Sea, with waves roaring in at heights of seventy feet.

But by now 'Tex' ('Big Tex' to distinguish him from the other American tour chief, bow-legged, tobacco-chewing 'Little Tex') was sending regular coded 'Eureka' signals to indicate that they had hit a 'yellow zone' – mud which turned yellow under a fluorescent light. And that meant only one thing – *Oil!*'

The reports came at a very convenient moment. By the spring of 1973 Britoil was nearly bust. With operating costs running as much as £10,000 a day, the Colonel knew that the kitty was drying up. In May of that year he had made two quick flights to Houston. As a result Hardman, representing the Oil Banks, bought into Britoil to the tune of twenty per cent. A visit on spec to Hamburg followed, terminating in discussions with Voelker Krause, the West German petro-chemical industry's boy genius, at Ludwingshafen. The result had been an injection of ten per cent of German capital. Britoil had been saved for another twelve months!

But as 1973 had given way to 1974, the oil stubbornly refused to surface. That winter the sides of the hole had caved in twice and gripped the drill strings causing 'fishes': a wearisome business of stopping the whole operation and clearing up the mess. They had 'a twist-off' – a major drilling mishap – with the drill-string broken far below the surface of the hole, which resulted in an even more difficult fish: the maddening, nerve-wracking job of fishing for the part broken off within the hole. To Colonel Hammond, confined helplessly to his 15th floor office of the Britoil Building, it seemed as if nature itself were actively fighting the operation; as if the very North Sea was challenging *England's Pride* for the control of the riches below its surface. And now for the last two months, with the German-American money draining away rapidly with not a single drop of oil to show for it, the rig had been plagued by accidents, go-slows, and non-delivery of vital equipment.

As Big Tex had rightly pointed out in his call, it looked as some damned union organiser were behind it all; and if that was the case, he was sunk. Hardman would hit the ceiling – the very mention of the word 'union' had him reaching for his little pink pills – and Krause, used to the sophisticated tactics of the German *DGB*,* would not be too happy either. While the thin bitter rain slashed the windows of his office savagely, the Colonel's worried eyes kept flashing back to the wall clock time and time again, as the hour of the crucial board meeting with Hardman and Krause and the rest came closer and closer. 'What the hell was he going to tell them? How was he going to get more money out of them to keep *England's Pride* going . . .?'

Deutsche Gewerksschaftbund – West German TUC.

4

Krause looked down out of Clarissa's window. A couple of dozen drenched men and women hurried down Park Lane, escorted by a bored policeman in a dripping cape. He turned his head to one side to read the words on their blood-red banner. 'International Marxists demand freedom for Ulster's workers!' Krause shrugged and turned away. It didn't mean anything to him. He glanced at his elegant wrist watch and wished Clarissa would hurry up. It was nearly eleven. At twelve he would have to have lunch with Hardman and he guessed that the American businessman was not going to make it a pleasant one for him. He sat down again and leafed through the trashy society magazines, their glossy pages covered with photographs of bowler-hatted women who looked like the horses they were usually holding. 'What a boring existence she must lead;' he muttered to himself in English. Yet he also knew that Clarissa Hammonds excited him, not only physically, but also because of her social background. She was from the top drawer. Her father had been a Lord; his had been a Saxon market-gardener, who had worked himself to death in the Hamburg municipal park of *Planten un Bloomen'* after the family had fled west in 1953, in order to send Voelker to the *Gymnasium* and, thereafter to the University of Goettingham.

She always seemed to be utterly careless – careless of her money, her looks (she drank far too much), her body (if the rumours related behind the unsuspecting Colonel's back were true). He, for his part, was a typical Saxon, careful, thorough, always planning for the morrow. His wife Renate had even accused him of being 'wooden', living 'only for his job and career', though as he had told her often enough at such moments of

33

accusation, which usually occurred when she had her periods, 'But my little cheetah, I'm only doing it for you – and the company.'

Suddenly the door to the bedroom opened and he dismissed the thought of Renate. Clarissa Hammonds was standing there, her pale face framed by her dark brown hair cut round to form a point level with her chin, her superb breasts emphasised to perfection by the tight sweater.

'Hello Voelker,' she said in her upper class voice.

He hurried forward and bent to kiss her outstretched hand. Clarissa looked down at the back of his cleanly shaven neck. What a predictable bore he really is, she thought. The calm voice, the correct opinion, the objective approach, with probably – for all she knew – sex twice a week on Wednesdays and Saturdays because one could sleep in on Sunday. He raised his head again and she smiled at him: a smile which he knew was insincere.

'Would you like a drink, Voelker?' she asked.

'A drink?' It's only eleven, you know, Clarissa.'

'Eleven *already*?' she mocked him. 'I've usually had my first gin and tonic by now.' She indicated the drinks table. 'Do be a darling and fix me one, if you don't want anything. There's ice in the thing there.'

Voelker, who had accepted his father's dogged Saxon conviction that a wife was there to serve her husband and never lifted a finger to help his Renate back at their Ludwigshafen company villa, went tamely over to the drinks table while Clarissa lit another of the forty-odd cigarettes she smoked in a day.

'You here for the board meeting?' she asked carelessly and coughed as she inhaled the smoke.

'Yes. I came over specially as soon as I received Hardman's telex. Besides, the German papers were full of it this morning.'

'Were they now!' she said with just a trace of cynicism

34

in her voice. 'The German papers — how madly exciting!'

Krause did not notice the cynicism. He handed her the drink with heavy gallantry and said: 'You're looking very good this morning, Clarissa.'

She took a deep drink. 'I suppose I'm bearing up fairly well seeing that I must have drunk enough Scotch to kill ten assorted highlanders at that boring dinner Harry took me to last night.'

'One shouldn't drink so much,' he said.

'One shouldn't live, but one does, Voelker.' She took another drink.

'Ah, but you are a woman — a very beautiful one admittedly — but still a woman, who does not understand the business world.'

'The business world, Voelker, is a drag — an utter drag.' Clarissa pouted. 'All this stuff about the North Sea and oil and everything. God knows how you can take it all so damned seriously! It bores the pants off me.'

'It keeps you in this,' he hinted gently, waving his hand around the luxuriously appointed room, 'your place in France and the boat and the rest.'

'It's the least one can do in a difficult world, scraping by on the basic minimum,' she said with a grin and finished the rest of her drink. She thrust the empty glass at him. 'If you would, Voelker dear.' She poked the end of her tongue through her teeth provocatively, well aware of the effect she was producing on him. He reached out a hand for her waist. But she dodged it gently. 'The *drink*, darling.'

Obediently he went over to the little glass and chrome table and began to make another gin and tonic. 'What would you do, Clarissa?' he asked carefully, not trusting himself to look at her, knowing that he was about to say something rather dangerous, but unable to stop himself, 'if all this had to stop — *suddenly*?'

'What do you mean?'

'What I have just said – if all this stopped. If there were no more money for the life you lead here?'

'For God's sake, don't be so pompous, Voelker! What exactly do you mean?'

'Well, my dear Clarissa,' he straightened up, the drink finished, 'this afternoon's board meeting could well decide the fate of Britoil and your husband's future too.'

Clarissa shrugged her beautiful shoulders and her breasts shivered delightfully under her tight white sweater. 'So.' She reached her manicured hand out for the drink. But he did not give it to her. Instead, he continued in the same subdued toneless manner as before, although his heart was suddenly beating like a trip-hammer.

'Hardman will undoubtedly turn the screws on the Colonel. He has had his day and Hardman knows he's winning now. He'll buy the rest of the board with an offer of fresh capital – and you know what that will mean? The Houston bankers will take over and your husband will have to go.'

He paused. Clarissa was silent. But the scornful smile had left her face, and her dark eyes were fixed on the old, faded photograph of the Colonel as a captain in the East Yorkshire Regiment, taken by some provincial garrison photographer just after he had been given his first company in 1943.

Krause licked his lips. He had not attempted anything like this, since the day he had tried to seduce the elderly, moustached *Frau Professor Heinze,* whose husband was to conduct his economics exam viva for the *Staatsexamen.*

'The Colonel has only one chance of retaining control of Britoil,' he said softly, still not looking at her directly, knowing that if he did, he would never dare to go ahead with his outrageous proposition. 'As you know, he owns twenty per cent of the stock. My group owns another ten. Together we could well swing the

36

rest on to our side and outvote Hardman. That is if—'
he broke off suddenly.

'If what?' she urged.

For the first time he looked at her directly. Still he
could not bring himself to say what he wanted to.

'Well, for God's sake, spit it out! *Pee or get off the
pot, Voelker!*'

The crudity of her expression did it. In a sudden
excited flow of words, he made his monstrous proposition, not pausing for breath, feeling himself beginning
to sweat although the elegant flat was cool by German
heating standards. Then it was out and he was standing
there, the gin and tonic still held in his carefully manicured hand with the ice already starting to melt.

Clarissa looked up at him, her dark eyes full of
amused shock. 'My God, Voelker, do you know what
you're trying to do – *you're bloody well trying to blackmail me into getting between the sheets with you!*'

5

The board room of Britoil was thick with cigar smoke. The elegant round table, which the company's secretaries had laid out so carefully just before lunch, was now a confused mass of papers, the white blotters already a mess of blue doodles and lists of figures, the Vichy water bottles empty, the ashtrays piled high with thick cigar ash and wet stubs. A similar change had taken place among the members of the board, too.

They had arrived in cool expectation, not realising – most of them – what awaited them. Now that cool expectation had changed to uneasy tension, as Hardman, the small, fat banker from Houston, had reeled off unpleasant statistic after statistic, punctuating every set of figures with a stab of his cigar in the direction of the Colonel, as if he really wished to grind its red-glowing end into one of the Britisher's faded blue eyes.

By now they had divided into two groups: the representatives of the people who had originally bought the 'Britpennies', which had set the company up and enabled it to buy the *Pride*; and the representatives of the insurance companies which had bought about twenty per cent of the stock from the original owners of the 'Britpennies'. The former, the Colonel guessed, were still not convinced by Hardman's harsh statistics. If he were lucky, they could still rally to his side. The latter had really bought Hardman's approach hook, line and sinker. No doubt the balance ledgers which they had for brains were already transforming the ugly red figures into black ones with the aid of the money that Hardman promised would come from Houston, if his suggestion were accepted.

As the Colonel saw it, the situation was evenly balanced at the moment. The only imponderable was the Boche Krause who sat at the opposite side of the table from him, his neatly trimmed blond hair as immaculate as ever, no sign of strain on his face. 'Ten per cent of the vote,' he told himself, 'and I haven't a clue what he's going to do.' He recalled the old phrase of the soldiers he had once commanded, who were probably long dead now, 'Ay, sitting there like one of bloody each, waiting for bloody vinegar!'

The board room filled with the animated hum of conversation as the directors talked to their neighbours or to one another across the littered table while Hardman sipped the last of his Vichy and lit another cigar preparatory to his final assault. The Colonel sat upright in his chair, as if he were back in the Mess at Catterick as a young subaltern frightened of doing the wrong thing, knowing at least that the terrible old majors, who were all of twenty-five and twenty-six, wouldn't think him too bad if he sat upright. He stared undisguisedly at Hardman, knowing what was coming. The man from Houston was going to attempt to get rid of him. Colonel Harry Hammonds had had his day. The time had come to send him out to grass.

Hardman rose to his feet awkwardly. 'Gentlemen,' he said importantly and cleared his throat to stop the chatter. 'Gentlemen, I feel that the time has come to make a decision. Britoil has been in business – real business – for two years. During that time it has drilled six holes at a cost of' – he hesitated and looked down at the paper in front of him – 'one million British pounds a hole. Thus we and the people we represent have invested six million British pounds in the floor of the North Sea. To what advantage? To no advantage – save to those types of fish which prefer to copulate in exceedingly deep holes.'

The insurance men laughed dutifully. The Colonel told him that Hardman's accountant's heart must already be beating faster in triumph.

'But those are the costs which every oil exploration company must expect to bear,' said Hardacre, one of the Britpennies' representatives from the north, 'We all know that.'

'Sure,' Hardman turned on him. 'Sure, sure – everybody knows that. No sweat too, if you're Gulf or Exxon. But we're Britoil and the dough is running out for us, Hardacre.'

Hardacre flushed unpleasantly. 'I have gathered that from what you have said – at some length – over the last half hour, *Mister* Hardman. But what can we do about it? The oil's there. We know it – everybody in the trade knows it. It is only a matter of time before it comes through and then our present financial problems will be solved.' He looked to the men on both sides of him and they nodded significantly.

Hardman was unmoved. He took a deep pull of his expensive cigar for effect; then said, 'And time, Hardacre, is exactly what we ain't got. According to my calculations this company will be completely broke by the beginning of next month if we don't make a strike within the next seven days.'

Hardacre looked up at him. 'But what then are you suggesting, Mr. Hardman? Are you suggesting that Britoil is finished? Or something else?'

'Well, not exactly. Our real problem is a twofold one – leadership,' he looked significantly across at the Colonel, 'and the money market's confidence in that leadership.'

It was just then that Krause spoke for the first time since the crucial board meeting had begun. 'I think that before we make any binding decisions, gentlemen,' he said carefully 'we should take a short break.' Before Hardman could protest, he pushed his chair back and rose to his feet. Almost automatically the others followed, even the insurance men. Colonel Harry Hammonds had a few minutes further grace.

Inside the board's dining-room the air crackled with hostility. Even the pretty young secretaries, whose skirts were so short that Big Tex was wont to crack after a visit to the HQ, 'Hell, in that goddam place you've got to be careful yer don't knock the coffee-cups off the table with it!' could not seem to appease the two factions with their sandwiches and drinks.

'Get me a double, Pat, please,' the Colonel said to his own secretary, the divorcee daughter of old Peters, his batman, killed at the beginning of the Reichswald.

'Bad, sir?' she asked, efficiently making the drink at the same time, her pretty face full of concern.

The Colonel knew she was utterly devoted to him. Ever since she had divorced her husband, she had been prepared to go to bed with him – she obviously didn't approve of Clarissa's goings-on and wanted to make it up to him in this manner. But he always remembered old Peters, preparing a cup of compo tea for him that bitter February morning when the Boche moaning minnie had opened up and the mortar bomb had ripped his arm away. He had bled to death in an hour. Somehow he felt that it would be a kind of betrayal of the man to go to bed with his daughter thirty years later.

'Bad,' he replied to her question. 'Bad, isn't the word for it! It's a bloody catastrophe!' He took a deep drink of the scotch. 'If it hadn't been for Herr Krause a few moments ago, my goose would have been cooked properly.' He glanced round the room, past the little circle grouped around Hardman. 'Where is Krause by the way?'

'I think he went to the loo, sir,' the girl replied.

'Oh, I see.' The Colonel finished the drink in one greedy gulp and handed the glass back to the secretary. 'You'd better give me another one, Pat. I'll need it when the chop comes.'

But the secretary was mistaken. Voelker Krause was not in the elaborate marble directors' toilet. He was telephoning Clarissa from the phone in the corridor. Swiftly he filled her in about the events in the board-room; then he hesitated, his courage almost deserting him. 'So you see, Clarissa, it has happened. Now the question is—' he broke off suddenly, leaving the sentence uncompleted.

'Now the question is whether you will go along with that bastard Hardman or whether you will support my husband?'

'Yes, that's it, Clarissa,' he replied unhappily.

'Well then vote for my husband,' she said. He guessed she had been drinking heavily over lunch again.

'And my reward?'

'Oh that,' she laughed carelessly. 'Of course, I'll let you fuck me Voelker – I don't think I've had a German for a while.'

Within five seconds of their reassembling, Hardman knew he had been defeated. The sour and worried looks on the faces of the insurance representatives told him that. The Colonel had told them Krause's surprising decision as they had entered. Now, enlivened by the two whiskies and a fresh burst of confidence in the future, he nodded to Hardman, 'Joe, I think you were going to say something.'

Hardman waved a pudgy hand in his direction. 'What is there to say, Colonel. You've won – *and lost*!'

'What do you mean, Mr. Hardman?' Hardacre asked severely.

Hardman shrugged and took a long draw at his cigar. 'It's pretty goddam obvious, isn't it. Britoil is broke and nobody I know of – at least – is going to advance us any more darn credit under these circumstances. According to my calculations, the Colonel has exactly seven days to find that oil of his before the bailiffs start closing in on us.' He closed his eyes, as if he wanted to blot them and Britoil out of his sight for ever.

Hardacre looked at the Colonel: 'What do you say to that, Colonel?'

The Colonel rose to his feet slowly. Carefully he looked around the room with the same direct stare he had used on his officers at an ops session when he was about to announce a new difficult operation. 'Gentlemen,' he said, 'my old brigade commander once gave me a piece of advice on how to make a speech. It was very simple – 'stand up, speak up, shut up.'

He smiled but nobody laughed. With his pudgy hand shading his eyes, Hardman groaned and muttered something which sounded like, 'Oh, my aching back!'

The Colonel's smile did not waver. He was completely in control of himself and the meeting now – and he knew it. 'Gentlemen, I'll follow that advice. Without being chauvinistic – though I'll admit to being what some people these days thing is a dirty word – a patriot – I formed Britoil so that the oil to be found under the North Sea went to this country. I do not want the company to be dominated by other interests, if I may express it thus without offending our foreign-born members? So I say to you, if we have only seven days to find that oil, we will find it within that period of time.' His voice rose encouragingly. 'We're too deep in now. Too many little people all over this country have invested their savings in us. And I'm not going to let those people down.'

He paused for breath, then delivered his final words, based on the decision he had made the moment that Krause had promised him further support: 'I shall be taking the Tyne-Tees to Yorkshire in exactly forty-five minutes from now. I'm going to take personal control of the shorebased operation.'

There was a murmur of surprise from the board. Even Hardman took his hand from his eyes and looked up, his face shocked. But the Colonel had no further time to waste on dramatic effects. In the next office, Pat was

43

already packing his gear, telephoning the hotel, contacting Clarissa, getting their tickets and the like.

Hastily he concluded: 'Gentlemen, the geologists tell us that the oil is there in our block. That is certain. *Now I'm going to make sure that the Pride strikes it, even if I have to get the drillers to dig it up with their bloody big hands!*'

6

Regierungsrat Herzner stared thoughtfully out of the window. The Rose Monday procession below was finally over. As usual in Catholic Cologne, the wooden floats had made fun of ruling Socialist-Liberal coalition in Bonn. Schmitt the Lip's characteristic forelock, Genscher's beer belly and Friedrichs' long mournful face had been predictably prominent. Wine, in its various forms, had come second to the politicians, despite the fact that Cologne itself drank beer, that awful flat beer to which he simply could not become accustomed. Looking along the street, filled with drunken, singing men in the powdered wigs and uniforms of the eighteenth century and equally drunk women, wearing as few clothes as possible despite the freezing cold, the *Regierungsrat* told himself that in Carnival-crazy Cologne the locals would drink anything at this particular moment in time. Herzner, who was Nollau's second-in-command and came from the protestant north, turned finally and shook his head in mild disbelief. 'I don't know, Mueller, I've been here four years now and I still can't get used to it. Heaven, arse and twine, there are women running around there in the main streets half naked – and it's going to snow again at any moment!'

Outside a drunken brass carnival band from one of the suburbs staggered by, playing '*Am schoenen deutschen Rhein*', followed by raucous cries of '*helau*' from the delighted revellers on the snowy pavements. Herzner sighed, sat down at his big desk and stared at Mueller waiting for the racket to die away. To him Gerd Mueller looked like a caricature of a bad caricature. Cheap working man's cigar clenched between his gold teeth, long ancient leather coat, broad-brimmed felt hat of a forties vintage, which he would have insisted on wearing in the offices if Herzner had allowed it. No wonder the young operatives called him 'Gestapo Mueller'* behind his back. And even if Mueller had heard it, he would have not minded; he was always dropping names such as Heydrich and Schellenberg and what Naujocks had told him about Salon Kitty, as if he had actually been a member of the SD† In fact, Herzner knew from Mueller's records that he had been a humble corporal in the Army's *Geheime Feldpolizei*.‡

But Herzner had come to realize over these last couple of years or so that Mueller's appearance was his strength. He looked so obviously the thick plodding flatfoot of the forties vintage *Krimis* and films that no suspect ever took him seriously. 'You mean it was *that* fat stupid bastard who shopped me!' they would exclaim indignantly when they were finally brought before him. *'But he looked such a joke!'*

But Gerd Mueller was no joke. After thirty-five years in police work, he was the most experienced man in the department – for this kind of job at least; the ex-*Obergefreiter der geheimen Feldpolizei* never gave up.

The blare of the off-key brass died away and Herzner said: 'All right, shall we start while the silence holds?'

'Have I the *Herr Regierungsrat's* permission to smoke?' Mueller asked, using the old indirect formula for addressing a superior.

'Oh, for God's sake, Muller, stop playing a game which died these thirty years ago!'

Herzner waited impatiently until Mueller had lit the cheap cigar stub with a great deal of blowing and coughing. 'Okay, Mueller, what's the story?' Mueller looked down at the notebook balanced on his knee. 'Weekly Aeroflot jet from Beirut landed at Frankfurt-Main this morning. About ten minutes later one of our black allies and defenders from the land of unbounded

*Head of the Gestapo who disappeared in 1945.
†Nazi Secret Service.
‡Equivalent to British Army Field Security.

46

possibilities,' he looked up expectantly and got the look of disapproval he had anticipated, 'reported a broken arrow. You understand the Ami jargon, *Herr Regierungsrat*?'

'I do. Get on with it.'

Mueller wet his yellow-stained thumb and flipped the page. 'I then proceeded to ascertain if there was any corroborative evidence for the aforementioned and discovered that one of the ATCs at Frankfurt tower spotted a similar Popov car at the time the TU 104 landed.'

'So,' Herzner looked down at the 'flash' on the Aral filling station killing and picked his front teeth.

Mueller watched him lazily through half-closed eyes. The pompous little ex-inspector of taxes, or whatever the hell he had once been before the *Sozis** had kicked him upstairs into Counter-Intelligence, knew that there was a connection between the broken arrow sighting and the autobahn murder, but he hadn't the slightest idea of how to start working out the connection. In a minute he would ask, 'well what do you think?' The political appointees who had sat in Herzner's chair for the twenty odd years since the *Bundesverfassungsschutz* always did.

'Well, don't just sit there, Mueller,' Herzner said irritably, 'that's not what you're paid for. What do you think?'

'The homosexual bit at the filling station was a plant. A couple of pictures of warm brothers, the scratches across the face, the scent. The Ivans just want to throw us off the track. You know what the average police officer is like. As soon as he figures a stiff is a warm brother, he steers clear of the case. Either he's not interested – so what's one more dead queer? Or he's scared to be thought interested. Perhaps his colleagues might think he fancies a bit of the other himself. You know, *Herr Regierungsrat*?' He licked the tip of his little finger delicately and drew it across his right eye-

*Socialists.

47

brow in an exaggerated female gesture, pouting his lips in what he presumably thought was a look of passionate enticement. 'So the Ivans think they can cover up by making Husak out to be a warm brother who took the Moskavitch unofficially from the Heidelberg park to cruise around the Frankfurt field to pick up some young kid working the pavement. After all, stations and airports are notorious places of association for that type of person. He succeeded and the kid turned out not to be the kind, or he was after Husak's cabbage. Did the embassy report that Husak's money had gone?'

Herzner picked up the message from the Soviet Embassy in Bonn, which lay next to the flash. 'Yes. He had a sizeable amount of money in his possession – it says here.'

Mueller laughed contemptuously with the cigar stub trembling back and forth on his lower lip. 'I'll go and shit in the wind! What kind of thick-headed dummies do the Ivans think we are? The KGB boys in Bonn must be losing their grip.'

'What do you mean, Mueller?'

'Well, sir, let's have a go at trying to tie this one up. Broken arrow at Frankfurt field and the murdered Czech dumpling-eater on the autobahn. Question one: what was Husak doing on the airfield – he obviously sneaked in from the Ami base on the other side? Answer: He was picking up somebody from the Beirut plane and it wasn't a piece of lily white ass in frilly white knickers. Question two: why had Husak to be murdered on the autobahn? Answer because that someone was important enough for the KGB to sacrifice their little dumpling-eating Czech cousin to cover his illegal entry into the Federal Republic.' He paused. Outside there was a snap and crackle of fireworks as some *Funkengarde** or other marched by, firing their popguns with drunken enthusiasm, in spite of the snow which was beginning to drift

*Carnival association.

48

down again. Mueller waited till the noise had died away. 'Now it begins to get difficult, sir. Question: who was that important passenger – or passengers? Answer.' He tapped his notebook with his heavy hand. 'According to the passenger list, *nobody*! Everybody who got on at Beirut, got off at Frankfurt. The *Grenzschutz* confirmed that.' He beamed at Herzner.

'All right,' the *Regierungsrat* said testily, 'if you're going to make a shitty point, make it!'

'You must allow us policemen to have our little pleasures. Little fishes are sweet as they used to say when I was a boy. The Ivan pilot made an unscheduled stop on his way to Beirut. Engine check – or something like that – was the excuse. Where? Wheelus Field near Tripoli. You remember the Libyans kicked the Amis out of there in the sixties. Wheelus Field, Libya – *Colonel Gaddafi's* Libya,' he broke off suddenly and let the *Regierungsrat* do the rest. He still has three years to go till his pension came up; it wouldn't pay to get on the wrong side of Herzner.

'*Gaddafi!*' Herzner sat up suddenly. 'Oh, you holy shit,' he cursed. 'You mean terrorists? Not another Munich!'

'Yes, our poor dear Jewish friends,' Mueller said, lowering his eyes in mock humility.

'Shut up!' Herzner said savagely. The terrorist attack on Munich station had caused a lot of heads to roll in the *Bundesverfassungsschutz*. For a week or so, it had seemed he might be going back to the Bonn *Finanzamt* himself. He considered for a few moments, his mind racing crazily; then he licked his suddenly dry lips and said: 'If I understand correctly, Mueller – and correct me, if I am wrong – you feel that for reasons known only to themselves, the Popovs have smuggled one or more terrorists, presumably Arab, into the BRD. In addition you feel that this terrorist – or terrorists – is so important that the Russians were prepared to murder one of their own men to cover up the transfer?'

'What do you want me to do – draw you a shitty picture?' Mueller said to himself. But he replied: 'Yes, that's about it, *Herr Regierungsrat*. I think I agree with your analysis of the situation.'

'All right, Mueller, what are we going to do about it?'

'Track back, *Herr Regierungsrat*. The Ivans smuggled him – them – in the crew compartment of that jet, and the crew are still in Frankfurt.' He allowed himself a slight smile. 'Suspected cholera, you understand.'

'Good – very good. They'll give you the information about our man?'

'*Give, Herr Regierungsrat*!' Mueller made the old German gesture of thumb against forefinger, as if he were counting notes. 'Those camel-copulators don't *give*, sir. They *sell*.'

'All right, you can have limited drawing rights on the reptile fund,' Herzner said grudgingly, his ex-tax inspector's soul rebelling aginst spending money. 'But the big question, Mueller, is – what is his – their – target?'

Mueller looked penetratingly at Herzner, the same old naked look in his eyes as that with which he had scared the crappy Frog resisters so long ago. 'Target, *Herr Regierungsrat*? I don't know, but just let's hope it isn't inside the democratic Federal Republic of West Germany.

50

DAY TWO: TUESDAY

'The whole of the warring nations are engaged, not only soldiers, but the entire population, men, women and children. The fronts are everywhere. The trenches are dug in the towns and streets. Every village is fortified. Every road is barred. The front line runs through the factories. The workmen are soldiers with different weapons, but the same courage.

Winston Churchill, Summer 1940

1

'*Rahim!*'

The Palestinian woke at once. Without even a gasp of surprise, his hand flashed under the pillow and whipped out the automatic. Then he lowered it carefully. It was the professor's daughter, dressed in a baby-doll nightdress, the indirect light from the corridor silhouetting the curves of her taut body, which seemed so slight, so innocent in comparison with the lush charms of the Arab woman he was used to.

'What do you want?' he asked in his careful German.

'You,' the girl whispered.

He had hardly slipped the pistol away before she skipped across the room and threw her bare arms around his neck and gave him a long open-mouthed girl's kiss. He responded as best he could, pushing the automatic more securely under the pillow. Then he pushed her away, feigning breathlessly.

'Please Fraulin Heidi,' he protested, 'you're choking me!'

She plumped down on the bed carelessly, legs spread to reveal the black V, breasts thrust out provocatively beneath the thin perlon of the baby-doll. She grinned lasciviously. 'I'd love to! You know you are so beautiful – like a thin, shaven Che'. She indicated the poster of the South American revolutionary which decorated the wall of her room – the *Herr Professor der angewandten Linguistik* at the local university, her father, who had been his contact the previous afternoon at the Karl Marx House had insisted he should take it.

He nodded, sizing her up with his black, blank eyes. Then he flashed a glance at his watch. It was after midnight and he was tired; it had been a long day. Yet, the professor's daughter could be useful. If you fucked them well – and she had wanted to be fucked all the long boring evening with her father, *der Herr Professor*, he had realised that – they usually were. Women, it had been his experience, especially European women, kept their brains between their legs.

'Come on,' he said.

She needed no urging, as he threw back the *Federdecke* to reveal his long naked body, heavy with muscle around the shoulders, matted with thick glistening hair at the chest and loins. 'Woo!' she whimpered and pressed her body, soft and yielding, against the hardness of his. He responded, as he had been trained to do at the school outside Moscow, feeling no pleasure save that which any professional performance gave him. He ran the tips of his fingers down the small of her spine, round her hip and trailed his fingernails along the soft inner flesh of the flat belly. She shivered and closed her eyes. Carefully but firmly he pushed her on her back, squeezing her buttocks, exerting and relaxing the pressure at quick intervals so that she gasped with both pain and pleasure. He bent down and pushed up her nightdress with his free hand. His wet lips carefully nuzzled her nipples. They swelled immediately, thick and dun and surprisingly erect for a girl of her age. He sucked the one and then other, giving them quick darting kisses. Her breath started to come in quick shallow gasps. He looked down. Her eye-lashes were trembling. It was one of the signs. He thrust his tongue in her ear and kneaded her breasts savagely. She grabbed for his organ and groaned with pleasure at what she found there. Now she was writhing from side to side on the narrow bed, as if he were already inside her, her loins frantic with desire. He let her wait a few more moments. The first time had to be tremendous; his instructor at the place outside Moscow had been very definite about that.

'Comrades,' he had announced as he had risen from the whore's exhausted body, his sex still proudly erect, not even breathing hard, 'your objective is not to receive

54

pleasure, but to give it. *Understand?* Make them feel that there has never been another man before this first time and that there can never be another man after you. Let me show you what I mean . . .'

She was making hectic little moaning noises now, the plea *'komm . . . komm . . . schnell . . .'* bubbling from her lips, the sweat standing out on her brow in gleaming pearls. In a minute she would be finished and he could not allow that to happen; it would be an anti-climax. It was time. Swiftly he thrust open her knees. Brutally he rammed home his sex into her body.

He rode her once. And another time, as the sounds of the Moselle city outside died away in the heavy falling snow. Then another time. Still he contained himself, as he had been trained to do. If necessary he could go on all night. Now she was completely crazy about him, ripping at his broad back, biting his shoulder, sucking at his mouth, as if she wished to draw the very life out of him, gasping incoherent phrases.

At about two in the morning, he pushed her away from him, lit a cigarette for himself and another for her. Then he leaned back, hands clasped behind his head, watching the blue smoke curl slowly towards the shadowy ceiling. Down below the wall clock ticked away the minutes of his life with metallic inexorability.

'Listen,' he said after a while, stubbing out his cigarette on the glass top of the beside table, 'do you know how he's going to do it?'

'Do what?' she breathed, still feeling his blazing heat inside her.

'Get me across.'

She shrugged. He could see that her nipples were still erect. 'My father – the great revolutionary – *heil Moskau* – keeps such things to himself. Party discipline, you know,' she added cynically.

'Party discipline,' the Palestinian thought contemptuously, what did these soft-bellied, limp-handed middle-

class European party pinks know of discipline? They were just playing at revolution. 'What do you personally think?' he said aloud.

'Professors of applied linguistics are not given to flights of imagination,' she said with the assurance of the teenager who has long seen through the pretence of her parents' world. 'The border between us and the Benelux is wide open. When father has had other visitors like you – but never so nice,' she pressed her stomach into his side to emphasize the warmth of her feeling for him, 'he usually takes them up to our weekend place near Pruem. Abouty fifty kilometres from here, and half an hour's walk from the Belgian frontier. I should imagine, Rahim, that they cross from there.'

'I see,' he said casually, although the plan she had outlined had left him aghast.

Outside there was no sound save the soft beat of the snowflakes on the window.

What were the Russians up to? he asked himself. It almost seemed as if they wanted him to be caught. First that absurdly transparent business with Husak. Now this turd of a German professor, leaving a trail a mile-wide behind him! It would be easy even for the German *Kripo* to follow what was probably a well-detailed escape route for the amateurish group of addled-brained university revolutionaries who made up the anarchist Baader-Meinhoff, the Second of June complex. The Herr Professor's well-known 'proletarian' deux-chevaux with its Trier number plate, a lonely weekend house to which any visitor would be noted, the proximity to the obvious frontier. It stuck out like a sore thumb.

The girl leaned forward and thrust her tongue wetly into his ear. Taking his organ in one hand, as if it were something very precious. she whispered hoarsely what she would like to do for him. He nodded his head in eager agreement, making his breath come faster, as if he were tremendously excited by the offer. Slowly she slid

56

her face along the length of his hard body, drawing her wet lips and tongue along the skin. He made himself react. Her mane of brown hair shrouded his belly. He gave a couple of fake sighs of passion and let her get on with it. When he thought she had excited herself enough, he thrust her over on her back and flung open her legs. He plunged into her like the trained stallion he was. This time he allowed himself to get finished, filling her writhing sweat-lathered body with his seed, though she had told him she could not take the pill.

Five minutes later she was fast asleep, her arms flung out in extravagant exhaustion. He gave her another five minutes but when she began to snore softly, he knew she was completely away. He disengaged himself carefully. She muttered in her sleep, but didn't awaken. Swiftly he dressed save for his shoes, slipping them in the pockets of his jacket. He almost forgot the automatic, but he remembered it in time. Just before he left, he turned at the door and whispered 'whore'. Then. 'And if it's a boy, call it Rahim.'

At their first meeting in Karl Marx's birthplace, the Palestinian had noted that although the girl's father was a perfect symbol of the middle-class intellectual revolutionary, from the pipe with the fashionably curved bowl to the roller-neck sweater of rough dark wool with holes at the elbows, his black shoes were highly polished. A man who obviously played both ends of the field. A careful man – after all he was a German *Herr Professor*. So whilst his car key would undoubtedly be on the table at the bed, where he slept at the side of his dutifully revolutionary wife – no bra, no wedding-ring, no opinion of her own save the currently fashionable one to which *'mein Mann'* subscribed – he would have a spare somewhere in case he lost the other. But where?

In his stockinged feet, seeing his way by the pale reflection of the snow outside, he searched the living room. It was heavy with the West European intellectual's kitsch of revolution – drawings of the Kent State shootings, posters of heroically posed Russian workers with anatomically impossible muscles, flags from 'international solidarity' and 'the people for peace' meetings all over Eastern Europe. But the typical icons of the parlour pinks hid no key.

He frowned and pushed his way into the kitchen: the truth behind the modish facade. It was militarily neat and *gemütlich* down to the home-made egg warmers, complete with embroidered hearts and flowers – a typical product of bourgeois German feeling for order. Swiftly he searched the kitchen drawers. Each knife, each fork seemed to be in its appointed place. Then he found them – a whole set of spare keys, each labelled in a careful German hand – *'Keller, Boden, Garage – Auto*!' He had it!

Two hours later, after a nightmare drive through the snow-bound mountain roads of the Eifel, he drove the bucking, bouncing 2 CV into a thick pine wood on the heights just above Pruem, where it turned off to the border village of Bleialf, the last one on the German side. He stretched his cramped limbs and stared out at the snow. It was belting down. The car would be covered within the hour. No one would be able to find it unless they were deliberately looking for it and somehow or other he felt the good *Herr Professor* would not be reporting the loss of his 'duck' to the police in any hurry. He grinned at the thought of the look on the German's face when he discovered his guest had gone in the morning.

He spent the next ten minutes burning the various car documents before tackling the passport, which was difficult. But finally, despite the driving snow, the thick sheets started to burn. He waited until they had disappeared into a mass of black hissing ashes; then he crushed them deep into the snow with his heel. Doctor Rahim was dead. He was anonymous and on his own again – they way he liked it. The thought made him feel good. In spite of the icy cold, he began to whistle as he set off towards the border. He should be there and across the couple of metres broad Ihren Bach – the border river – before dawn. No border guard in his right senses would be out looking for suspects on a night like this.

2

Big Tex's tour had its first 'fish' at dawn.

Outside the cold was hardening again. It closed in on the men who had been working all night with steely fingers, groping cruelly for the blood in their veins, while the new wind came howling in direct from the North Pole. As the old shift moved stiffly about their tasks, silhouetted like a collection of ancient ghosts against the grey mass of sky and heaving green water, they told themselves there'd be another of the North Sea's terrible storms before this day was out. But the 'fish' beat the impending storm to it. Just after seven as the cooks were serving the first steaks and chips of the day and which they would continue to serve at hourly intervals for the rest of that day, the rotary started to spin faster and faster. The green luminous hands on the torque recorder, the weight indicator and the various mud pressure dials began to slacken off alarmingly. The driller reacted quickly enough. He braked the console and shouted a warning.

This particular crew was just going off duty and they knew that Big Tex would hit the ceiling when he found out. Less than twelve hours of the new tour and their first 'fish' already. After some mumbled discussion among themselves, the bright white lights gleaming on their shiny, oil-dirtied faces, they decided to give it another couple of turns, while the driller checked at the dials at the console. But it was no use. It was a fish all right.

'Jesus H Christ,' groaned the driller. 'Big Tex'll have the goddam nuts off'n us for this!'

But surprisingly enough the leathery-faced 'pusher' contained his temper. He checked the driller's notebook and appeared satisfied with it. Kicking a coke can out of the way – his only sign of irritation – he went over to the rotary and stared at it thoughtfully. Then he went over the drilling records, which gave the details of the bit-size, the drilling speed, mud pressure etc, and finally decided it was not a simple twist-off with the broken section left free in the hole.

He sighed and said to the assembled crew, 'Okay, boys, I guess we've gotten a cave-in. The pipe's stuck in a bad place and we've got a deviated hole. Better get some sack-time. The new shift can take care of this particular baby.'

All that morning Big Tex directed the operation to recover the broken part. He cupped his hands around his mouth, shouting above the ever mounting wind, and had the Bowen overshot lowered in place, while the green sea heaved and swayed below and high, curling foam clutched at the rig with greedy fingers. Big Tex hoped that with the aid of the specialised tool, he would be able to engage the broken pipe and draw it up.

But with the spray running down their wind-reddened faces, their overalls thick with wet mud, the shift was forced to give up. The Bowen was not gripping. With an effort of will Big Tex controlled himself, his voice hoarse with shouting, his hands black with oil and mud. Nearly half the shift was gone and they had not yet drilled an inch of goddam rock.

'All right, guys,' he yelled above the wind, 'let's run down a washpipe and see if we can get the bugger free with that!'

There was a series of groans from the men on the heaving, muddy deck. The wash-pipe, which Tex hoped would wash the broken part with mud so that it would slip out more easily, involved a lot of back-breaking, heavy work, tough even for the former coastal fishermen among them who were used to dragging in nets, laden with fish and weighing tons. Reluctantly, their cracked hands frozen and unfeeling, they started to break out the new gear, hating what was to come.

The afternoon passed in a leaden, dogged, brutal slog.

61

The elements did not help either. Time and time again the wind whipped bitter flurries of icy spray across the deck, lashing their frozen faces, turning their hands into numb lumps of flesh, scarcely able to hold the icy tools.

Tempers began to fray. A roustabout dropped a wrench on his foot and cursed his mate fluently and at length, although roustabouts dropped wrenches on their feet all the time. The cooks served coffee for the Americans and tea for the Yorkshire East Coast men. Both Americans and British complained the drink was 'like goddam washing up water and as cold as a well-digger's ass!' They threatened to do something anatomically impossible to the frightened cook with his urn. He scuttled back to the safety of the galley, as if he thought they really meant it. An hour later Jacko reported that the daily chopper bringing in the mail and other supplies was delayed because of the bad weather – and was received with an angry barrage of abuse.

Then they lost the overshot and Big Tex, who had been fighting to control his temper the whole long miserable afternoon, blew up. 'Listen, you bunch of incompetent knuckleheads,' he roared angrily above the roar of the wind, 'you lot of short-assed dummies. I'm now gonna go to the head to take a long crap. But by Jesus H Christ, when I come back, I'll expect you to have recovered that goddam overshot.' His face brick-red with rage, the veins standing out at his throat and temple, his huge fist clenched threateningly, he added, 'and if you haven't, I'm gonna feed each and every one of you dumb apes a knuckle sandwich personally – and with pleasure. *Now pop to it!*'

When he returned half an hour later they had retrieved it. But now their mood had changed from open anger to a sullen, glowering resentment. Grimly they indicated to each other what should be done by sharp angry nods of their white helmeted heads. The floormen concentrated on working the break-out and back-out tongs, shouldering aside the dripping 120-foot lengths of pipe hanging from the elevators, with restrained fury, while the roustabouts hosed oil and mud from under-foot, swishing the icy jets of water from side to side as if they wished to wash the whole accursed rig into the sea.

They worked on doggedly without any attempt to break the taut brooding silence among their ranks. Haul over the tongs, kick the hose from the hole, boot the slip into the hole so that they could clamp on pipe, fix it with the tongs, strain and release as the drillers gave a quick pull to break the joint. Over and over again. With back-breaking, sweating, straining, gasping regularity. Thousands of feet of muddy dripping black piping hauled up from the clinging green depth of the sea. Hour by hour.

Big Tex, withdrawn into a stony silence now and chomping stolidly on a wad of black chewing tobacco – a habit he had picked up in the old days when you couldn't smoke on deck – saw that the sullen-faced crew were making progress. Yet at the same time, as the fury of the wind began to rise to an alarming crescendo, he knew that something had to give – and give soon.

Great masses of green water were battering the *Pride* now. The howling wind was blowing a continuous stream of white foam across the swaying pipe-littered deck, so that the toiling, straining men appeared to be working in a snow storm. It was every man for himself, cut off in his own terrible little world of back-breaking labour. Time and time again, Big Tex narrowed his eyes against the bitter, spray-filled wind and glanced hastily at his watch, telling himself they couldn't take much more of this. He'd give them forty minutes more . . . thirty . . . twenty . . . fifteen . . . ten minutes . . . And then it happened. Longbotham was on the elevators, a big beefy, normally good-humoured ex-trawlerman from Hull, who worked all weathers with his sleeves rolled up his brawny, musclar arms, to reveal a line of nubile, blue-tattoed ladies, moving obscenely every time he flexed his powerful muscles. But growing careless, even his enomous strength crumbling under the strain, he let the elevators drop past their usual point. They hit the derrick floor with a frightening crash, only a couple of feet from a startled floorman.

The floorman jumped back in alarm, his face as pale as his white hard hat. 'What the hell are you up to, Longie?' he yelled, more in surprise than anger. 'Yer nearly nobbled me there, mate.'

Big Tex was not so gentle with the ex-trawlerman. He exploded at this fresh evidence of his tour's carelessness.

'Christ on a crutch, Longbotham,' he yelled above the roar of the wind. 'What the hell's wrong with you, you big lug!'

'Maybe the clutch slipped,' Longbotham said sullenly. 'Anything could happen on this sodding rig.'

'And maybe you weren't doing your job properly,' said Big Tex, his eyes narrowing dangerously.

'Are you accusing me of negligence, Tex?' Longbotham asked slowly, as if he wanted the men standing around watching them to hear.

'What do you goddam think – inviting you to tango with me!'

Deliberately Longbotham blocked the brake and stumped across the wet, muddy floor in his flapping gumboots. 'Mr. Watson,' he said with heavy menacing formality, his bare arms crossed across his chest, 'I would like you to take that back. It is a very serious accusation, you know.'

'*Take it back* – in a pig's ass, I'll take it back!' Big Tex roared. He grabbed hold of Longbotham's shirt front and dragged the big man close to him. 'Listen,' he bellowed in the Hull man's face. 'Either piss or get off the pot! Now are you gonna go back to that goddam console or am I gonna suspend you – without pay? And buddy, you'd better believe it – there's nothing I'd like to do better.'

Longbotham broke his hold with an upward motion of his big arms; and Big Tex let him do so.

The side of Longbotham's beetroot face was trembling with rage. 'Listen yersen, yer shitty Yankee bastard. You can't push me around like that! You sodding Yanks think yer own the place with yer big talk and yer fancy ideas. Well, put this into yer pipe and smoke it. The lads is not going to stick it no more. Working all sodding hours. Short-handed, sweating yer guts out for bugger all! The fish is still down there and I don't sodding well care if yer never get it up again—'

It was then that Big Tex hit him. A quick slug in his fat belly, the product of too much Taddy Ale. He gasped and doubled up violently, retching thickly, his National Health teeth bulging out of his gasping mouth. When Longbotham was almost level with his own heaving chest, Big Tex brought up a tremendous uppercut from the waist. Longbotham shot backwards. His gumboots left the deck. The next instant he smashed into the side of one of the elevators. His head lolled to one side. With a low groan, he lost consciousness.

There was an angry murmur from the watching men. Big Tex ignored it. It wasn't the first time he had dealt with such situations in the same short, swift manner. He walked over to one of the deckmen holding a hose, from which the water dribbled on to the slippy deck. Without a word he pulled it from his hand and turned the power full on. A jet of ice-cold sea-water hit the unconscious Longbotham in the face. He spluttered frantically and came to at once, fighting off the jet with his hands.

'All right,' Big Tex barked, 'haul ass, you knuckle-headed bastard! I'm suspending you.'

Without a second glance to check whether his order was being obeyed – he knew it would be – he turned and walked back to his crowded little office. The matter was settled for good, as far as he was concerned.

But for once, Big Tex had miscalculated. Fifteen

minutes later Jackson, the bespectacled little radio operator, burst into his office without knocking, his hand clutched to a badly bleeding nose.

'*Tex*,' he gasped urgently, making the 'x' in the big American's name sound like an 's' because his mouth was full of blood.

'What is it, Jacko?'

'They forced their way into the radio shack and made me call him up on the radio phone. I told them it wasn't allowed by company rules, but—'

'For Chrissake, Jacko,' Big Tex interrupted him with a curse, '*who* did *what* to *who*? And willya wipe that goddam hooter of yours. Ya sound like a goddam Times Square queen with that stupid darn lisp!'

'Well, I'd just checked on the situation with the chopper. The Jolly Green Giant is going to try to bring it out.'

Big Tex nodded his head as he absorbed the information. The Jolly Green Giant, a huge ex-US Army warrant officer who had flown an Air Evac chopper in Vietnam, was one of the most popular fliers in the Company. He had risked his neck a dozen times over the last few years to fly supplies out to the rig through the weather that none of the other pilots would tackle. 'Yeah, get on with it.'

'And then I was about to set up the routine sixteen hundred hours transmission in code for the Britoil House lot when the whole bunch of 'em burst in on me. I couldn't—'

'Who burst in on you?' Big Tex rapped.

The radio operator shrugged helplessly. 'A whole gang of them – drillers, floormen, roustabouts. Everybody, all shouting and pushing and everything. Honest, Tex, I didn't have a chance in hell. Believe me.'

'Okay, Jacko, I believe you – don't wet yer knickers. What happened then – what did they do?'

'They forced me to use the radio-phone to call him. They told him they wanted him to represent them on

66

account of how they were going to take industrial action. What could I do, Tex? They'd already punched me in the nose and they looked as if they were going to stop at nothing. I had to give in—'

'For crying out loud Jacko! *Who? Who did they call*?'

The radio operator gulped, as if he needed plenty of oxygen before he dare even mention the name. 'Harehill – *Joe Harehill*.'

Big Tex had only met the untidy labour leader once, though he had read about him often enough in head office's confidential memos to section heads. According to the security men in the Britoil Building, Harehill could well be a communist, one of the small cell which had infiltrated the TUC structure so efficiently these last few years. Big Tex thought otherwise. To him it seemed that the labour leader with the cunning pale eyes, whose declared aim it was to unionise all the oil rigs working off the North Sea coast, was a guy on the make, trying to get his name in the papers, escape the provincial obscurity of his union's Hull office into the big time of the British capital and all that meant to the average guy in the UK. All his life he had seemed to meet guys like Harehill on both sides of the fence: cynical manipulators of the truth and people, with only one aim in sight – how to get the biggest slice of the cake for Number One.

'And what did he tell them?' Big Tex asked, forcing himself to be calm.

'He told them to down tools straight away, Tex, until *he* saw they got their rights,' Jacko answered fearfully.

'Oh Jesus H Christ, *that bastard*!'

67

3

Mueller plodded heavily up the hill towards the University. He could have taken a taxi from the station. But he had a spare taxi bill for the account when it came to settle up his expenses at the end of the month. This way he would make three marks fifty. Not much, he told himself, but another brick in the house he was buying for his retirement in Spain.

As he ploughed his way through the slush, he considered the situation. It hadn't been too difficult to get a lead on the man. The Frankfurt *Kripo* had hauled the first steward out of the second steward's bed at dawn and accused him of bringing in a consignment of 'hash' on the Beirut flight. That had scared him shitless. Then they had let up a bit – the old Hamburg salad technique, he called it, sour one minute, sweet the next – saying they wouldn't be too hard on him if he were prepared to help them. All flashing teeth and big Arab hooked nose, he had been prepared, but he had clammed up immediately, once they mentioned the illegal passenger. Finally he had been forced to take over himself – though he had wanted to remain in the background; the Arabs had long and bloody memories. The slush money from the reptile fund had done it, and he had his description: a Palestinian, no name, about one meter, eighty-two tall, perhaps thirty years of age. Quiet, softly spoken. No particularly strong characteristics – save one, the man's eyes. The steward had shuddered violently when he had mentioned them, but the only words he had found to describe them were, 'They are frightening, sir, *very frightening.*'

While he had been working on the queer steward, the autobahn police had been checking all the autobahn exits on a stretch from Frankfurt south-west to Cologne and south-east as far as the border. 'After that, those fat Swiss cheese-eaters can have him,' he told his contact with the autobahn police. 'My guess is he's using the Polish goose or the Hungarian salami as his means of transportation.'

His contact had understood at once. The Polish and Hungarian trucks carrying food for the West German market were a law to themselves, only leaving the autobahn when they delivered their goods. Otherwise they could criss-cross the Federal Republic without hindrance. The Russians used them frequently to supply their agents.

Just before midday, the Rhineland-Palatinate autobahn police came through with a report. A Hungarian truck had dropped a hitch-hiker at the Koblenz turn-off. The local Mainz branch of the *BVS* had followed it up and struck lucky. A counter-clerk at the main railway station had remembered the Palestinian. He had bought a first class ticket to the border town of Trier and he had thought it unusual. Foreign guest workers, as he took the Palestinian to be, normally were so tight with their money that they would never waste any on a first class ticket.

Mueller beamed when he heard the news and lit a fresh cigar to celebrate, although he was trying to limit himself to ten daily – if he ever wanted to get that house in Spain, he had to. Things were beginning to shape up. A quick telephone call to Trier and he had the name of his most likely man – Herr *Professor Hermann*, who taught something called 'applied linguistics', which sounded to Mueller like some kind of sexual perversion. Now as he turned into the drive of the new University, he could hear them chanting and speaking. Talk – talk – talk. Big words in high-pitched, important lecturers' voices, which he only half understood. He sniffed at the look on the unwashed, long-haired serious white faces on both sides and said: 'Like a shitty education factory.'

He bumped into an elderly, one-armed man in the uniform of the *Bundespost*, pushing a wicker-work cart. 'Admin, mate?' he was always friendly to veterans, though they would screw you just as much as the new boys would.

The postman jerked a thumb over his blue-clad shoulder. 'Last block – well it was last time I was up here. Yer never know, of course. They –' he clenched his fist in the communist salute momentarily to indicate who 'they' were – 'took over again the week before last.'

'Thanks and Heil Moscow,' Mueller answered.

He plodded on through the slush. 'Professor Hermann?' he asked the wizened porter in his cage, eyeing the blood-red streamers decorating the walls, which proclaimed: *'Red Cell History Demand Freedom for Student Comrades in Chile'* and *'Red Cell Socio-Political Science Demand Release of Greek Students from Colonels' Fascist Dictatorship'*. 'There's a lot of demanding going on here,' he added, in no way worried. He was off to Spain as soon as he retired.

'Lot of warm brothers,' the porter said scornfully. On his lapel he bore the badge of the NPD. 'Should go home and sew themselves frocks. Last door on the right, mate.'

Mueller ignored the usual notices, including the obligatory 'Consultations Mondays and Fridays, mornings only – Doctoral candidates Wednesdays.' He knocked and walked in without being asked.

Professor Hermann looked up from behind his desk. He was dressed in a scruffy pullover, his face unshaven, his thin hair reaching to his shoulders. Behind him his yellow suede jacket, with long fringes running down the sleeves, was draped carelessly in the approved 'proletarian' fashion over the chair. 'Buffalo-shitting-Bill,' Mueller told himself contemptuously.

'Did you knock?' Herman asked.

'Yes I did, *Herr Professor*. But I didn't do so loudly.

I thought I might disturb your academic deliberations.'
Again Mueller's obvious irony was wasted.

'Oh, I see,' Herman answered somewhat mollified.
'Who are you? What do you want?'

Mueller showed him his 'dog licence'. Since the
Baader-Meinhoff affair, the Professor was used to such
visits; Mueller's visit didn't disturb him. 'Ah,' he said,
'the Gestapo has arrived. What can I do for you, *Obersturm*?'

'Very sure of yourself, aren't you, my little schoolmaster,' Mueller told himself. 'But we shall see how sure
you'll be when I've finished with you.'

'*Obersturm* wasn't a Gestapo rank, Herr Professor —
just for your information. It was an SS and SD rank.'
He paused a moment and fumbled with his cigar deliberately. 'Damn thing will never light properly! You
see I was in the SD.'

The Professor threw down his pen in irritation. 'My
good man, your past — unsavoury as it is undoubtedly,
doesn't interest me one little bit. What do you want to
see me about?'

Mueller puffed his cigar again, then he breathed out a
stream of blue smoke in apparent contentment. 'Do
you know what Professor, I was a policeman under
Adolf, and I was a policeman under Konni* and now
I'm a policeman under the *Sozis*. I'm what you might
call a survivor. I suppose when your lot take over, I'll
still be a cop — if I haven't retired by then. After all
your lot especially appreciate a good policeman.'

Hermann waved his hand in a gesture of intellectual
irritation. 'Oh, for God's sake, man, don't beat around
the bush, get to the damn point.'

'Of course. I understand. You are a very busy man.
You have to get on preparing a better world for us all
— whether we like it or not, eh?' He flashed the professor a gold-toothed smile. 'Then I'd better get to the

*Konrad Adenauer, the conservative West German chacellor.

71

damn point, my dear professor, otherwise I'll never pass my examinations and become a solid citizen.' He leaned forward suddenly, his face hard, the cigar clenched between his fat fingers. 'Where's the Palestinian?'

'What Palestinian—' Professor Hermann's indignant reply changed to an anguished yelp as Mueller pressed his glowing cigar end on to his outstretched hand.

Mueller did it again and in the same instant grabbed him by his ragged pullover. 'Listen, schoolmaster, I don't like your sort. You know Goering once said – "when I hear the word intellectual, I reach for my revolver". I feel the same. Now I'm going to ask you a couple of questions and I want a couple of answers – pretty damn quick!'

In the end Mueller had no problems. The Professor told him what he wanted to know: how he had contacted the Palestinian in the *Karl Marx Geburtshaus*; how he had taken him home and had planned to slip him over the border as soon as his lectures were finished today; but how he had disappeared with the 2 CV before dawn.

'Number?' rapped Mueller.

Professor Hermann told him. Mueller noted it and called Bonn Customs HQ immediately. Within ninety seconds the new *Zoll* computer system, installed after the Baader-Meinhoff killings, would have it flashed to every border crossing in West Germany. He lowered the phone. 'And his mission?'

Herr Professor der angewandten Linguistik Dr. Hermann, corresponding member of the *International Review of Applied Linguistics*, sometimes visiting professor at the Universities of Essex and Edinburgh and MIT, spat out his answer venomously. 'I don't damn well know, but all I hope is that it is to blow your whole rotten system here in the west sky-high.'

The Palestinian crossed the Belgian frontier just beyond the snow-bound little village of Schoenberg. Carefully he scrutinized the border village nestled around the onion-towered Baroque church. Nothing moved, save for the lazy blue curl of smoke from the white, heavy, slate roofs. The villagers were hugging their tiled stoves this cold February day. It was safe to go on. Swiftly he doubled across the little, tree-lined Losheim-St Vith highway and disappeared into the firs on the other side which marched up the steep hillside towards his objective, Herresbach. And then the snow too started to fall again, blown into a mad blinding frenzy by the harsh wind which always blew in the Ardennes. Within minutes he was lost in a howling white wilderness, gasping for breath like an asthmatic old man, his eyes narrowed to slits against the driving snow. Desperately he struggled on. The going was terrible. He couldn't see a metre ahead. The snow-bound fir branches tore at his clothes, lashed at his face but he forced himself not to give up. According to his map, the tiny hamlet was not more than a kilometre away on the other side of the hill. Ten minutes' march – even in the terrible snow storm, not more than twenty minutes.

Thirty minutes passed and still he was in the middle of nowhere. An hour: he stopped, sobbing for breath and colder than he had ever been in his whole life. He leaned against a tree weakly, the snow flurrying all around him savagely. For a moment the wind dropped and he could see ahead. What he saw nearly made him break down and cry like a silly schoolgirl. He was back on the St-Vith-Losheim road, back where he had started an hour before. He cursed bitterly in Arabic and felt the strength leave of his legs.

Desperately he fought off the desire to lie down and rest in the snow. With hands that felt tremendously thick and clumsy, he sought the benzedrine his chief, the Doctor, had given him just before he had set off on the mission. How long ago that seemed, in a world, bright with hot sunshine, unlike this damned white wilderness. Fumbling with the tube with violently trembling hands,

73

he finally managed to get the lid off and raise a tablet to his swollen, cracked lips.

It was just then that the man in dark-green cape loomed out of the whirling flakes and said first in French, then in the more familiar German: *'Haende hoch!'*

The Palestinian looked at him in open-mouthed stupidity, then he saw the sleek pistol which the green-caped Belgian border guard held in his gloved hand and did as he was ordered.

Corporal Jean Henkes had just been going off duty when the message had come through to his German neighbour in the wooden shack of a customs post they shared on the hill above Schoenberg. The old days when Brussels deliberately sent Walloons to the frontier who couldn't speak a word of German, save perhaps *'Nazi Schwein'*, were past; now most of the Belgians were from the three German-speaking border cantons of St Vith, Malmedy and Eupen, and Heinz had shown him the exciting message immediately, saying: 'Jean, if we only find this bastard, we'd be out of this damned boring dump – *smartish*. It'd mean promotion.'

Now fifteen minutes later the man for whom the whole border between Trier and Aachen had been alerted was standing facing him, his hands raised in the air, his white-burdened shoulders bent in exhaustion and defeat. Suddenly Corporal Jean Henkes did not know what to do; he had never apprehended anyone like this before.

Then he remembered the American police series he liked to watch on the German Second Channel, which all the border people tuned into instead of Brussels. On the TV the smart young Ami cops 'frisked' their suspects after making them turn round and lean with their hands touching a wall. But there was no wall here. He solved that one by using a tree instead. 'All right,' he snapped, sounding more confident than he was feeling. 'Turn round.'

The weary Palestinian did as he was told, and waited – apparently completely broken now – for further orders.

Henkes felt a growing confidence. The suspect was acting just like the TV actors. 'Now put you hands on that tree. Higher!' He raised his gun threateningly. 'And spread your fingers out – *quick*!'

Slowly but obediently the Palestinian followed the directions. Henkes allowed himself a smile of triumph. Perhaps the German Heinz was right after all; he might get a promotion. Still holding his pistol firmly in his right hand, Henkes reached forward with his left carefully and cautiously tapped the Palestinian's pocket. But Corporal Jean Henkes, father of three boys who loved to join them in the evening as they crouched around the TV, had not watched carefully enough. He allowed the Palestinian to keep his legs together and instead of approaching him from the side, he did so from directly behind. It was a fatal oversight. As the pep pill began to pump new energy into the Palestinian's blood-stream, he sucked in air and judging the Belgian's position exactly, lashed out with his heel.

The vicious blow caught Henkes right between the legs, as the Palestinian had judged it would. He dropped, his mouth open wide in a thin scream of agony, his hands frantically seeking his crushed testicles, the pistol falling to the snow. The Palestinian did not give him a chance. He spun round and brought up his knee. It connected with Henkes's chin. His head clicked back. He was dead even before he hit the snow.

But the Palestinian was not leaving anything to chance. As the snow storm started to peter out, he bent down over the border guard sprawled extravagantly between the trees. He thrust his right hand round Henkes' neck and gripped his own left arm beyond with it. His left hand he placed against the back of the Belgian's carefully-trimmed head. He grunted and gave the head one short vicious twist. Against the howl of the Ardennes wind, the crack of the cervical column snapping was virtually inaudible.

Ten minutes later he was sitting at the bare wooden table in the dark kitchen with the crucifix on the wall above the green-tiled stove. He was eating the fried potatoes and eggs from a great black frying pan, while the one-armed man, who was his second contact, watched him almost affectionately, telling himself that this was how it had been in the great days when those young men, with the gleaming silver runes on their collars who were long dead, had come out of the line and fallen on the food from the kitchen bulls' 'goulash cannons'* like the wolves they were . . .

*Wartime German Army nickname for mobile stoves.

4

Big Tex thrust open the door of the radio shack and said quickly, 'It's only me Jacko, don't cream yer drawers.'

The radio operator was sitting on the shapeless stained mattress which Big Tex had ordered him to take out of the crew dormitory and put in the shack. He took his blood-stained handkerchief from his nose and said thickly, 'It's started bleeding again.'

'Tough tittie, Jacko,' the big American answered unsympathetically, 'complain to the chaplain.' His eyes swept quickly round the cluttered shack. The only way the bastards could get in was through the door and he had ordered Jackson to let anyone who tried to do that have it with the wrench he had given him fifteen minutes before.

Satisfied, he said: 'Okay, Jacko, this is the deal. You don't leave this shack from here on. When you're tired, hit the sack on that,' he indicated the mattress. 'I'll bring you your chow at the usual times. Savvy?'

The radio operator nodded.

'Good. Now nobody – but nobody – is going to send another message off'n *Pride* without yours truly giving his permission.' He jerked a thick thumb at his own massive chest. 'And if that bastard of a union organiser Harehill tries to call on the radio-phone, tell him to shove his union badge up his fat ass, get it?'

'I get it, Tex, but what are you going to do?'

'Do? I'm gonna seal this rig off until those bastards out there are back at work.' He glared at Jackson, as if he were Harehill and his powerful million-strong union. 'And I'll tell you something else, Jacko, this lousy tour is gonna strike oil whether they know or like it or not. I've been in this industry nearly thirty years and I've never been stopped by a machine or man yet. I've never quit yet and I don't aim to, even if I have to bore so many darn holes that the sea runs out.' He paused for breath, his leathery face almost crimson, his chest heaving with rage. 'Okay when I leave here, you lock that door behind me. Then send this message – you don't have to bother to code it. The whole goddam industry can know for all I care.' He passed the crumpled piece of paper to the radio operator.

Jackson read it through quickly. It was a typical sample of Big Tex's plain, matter-of-fact prose. 'Further to tel call. Situation well in hand. Do me a favor, Colonel, and get that guy Harehill off my back. Watson.'

Jackson was a product of *Conway* and the Royal Navy. He looked at the big American with a worried frown on his blood-stained face. You didn't send uncoded messages like that. 'Do you want me to tidy it up a bit, Tex?' he asked anxiously.

'Tidy it up!' he exploded. 'Say, give me that goddam message. 'He grabbed the paper from Jackson's hand and taking out a stub of pencil slashed at it angrily, then added something else. 'Now,' he shoved the paper back at Jackson, 'send it like that – and brother, believe you me. I'll have you by the short and curlies if you don't.'

Aghast the radio operator stared down at the amended message. Where the word 'guy' had been, the big American had substituted 'mother-fucker'. Jackson groaned aloud. It had never been like this in Royal.

Big Tex had been brought up the hard way. He had run away from his parents' poverty-stricken farm at the height of the Depression, riding the rods, fighting off the bindle-stiffs in the tar-paper camps when they were high on 'dago red' and horny, standing for hours for hand-outs in the bread-lines. In '39 he had had enough; he joined the Regular Army – infantry. In '42 when the First Division – the Big Red One – shipped out he was a sergeant. After the big-bug-out at the Kasserine Pass, they gave him a battlefield commission. Thereafter he fought in Sicily, Purple Heart and Silver Star. France, again Purple Heart and Silver Star, plus a mild dose of clap. Belgium. The big Red One had been through it without even knowing it. Aachen, another Purple Heart and the Distinguished Service Cross. But the Huertgen Forest had stopped him. He had woken up briefly at an aid post at a place called Schoenberg, wherever the hell that was. Paris had followed and London. But this time it was over. On the same day that Patton's Third Army linked up with Hodges' First and nipped off the Bulge, he found himself the possessor of a good conduct discharge and an AWOL bag filled with medals, for which he could think of no possible use, staring into the Texan sushine, wondering what he should do next.

Oil! It was the natural thing to do in the Lone Star state. That or steers. After working his way through as many waitresses, women war workers and Army nurses who were impressed either by his war record or discharge pay, he enrolled at the University of Texas on the GI Bill. He failed the course, but he still stuck to his intention to work in oil, if not as an engineer then as an ordinary hand.

The years passed. He worked everywhere. The Gulf, the Canal, the Near East. The heat, the dust, the strain, the hard work and even harder living etched themselves on his face as if they were marks on stone. He was now nearly fifty. A big man, two hundred pounds of hardness and muscle, kept going by work and Old Crow, knowing no home and no family save the rig and the tour, living solely for success.

But in spite of his plain-speaking, Big Tex was no fool. As he walked across the deck with the arc-lights swinging wildly in the wind, feeling the invisible presence of the sea outside in the motion beneath his feet, he knew he couldn't tackle the tour as a group and quell them by brute force. That was out. Dough wouldn't buy them either at the moment. They were too angry, resentful, full of hurt pride and vanity to allow themselves to be bribed. Perhaps tomorrow, when they had cooled off, things would be different. Plenty of 'green' was usually the medicine that cured most illnesses. Except that would be too late. He wanted them working again tonight. He knew that the board was ganging up on the Colonel. If the *Pride* didn't come through with the oil soon, the elegant Britisher, whom he had come to admire and like, would be given the old heave-ho. In the oil industry whenever it came to a showdown between the accountants in the head shed and the guys in production, the accountants with their crummy balance sheets and their rationalization schemes always won. He paused at the starboard mud pump, his face an unnatural green in the flashing light of the arc. What the Sam Hill was he going to do?

And then he had it. *Of course.* He'd frighten the bastards back to work. He walked quickly across the deck to the shed and took the key, which he always kept personally, out of his pocket and opened the steel door. A faint bitter smell of almonds assailed his nostrils. He coughed and swung the door closed behind him. He locked it and turned on the light. A bright red sign sprang into view EXPLOSIVES – DANGER. NO WELDING WITHIN THIRTY FEET. He nodded and walked over to a long metal cylinder perforated lengthwise with eight holes. It reminded him momentarily of the barrel of the crappy Kraut spandau which had stopped him for good in the Huertgen. But this particular cylinder was even more dangerous. It was a gun perforator, which the driller lowered into the rock and fired bullets to accelerate the flow of oil. And in the case stacked behind it there were more of them, plus a couple of back-off shots, a fishing tool which was used together with explosive. For a moment he rubbed his unshaven chin, feeling the stubble crackle against the callouses of his palm. Then he got down to work.

It was Longbotham who spotted him first. He wandered out of the crew's dormitory, a can of *Long Life* in his hand and watched in silence, as Big Tex knelt above the hole. The American knew he was there. For the last five minutes he had been making enough noise to attract the stupid bastards outside. But he didn't let Longbotham know that. Instead he continued working on, packing in the gelatine with the back-off shot, so that even the big knucklehead of an ex-trawlerman could figure out what he was going to do.

Longbotham came back a few moments later with the rest. Silently they crowded around the door to their quarters while Big Tex finished off and wiped his hands on the front of his dungarees. With a grunt he straightened up and faced them. There was no sound, save the creak of the arc lights and the faint high-curling hiss of the foam blown off the waves.

'What yer gonna do?' Longbotham asked.

'Talking to me?' Big Tex asked easily.

Longbotham reached forward and grabbed the unlit cigarette out of the mouth of a little floorman before he could apply a match. 'Have yer gone bloody barmy!' he yelled and threw the cigarette on to the wet deck in rage.

Longbotham licked his lips. His face was ashen and unnatural-looking under the bright white light. 'What yer gonna do with them back-off shots, Tex?'

'What do you think? You guys have withdrawn your labour – isn't that what you union guys call it?' His faded blue eyes swept their pale serious faces. 'So,' he shrugged carelessly, 'what's a guy like me to do? After all I'm a boss's man. They hold me accountable for what goes on during this tour at the head shed.'

'For Chrissake,' Myers, a cock-eyed junior galley man who subscribed to health-and-strength magazines and whose bunk space was covered with multi-coloured beefcake, snapped, *'what the hell are you up to?'*

81

'I'm going to get up the fish myself – with that.' He pointed to the gear he had packed into the hole.

'Are you off your rocker!' Myers shrieked, his voice suddenly high-pitched, and hysterically feminine. 'You bloody well know as well as we sodding do that we've got a soft bottom here!'*

'Sure, Myers,' Big Tex answered. 'But what else can I do? I'm paid to get on with the job – and that crappy fish is in the way.' He shrugged. 'In this business, a guy's gotta take risks.'

'But not risks like this,' Myers said, his eyes full of fear. 'An explosion and the soft bottom could shift away before you could say Jack Robinson. What then? The spuds could go and we'd be up the creek without a sodding paddle.'

'Yeah, what about the *Sea Gem* in sixty-five.'† Longbotham growled. Myers licked his lips and looked at the rest. 'Listen, lads. If the spuds go, the whole sodding rig goes and we've had it . . . We can't let the Yankee bastard get away with it.'

It was a situation which Big Tex liked, and understood well enough how to handle. It had happened to him often enough in the past thirty years. It was the problem of the individual versus the mob. If you allowed them to gang up on you as a mob, you were finished. But if you kept them as individuals, you could win through. Deliberately he brought the big wrench out of his pocket.

He spat drily. 'Who's gonna stop me, gents?' he asked challengingly. 'What about you, Myers?' He didn't even wait for a reply. 'You Longbotham?' The ex-trawlerman lowered his eyes and sucked his swollen lip; he said nothing. He had had enough earlier on.

'Or you North? . . . You Stevens?'

But there were no takers. They all knew and feared his temper.

*At the bottom of the sea.
†Capsized December 27th 1965 off the Humber.

'For Chrissake,' Myers yelled beside himself with rage. 'We can't let him get away with this!'

'Why don't you have a go then, muscleman?' Long-botham asked, not taking his gaze from the muddy, swaying deck. Big Tex knew he had won. But he stuck the wrench back in his pocket and looked at the hole for a long moment, as if he were thinking hard, then said almost casually. 'What do you say, fellers? Shall we hack it again? I guess we've had enough stand-down time for this one day . . .'

But the *Pride's* crew were not fated to work much more that particular day. Just before dark, the long awaited storm descended upon the rig with its full fury. A Force Eight wind came tearing in from the north-east at sixty miles or more an hour. It hit the *Pride* with an exultant scream. Loose equipment slithered crazily across the deck. A derrick brace snapped and slashed through the air a foot above Big Tex's head. He screamed a warning. But the wind snatched the words from his mouth and buried them in its mighty roar.

The men scrambled for cover, working their way up the heaving deck, the wind whipping at their clothes, as if they were climbing a steep mountain slope. The wind snatched viciously at their helmets, and flung them to the deck, where they rolled metallically back and forth, playthings of the storm.

In the end Tex gave in. Fighting his way to the radio shack, he shoved the frightened Jacko out of the way and bracing himself against the heaving deck, bellowed into the public address mike: 'Now hear this . . . hear this! Everyone off the deck! Stand down everybody!' With a grunt of anger he thrust the mike back into the radio operator's hand, mumbling, 'I don't know Jacko, but I think there's a jinx on the goddam *Pride*. Now gimme a slug of that hooch you've got stashed away in your locker, before I go goddam ape!'

The storm was taking over. Sometimes the tearing wind came in with a kind of whinny; sometimes as a red-hot angry sighing. But mostly it struck the rig with a furious scream, throwing up solid green walls of water, as if it wished to thrust it into the depths for good.

In the Mess all conversation had ceased. The men even stopped drinking. Numb and scared they sat there on the swaying benches, beer cans clutched in white-knuckled fists, while mugs, tin plates, empty beer cans clattered back and forth unheeded across the metal floor.

Inside the radio shack, Jacko was crouched over his receiver, the sweat pouring off him with fear as message after message reporting fresh disaster, came crackling in over the air. Behind him, braced against the side of a metal table, Big Tex sipped the radio operator's cheap whisky in gloomy silence, silently cursing the great storm.

One of the cooks flung open the door. Papers flew everywhere as the surging wind followed him in. 'Great balls of fire,' he breathed, 'I thought I'd never make it, Tex. The bitch had me off me sodding feet twice.' He brought a sodden package of sandwiches from beneath his oilskin. 'Corned beef butties,' he said apologetically. 'The stoves is out and we're getting short on tinned meat. When's the supply chopper coming in? We need fresh grub.'

Big Tex bit off the angry retort just in time. After all the hashslinger had risked his neck to bring them some chow, though God knows who would want to eat in the middle of this storm. 'Thanks,' he said, taking the limp sandwiches from the cook. 'Sit down, Tubby, and wrap yourself round this!' Bracing himself against the table, he poured the fat cook a generous slug of Jacko's whisky.

'Thanks, Tex,' the cook breathed gratefully. 'I need

84

it, I can tell you. I thought my number was up a couple o' times out there.' He took a hasty drink of the fiery liquid. 'And the chopper, Tex?'

'No deal. Not even the Jolly Green Giant could get through this. He's stupid enough to try, but – 'He broke off abruptly. At the receiver, Jacko's hunched shoulders had tautened. With sudden energy, he was turning the various dials in front of him furiously. 'What is it, Jacko?'

For a moment Jacko stared at him, as if he did not understand. Then he clicked on the amplifier switch. Above their heads, the loudspeaker crackled crazily. For a moment Big Tex could not understand the wild metallic static. Then suddenly the broad cheerful voice came through loud and clear. 'Hello, you greaseballs down there. What ya doing – having a little tea-party or something? When ya gonna turn on the landing lights so I can make my approach? Or are ya gonna make this one difficult for a poor old clapped-out vet of the great war to save South-West Asia for democracy and ITT?'

'Christ Almighty,' Tex exploded. 'It's the Jolly Green Giant!'

He pushed Jacko from the receiver and grabbed the mike. 'Listen you crazy nut, you can't land here. The rig's going up and down like a goddam yo-yo! *OVER*!'

'Is that you, Tex?' the Jolly Green Giant's voice boomed cheerfully from the loudspeaker over his head. 'What's up with you – losing ya nerve or something? Easy as peeing into a pot. But I need lights. *OVER*!'

'Listen, you goddam crazy bastard,' Tex roared into the mike, 'Get ya goddam ass outa here – quick. *OVER*.'

'But I've got a vital cargo, Tex. Mail, hash so that those hashslingers of yours can make their usual shit on shingle* – and *beer*. And ya know there's nothing too good for the boys in the service. Now are ya gonna put

*Hash on toast.

those goddam lights on, or am I coming in blind? *OVER AND OUT!*'

The amplifier died and Tex stood there white-faced with shock, his mind racing wildly. He knew the Jolly Green Giant, who had gotten his name from the big choppers he had flown in Vietnam, meant every word he said. The chopper pilot, as big and easy-going as he appeared outwardly, had been turned into a fanatical do-gooder by what he had seen in the combat zone. Some said that his first experience of a 'seek-and-destroy' mission which had taken him out of operations into Air Evac and left him with a three-inch square silver plate in his skull had turned him slightly crazy. Tex knew otherwise, the ex-Army chopper pilot was not nuts; he was simply a guy who now felt he owed the world a debt and was prepared to pay it even if it cost him his own life. Food, mail and beer were important for the men of the *Pride* – and the Jolly Green Giant would see they got them.

'All right, Tubby, get back to your quarters! Jacko,' Big Tex turned to the scared radio operator, 'raise the crazy bastard and tell him I'm putting the lights on on the pad.' He swallowed quickly. 'Then sound the general stand-to. This is gonna be a hairy son-of-a-bitch!'

It was a mad, howling world. Above them the wind screamed shrilly through the derricks. Below the sea lashed itself into a demonic fury, rocking the 20,000-ton rig from side to side as if it were a toy Meccano set. But the grim-faced men waiting on the circular chopper platform beneath the twin derricks, with the wind snatching at their clothing, holding on to their hard hats with frozen red hands, noticed neither wind nor sea. Their attention was fixed on the streaming white circle of light thrown out by the swaying arcs and the searchlight they had hastily rigged up as a temporary beacon. The Jolly Green Giant must come down soon.

86

And then? None of them liked to think of the possibilities.

Time passed leadenly. The wind veered against the cross-tides. The *Pride* started to shake more violently.

Jacko cupped his hands about his mouth and bellowed: 'For Chrissake, Tex, can't you do something? He couldn't land on this platform in this sea – even if he had Christ and the twelve Apostles sitting beside him in the cockpit!' Big Tex, clutching the loud-hailer tensely while the spray streamed down his crimson, stony face like bitter tears, shrugged his big powerful shoulders. There was nothing he could do or say. For the first time since that October long ago when he entered the pine forest at the head of a company destined never to come back, he began to stumble through the 'Hail Mary'.

It had just got to 'hallowed be Thy name,' when the cry was taken up on all sides. '*THERE HE IS!*'

Big Tex opened his eyes and there it was – a dark whirling object at the edge of the white swaying circle 150 feet above them. He pressed the catch on the loud-hailer. 'In the name of God, go away, you dumb bastard! Do you hear me – go away!'

The Jolly Green Giant's cheerful voice drowned the sound of the rotor. 'Gee, now ain't that a nice friendly welcome – and me, bearing gifts, as it says in the good book.'

'Jolly Green—'

The chopper pilot broke into Tex's desperate plea. 'Stand by.' His voice was suddenly very professional, 'I'm going to make my approach now. I'll try to catch the bastard on the upsurge. From up here, the s.o.b. looks like a Coney Island roller-coaster. 'Kay, here we go.'

Words died on Tex's lips as the chopper dropped a good hundred feet. For a moment it hovered there directly above, drowning out the roar of the storm with its clatter, setting the empty beer and coke cans on the platform off on a metallic crazy dance with its downward thrust. Tex held his breath, trying to gauge how the rig would react by the roll. As soon as it swung upwards, the Jolly Green Giant would plummet down and try to catch the landing platform at an angle. If he misjudged, he could well hit one of the two derricks with his prop or miss the rig altogether and plunge right over the side into the raging sea a hundred odd feet below.

'*Here we go!*', the Jolly Green Giant's voice cut in their tense silence. Like a gigantic black hawk, the chopper plummeted downwards, drowning out the white glare of the arcs and the pounding of the sea with the deafening clatter of its engines. Tex thought his eardrums must go. He opened his mouth instinctively and screamed. And then the rig lurched *downwards*.

'Holy Mother of God, he's had it,' someone yelled as the chopper shot right past and disappeared over the side of the rig into the outer darkness.

'I knew he couldn't do it!' Jacko cried.

'Knock it off,' thundered Tex. 'I want volunteers to go over the side of spud B to get—'

But there was no need for a rescue party. With a tremendous roar the chopper flew up from beneath the rig, revved frantically and veered off to the south. The tense men on the platform could hear the Jolly Green Giant gunning the engines somewhere in the outer darkness. A moment later the chopper was hovering over the *Pride* again and the Jolly Green Giant was bellowing. 'That was a bit nip an' tuck. 'Kay, here we come again!'

In spite of the freezing cold, Big Tex could feel the sweat trickling down the small of his back and his fists clenched themselves into tense damp balls as the pilot brought down the chopper a second time.

This time the pilot was inching his way down, feeling for the deck with his undercarriage, fighting the wind so that it could not blow him off course. One hundred fifty feet . . . a hundred . . . seventy-five . . . Now the big chopper was poised between the two derricks directly above them, its rotor whirling crazily at full revs, as the Jolly Green Giant tried to keep the plane in position.

Next to Big Tex, a hoarse Jacko cried: 'He's gonna do it! The big bastard's got the luck of the Irish . . . He's gonna bloody well do it!' And then a gust of wind shot against the rig. It heeled violently. The nearside derrick bent towards the hovering chopper. *'NO!'* screamed Big Tex. But there was no saving the plane. Metal ground against metal as the first blade of the rotor snapped. The chopper lurched violently, but still kept flying. The next blade went. The chopper started to veer crazily to port. The third and forth blades went.

'Oh my sodding Christ!' a roustabout screamed, horrified.

'SCATTER!' bellowed Tex.

They sprang for cover. The next instant the stricken plane plummeted downwards. It hit the deck with a bone-jarring crash. The nearside leg of the platform buckled. Men dropped over the side. With a throaty crump the chopper's port gas tank exploded belching black oily smoke, flecked with fire. The Jolly Green Giant's funeral pyre had already been lit.

They managed to get him out of the tangled charred mess of beer cans, smoking letters, burst tins of corned beef, whose contents had been fried to a crisp dark brown by the fire, half an hour later.

'Do you want to see him?' Jacko asked gently, coming into the control shack whence Big Tex had directed the fire fighting operation. Outside the storm was dying.

'He's dead, isn't he?' Jacko nodded numbly. 'Then I don't want to see him.' Suddenly rage overcame the big American. His face flushed with rage and he brought his fist down on the metal table with such force that the papers on it flew a foot into air. 'Jacko,' he cried, 'what's wrong with this goddam rig . . . what's goddam wrong . . . ?'

DAY THREE: WEDNESDAY

'But the old world was restored and we returned to the dreary field and workshop and the immemorial feud of rich and poor. Our victory was our defeat.'

Herbert Read: To The Conscript of 1940

1

The one-armed ex-*Waffen* SS man spotted the road block first. They were rolling down the rutted road to Malmedy on his ancient motorbike and sidecar on the first stage of the eighty kilometre drive to Liege where the Palestinian would take the train to Brussels. He came to an abrupt stop and whispered urgenty, '*Gendarmerie*!'

At the bend a couple of hundred metres further on, a black Renault truck was parked in a cut, its radio mast whipping in the wind. Four men in dark uniforms were grouped around it, their backs to them, smoking and stamping their feet in the icy cold. One of them had a machine-pistol slung around his neck.

'They haven't heard us,' the one-armed man assured him, 'the wind is coming from the opposite direction. Besides,' he sneered, 'all that yer average gendarme hereabouts thinks of is his belly and making children for Holy Church.'

The Palestinian on the pillion seat released his hold on the other man's waist and felt for the automatic. 'What are you going to do?'

'Always assuming that the gendarmerie are lazy swine, which they are, my guess is that they've sealed off that hill line up there from St. Vith to Malmedy. It was the old German-Belgie border before Versailles. Then they won't want to be farting around in the hills and woods in this kind of weather. They might get their big policemen's paddle-feet cold. So what do we do?' He swung himself off the seat and gripped the handlebars firmly. 'We go off the road here and take the trails through the woods to Stavelot. We can pick up the Spa-Liege road there.' He grinned at the Palestinian, his gums bare of teeth where the *Witte Armee** men had kicked them out after the surrender in 1945. 'Come on son. We'd better start pushing.'

The ex-SS smuggler was driving all out now. The Palestinian, his face whipped by the icy wind, asked himself how the smuggler did it with one hand missing. The bike's tyres shrieked rebelliously, as they hurtled round corner after corner on the winding fourth class road that led over the heights towards Stavelot. But lurching, braking, skidding, cursing and accelerating again, the smuggler somehow managed to keep the bike from shooting off the road over the steep drop half a metre to their right.

Telegraph poles loomed up. Matchsticks reaching for the leaden-snow-heavy sky glimpsed between the line of firs. 'Reach in the sidecar,' the smuggler bellowed without taking his eyes off the road. 'Steel spikes right on top.'

Letting go with one hand, the Palestinian groped in the sidecar. On top of what seemed a sack of scrap metal, he found a pair of steel spikes with leather thong attachments like the ones they had used as kids to cut the Israeli telephone wires outside the border Kibbutzim.

'Got them,' he yelled.

'Good, we might need them, if—' he broke off. 'Cyclists coming up!'

Two lights bobbed toward them in the forest gloom. The Palestinian could make out the dark uniform and the rifles slung over the gendarmes' shoulders.

The smuggler crouched over the handlebars. 'Typical Belgie, going to war on a bicycle, just like they did in forty.' He hit the accelerator. 'Hang on.' The motor howled. The bike shot forward. The two cyclists saw them. They shouted something. The one nearest to the drop tried to steer and unsling his rifle at the same

*Armed Belg. resistance group in World War II.

time. The motorbike crunched into his front wheel at sixty kilometres an hour. The policeman screamed. As the motorbike bucked and rocked beneath the two of them like a wild horse, the policeman sailed over the edge and began the long descent in a clatter of rocks. A wild angry shot bounced off a kilometre stone harmlessly. Roaring onwards, the smuggler sounded his horn twice in contempt. '*Scheissbelgier*,' he cursed. 'Never could shoot!' The next instant they were round the corner and out of range.

But still the smuggler was taking no chances. A moment later he brought the bike to a screeching halt and sprang off like a man half his age. 'Quick,' he ordered. 'Get the sack open and spread what you find there across, while I get up the post.'

He fixed the climbing spikes on to his boots and shinned up the telegraph pole, shears stuck in his belt, hauling himself upwards with his powerful muscular right arm with the effortless ease of a monkey. The Palestinian opened the sack. It was filled with heavy-metal spikes, whose purpose he guessed immediately: to rip open the tyres of any vehicle following them. Swiftly he scattered them across the road and grabbing handfuls of snow scattered the white cover over them the best he could.

Hardly panting the smuggler dropped to the ground and nodded his approval. 'Stop anything those crows' feet would. There's many a kilo of coffee I've got across the frontier thanks to those little babies in the old days. If one of those gendarme cars tries to follow us, it's in for trouble. Come on, let's get on. It's a long way to Liege yet.'

Two hours later they crawled into the suburbs of the sprawling industrial town on the River Meuse without having seen another police patrol. As they rattled slowly across the slippery wet *pavé* that led through the grimy factory district on the east bank, they relaxed, knowing they'd made it. The smuggler spotted the filthy little red-brick *Café de la paix* where the Palestinian would meet the Algerian with the new papers and instructions for Brussels and pulled up. The air was suddenly heavy with the sharp pungent spices of the Middle East and they could hear the faint nerve-twisting sound of Arab music coming from behind the thick felt curtains which covered the fly-blown window with its fading appeal to '*Buvez Stella Artois – la Bière Belge*'.

The smuggler wrinkled up his nose and lit a *Boule d'Or* quickly. 'What they cooking in there – *old camel shit*?'

The Palestinian did not resent the insult to his people. The smuggler had done a good job. He took out the bundle of money agreed upon in Beirut by the Chief and handed it to the smuggler. His red face beamed and he breathed out a stream of blue smoke. 'Good – in marks.' None of your Belgian franc shithouse paper.'

'Is that why you do it?' the Palestinian asked, getting off the pillion stiffly.

The smuggler tucked the money away carefully inside his leather jacket. 'Why else?' he answered easily.

The Minister with the dull red ribbon of the Resistance Medal in the button-hole of his black jacket frowned at the report on the big Louis XV table. The only sound which broke the respectful silence was the ticking of the ormolu clock on the marble and gilt Baroque mantelpiece. A traffic policeman had stopped the smuggler for speeding just outside Spa. He had asked for the one-armed man's *permission*. He refused. He had insisted that the policeman should speak the third official language in Belgium – German; hadn't the King himself used it in his last New Year speech to the nation, at least for a couple of sentences anyway? The harassed traffic policeman had not been able to speak more than a few words of Dutch, not to mention German. A heated exchange of words had developed, the red-faced policeman speaking French, the smuggler obstinately sticking to German. The argument had resulted in a visit to the local *poste de police* opposite the nineteenth century *Hotel Britannique*, where the smuggler had suffered an 'unfortunate accident', as the report put it delicately. Thereafter he had begun to talk French – and more.

'*Sales melons,*' the Minister cursed to himself, using the French *colons*' contemptuous term for the Arabs. Didn't Belgium have enough problems already with half a dozen radical groups, Walloon and Flemish, ready to jump at each others' throats at a moment's notice, not to mention the usual ragbag of Anarchists, Marxists and the like? He sniffed and looked up at the Boche who had been summoned from Trier at his express order. The man looked like an idiot, like something from one of those terrible French movies on the war and resistance.

'Tell the German,' he said to the interpreter standing at the side of his desk, 'that he has been brought here to identify the terrorist. He is the only one apart from the Hermann girl he questioned and the smuggler, who is no position to do so, who can identify the man.'

The interpreter bowed and put the Minister's words into German, rolling his 'r's' like an Alsatian or Luxemburger, while Mueller listened, bemused by all that had happened to him in the last two hours. He had hardly had time to slip on his shirt, drying over the central heating in his hotel room, before they had rushed him to the waiting *Bundeswehr* chopper at the local depot. Now he was in this elegant ministry on the hill overlooking Brussels, with frock-coated ushers at the door and stripe-panted flunkies in executive gold-rimmed spectacles everywhere. In a place like this, not even he dare light one of his cheap cigars.

'And tell the German too that he is concerned solely with the identification. Our own men from the Sûreté will take any further action.'

Before the interpreter could start, Goosens, the

Ministerial Assistant, came in through the elegant white-and-gilt door. 'Minister, they confirm that the dead policeman, Henkes, was killed by the terrorist.'

The Minister's habitual frown deepened. That complicated matters. But if they could get the *melon* off Belgian territory before the press got hold of the matter it would be better. Let the French deal with him – they were used to this sort of thing. They would be able to stand up to the usual terrorist blackmail more efficiently than poor little Belgium.

'Thank Goosens,' he said, 'and state categorically we want no trouble. Our concern is to get the terrorist off Belgian soil.'

Mueller absorbed the information and then asked the interpreter, 'Where am I supposed to take up my post?'

The Minister who had learned his German at Buchenwald, but had stubbornly refused to speak it these last thirty years answered the question himself: '*Gare du Nord*.'

The Palestinian spotted them as soon as he got off the Liège-Brussels train. Two big men with hair cut too short and big black dependable shoes on their feet, watching the crowds over the tops of their newspapers. He saw a fat, elderly man standing at the buffet stall eating a *tartine beurrée* and a couple of hardboiled eggs. He looked like a cop too, he was so obvious that he didn't have to worry about him.

He hesitated a minute, pretending to fiddle with the canvas grip that the Algerian had given him and he saw the two big men's eyes focus on the grip at once. Then he saw his own contact. A shabby little man in a faded blue suit and wearing an English-type cloth cap, just as the Algerians had described him, reading *La Meuse*, the Liège paper, the agreed signal. He gripped the bag more firmly and began to walk out of the noisy, echoing station, wondering whether they would stop him now or later. The two big men let him pass without glance. The contact burried his face deeper in the provincial paper. Only Mueller, who had signalled the men from the Sûreté, showed interest. He slipped the rest of the bread and one uncracked egg in his pocket and stared after the Palestinian, as if he were wondering what to do next, hand carefully on the outrageously dear egg. Then in an instant things had started to move. The two Sûreté men dropped their papers on to the wet concrete. The fat German followed. The Irishman dropped his newspaper into the trashbin and followed suit.

The Palestinian passed outside into a cold foggy Brussels, the passersby huddled in their coats, their breath greyly clouding the bitter air. He had no idea where he should go; in the last years he had been to most continental European cities but never to Brussels. But he knew that he had to shake off the men on his back so that the contact could get to him without trouble. In Beirut they had had little training in shaking off a tail. Their operations rarely were of such nature where tails were involved; they were usually quick, violent and dramatically brutal. But he did remember the chief, the Doctor, pointing out that one should convince the tails that one suspected nothing, before 'hooking them off' with a swift surprise.

He walked for about ten minutes pondering the problem. In spite of the hour, the streets were surprisingly empty, due probably to the bad weather. There was obviously little he could do there. He dropped into an open-fronted bar in the Rue Neuve and had a *café filtré*, staring at the *Mannikin Pis* above the counter and wondering with his habitual puritanism why such an obscene statue of a naked little boy urinating publically was placed thus. Did it mean the fat, greasy owner was homosexual? Leaving the cup half empty and throwing a 100 franc note carelessly on the counter, he went out. 'Hey, your change!' the fat owner yelled, but when the dark-skinned young man did not respond, he shrugged and said: 'Stupid foreigner.' Knowing they were still after him and still demonstrating to them that he knew nothing, trying to lull them into carelessness, he sauntered along the store front. At the corner he had spotted the display flags of a large store. 'English week,' they proclaimed. 'Try the grand specialities of the English kitchen, try the grand cheese, the English whisky!' The flags were decorated with the Union Jack, the wrong way round.

The Palestinian turned in casually at the entrance, feeling the hot air hit him in the face. He loitered in the entrance staring with unseeing eyes at the displays of women's panties labelled *'Occasion!'* In the store's anti-theft mirror in the corner, he could see the two big men. The fat one in the absurd, ankle-length leather coat was not with them. He pushed on through the solid heavy-built Belgian women holding panties that were much too small for them against their ample hips. He passed through the snack bar heavy with the smell of raw onions and mincemeat. He climbed on the moving staircase. A long row of tinned haggis in tartan-coloured containers met his eye decorated with a sign, announcing that this was 'the typical nourishment of the Scot'. He paused and stared at them blankly, wondering idly what kind of food they could possibly contain. The two men were still behind him.

He wandered on into the clothes department. He ran his dark eyes along the crowded counters. British woollens were obviously a good buy. Young men were everywhere, feeling the quality of the cloth, preening themselves in their new acquisitions before long mirrors, engrossed in earnest discussions with women holding their jackets. He looked at the line of changing cubicles which ran along the opposite wall shielded from the entrance by the racks of clothes. Here and there there were the over-coats of the men trying on new suits in the cubicles lying on chairs or carelessly hung from the edges of the racks. It was now or never.

Carefully he drifted towards the racks, trying the feel of a jacket here, looking at a suit there, hoping the tails would think that this was where he would pick up his contact. He came level with the edge of the rack closest to the cubicles and ducked. Moving at the double, crouched low, he whipped up an overcoat and the leather cap lying beneath it. A moment later he was in the nearest cubicle. His own coat went into the bag and dropped on the floor. He slipped on the other coat, hoping desperately that it wasn't too small for him. Thrusting the cap on his head at a jaunty angle and tucking his long hair into it, he stepped outside. The change had taken exactly one minute.

Boldly he elbowed his way out of the crowd. In the anti-theft mirror, he could see the two tails casting anxious glances to right and left. Once outside, he thrust back the fire exit door. It clanged hollowly behind him. An odour of stale food assailed his nostrils. A skinny girl came out of a door, her dress up around her waist, pulling at her slip. She shrieked when she saw him and he bolted past her, taking the steps two at a time. A pile of boxes leaking straw barred his way. He leapt over them. Far above him he heard a cry of rage. The next instant, he crashed open the door to emerge into a cobbled smelly yard. He clattered across the cobbles.

'Over here,' a voice shouted in English, but an English of a kind he had never heard before, 'the car's waiting.' The little man in the shabby blue suit and cloth cap made the 'th' sound like a 'd'. A green Volkswagen was parked there, the driver gunning the engine wildly. The little man bundled him in and shouted, 'Don't worry, we'll take care of the fat Jerry!' The next instant the driver was racing the Volkswagen out of the side street into the main boulevard, ignoring the irate cries and horns of the other drivers. A moment later it had disappeared into the thick stream of traffic heading west towards the motorway that led from Brussels to the coast.

The Irishmen cornered the German ten minutes later. Like the good policeman he was, he had not been fooled by the Palestinian's apparent casual air. The Belgie Sûreté men had been too obvious. The Palestinian had spotted them all right. When they had followed him inside, he had remained outside. Then as an afterthought he had moved with considerable speed for a man of his years and bulk towards the rear of the big building just in time to spot the green Volkswagen. He had got the number and was hurrying up the back street looking for a telephone box when they converged upon him out of the two doorways.

The rubber police club glanced off his temple. But he had started back in time and they didn't knock him out as they had intended. Instinctively he kicked out. The man with the club went down, grabbing his testicles. The blood poured down his face as he grabbed for his automatic. It was nearly thirty years since he had last fired it in anger, but he had not lost his touch. The automatic exploded ear-splittingly in the narrow confines of the tight back street and one of the Irishmen screamed thinly.

Their first bullet wrenched his kneecap off. Mueller sat down suddenly gasping with pain. But he had still not dropped his automatic.

'Stop that bloody firing,' a voice yelled angrily, as the red waves of pain threatened to drown him. Mueller tried to level his gun. A glancing blow struck it from his hand. It clattered to the wet cobbles.

'*Nein, bitte nicht,*' he cried as the remaining three crowded in. '*Ich bin beinahe soweit . . . die Rente, wissen Sie—*'

His plea ended with a scream as the little man in the faded blue suit kicked him. A rib cracked and stabbed into his lung like a needle. He screeched thinly with pain. The world was revolving in front of his eyes now in hazy circles. A knee jolted into his face. He no longer felt the pain, nor the warm blood trickling down his fat double chin. He thought of the house in Spain and a stream of monstrous atrocities bubbled from his grey, pain-racked lips.

'Aw, fer sweet Jesus' sake, Paddy,' someone said a long way away. '*finish him*!'

Hands grabbed him and forced back his head, tugging at his cropped hair. A faint prick. Deeper. Then the knife slashed across his throat and his scream died in a thick bubble of choking blood.

When the two Sûreté men found him minutes later and turned him over out of the puddle of blood, they gasped with horror. '*Mon dieu*,' the bigger of the two gasped, 'the Boche do bleed, don't they!'

2

That midday things started to go right on the *Pride*. The fish was dislodged. Hardly daring to believe the evidence, of their own eyes, the sweating, mud-stained crew watched as it was brought up. A jubilant Big Tex roared: 'Swell, boys . . . really swell!' He threw off the exhaustion of a night spent without sleep, promised the shift a barrel of beer if they got the drill started by nightfall, and ordered Jacko to radio the Colonel with the good news at once.

Standing in the midst of the industrial mess of pipes, mud pumps, cement mixers, Big Tex watched proudly as the standard unit of three floormen and a derrickman started putting down the ninety-foot length of pipes. Without timing it, he knew from experience that a keen unit could lift, position, lower and fix each pipe, weighing half a ton in 55 seconds. Attuned to each other, knowing how quick, how deft, how accurate their mates were they worked without words, saving their breath. They did not exactly run; but, as he told himself, realising that they'd gotten the old spirit back again, 'they're not too goddam far off it!'

Ninety feet of pipe a minute. Five hundred an hour. A thousand every two. Darkness fell. Still they toiled on. It wasn't time for the new shift yet. The lights went on, the arcs swaying in the wind. High above them the red light burned on top of the derrick. Beneath them they heard the straining sound of steel, screeching and squealing under the pressure of the waves. The cooks brought up hot cocoa and they worked with a mug in their hands, or if they needed both hands for their task, with the mugs of cocoa balanced on a drum or crate, taking the odd quick scalding sip between operations.

It was nearly seven o'clock and Big Tex knew it was

time to stand the crew down. 'What about it fellers?' he asked, pushing back his hard hat to reveal the red wrinkled line about his forehead. 'Want to call it a day? Time for chow?'

Big Longbotham, still working in his shirtsleeves in spite of the night cold, laughed, 'What's up, Tex – can't yer stand it, mate? Getting too old?'

Big Tex grinned. 'I can stand it as long as you can, *mate*. But a man has got to take a piss now and again when you get to my age.'

'Sodding arse-crawlers,' Myers growled at the derrick.

As Big Tex strolled off to the latrines, someone called after him happily, 'And watch it don't come off in yer hand, Tex. You know what they say about wanker's doom!'

Big Tex chuckled and waved his big hand at the grinning crew. In the latrine, he went through the long-winded business of getting his dungarees open and his zipper undone. Standing, his legs astride, he poised himself at the bowl and was about to pass water, when the diesels started. He grabbed for the handle above the bowl as the deck below him trembled violently. 'Christ on a crutch!' he roared delightedly.

The next instant he heard the first excruciating screech of the brake on the drilling drum, but to Big Tex standing at the latrine bowl, the howl sounded like Beethoven and the Beatles rolled into one, because it meant just on thing: they had started drilling again!

Leaving his flies undone, he ran wildly out of the latrine, his gum boots flopping absurdly. He burst into the radio shack. Jacko, already a bundle of nerves from the night before, swung round from the crackling receiver. 'What's up, Tex? What's happened?' he asked. He caught a look of the big American's happy unshaven face. 'We haven't struck oil, Tex, have we?'

'Not yet, Jacko,' Tex roared his tired craggy face wreathed in a huge smile of delight and achievement. 'But we will – we will.'

He cocked his head to one side. 'Don't you hear it, you deaf little bastard?'

'Hear what?' Jacko queried, the fear returning to his eyes. 'Not more trouble?'

'Hell no!' Big Tex bellowed. 'What's the matter with you. Can't you goddam hear – the drill's working again. Now get this down in code and send it to the Colonel toot sweet.' He licked his dry, cracked lips. 'Drill working again. Stop. Helicopter smash cleared away. Stop. Prepare to pay for one barrel – no stop that Jacko. Make that – prepare to pay for one *big* barrel of best limey beer. Stop. God willing and the gear holding out, we'll strike pay dirt and oil in the next forty-eight hours. Stop . . .'

The *Pride* blazed like a lighted ship at sea, its upper decks bright with red and white arc lamps, swinging gently in the night wind. Below the sea was calm again. The last traces of the storm had vanished now, and the only reminder of the previous night's tragedy was the blackened, buckled landing platform. Even the Jolly Green Giant's body had vanished, flown off by the first relief chopper, for Big Tex knew his East Coast fishermen. They would not have worked easily with a dead man on board, however much they might have liked the person when he had been living. The fishermen were a superstitous bunch at the best of times.

Big Tex, freshly showered and shaven, made his last inspection of the rig before he turned in for the night. He descended the ladder into the mud chamber and checked the tank full of clay-coloured mud and chemicals, which was the life-blood of the drilling operation on a rig. During drilling it was forced down between the wall of the hole and the drill. There it kept the drill true and helped to remove the fragments of rock which the drill forced up from the rock bed so far below. Without it no drill in the world, however powerful, could function for more than a couple of minutes. The highly complex mud looked okay to him and the mud balance, which ensured the accuracy of the whole drilling operation was perfect. Satisfied, he paused there on the slightly vibrating ladder and listened to the screech of the brake on the drilling drum, the steady throb of the diesels, the swish of the ever-present sea, and the steel music of the straining structure below him. To most people it would sound like the devil's own music – hellish. To him it was beautiful. Slowly and tiredly he mounted to the deck. The new shift were too busy to notice him. He watched them for a moment or two and walked slowly to the rail where Jacko was smoking his last cigarette before he turned in for the night.

'Hello Jacko,' he said. 'Having a last butt?'

Jacko nodded silently. Together they leaned over the rail and stared at the water gleaming a cold silver in the light of the sickle moon on the horizon. The blue smoke of their cigarettes ascended in lazy circles as they listened to the soft surfing of the water far below.

'What you thinking, Tex? About the Jolly Green Giant?'

'Ina way – in a way. Last night you and me thought he was crazy risking his life to bring in a few lousy letters and a couple of cans of beer for the guys on the rig. I guess most people on the shore would think that anyway. But I don't know.' He rubbed his hands through his cropped, greying hair. 'But perhaps the poor bastard wasn't so crazy after all. He knew what kinda guys they really are, most of them anyway.' He turned and stared thoughtfully at the men working in the bright arc of light. 'You see, Jacko, they're really pretty unusual Joes. I don't know anybody who works like them any more. And under what lousy conditions too! That's why it's getting harder and harder to get 'em. I mean what kind of guy in his right mind would work a twelve hour shift, then have a shit, shave and shampoo, and sleep another eight hours before grabbing some of that crummy chow dished up by those cooks and going back to work for another twelve hours? And that for fourteen days on end, with no betting shops, no goggle-box, no pubs – and no nice little wife waiting for you between the sheets at night with a hot pussy.'

'Why do you do it then, Tex?' Jacko ventured.

Big Tex shrugged. 'Jesus, how would I know? The dough perhaps? Perhaps it's the last challenge – the only place in the world, apart from the military (and they're pretty soft these days so they tell me) where you're on your own. A gang of guys who are working to a common aim like in the war, fighting the elements and nature and not another guy with a cannon. Aw hell,' he said, 'it's too hard to explain and too goddam late!' He flipped away his cigarette butt. It curved a tiny red arc into the air and disappeared over the side of the rig. 'Come on, Jacko, got to get in some sack time. It's gonna be a long day tomorrow.' He took a last look at the night shift of the men toiling on the drilling platform. 'A bunch of good Joes, Jacko – take it from me.

Myers waited till the two of them had disappeared towards their cabins, then rose from behind the heap of piping behind which he had ducked when they had unwittingly interrupted his off-duty prowl around the rig. 'Silly bugger,' he muttered contemptuously. 'Good guys!' He spat scornfully on to the deck and then turned away, slipping silently in his ragged rubber tennis shoes from bale to bale.

3

While Brussels prepared for sleep, they sat in the dirty flat littered with their propaganda and dirty beer glasses and talked. To be exact they talked and he listened, telling himself contemptuously that they talked as much as the despised Egyptians. But when the little man in the faded blue suit came in and reported that the man the fat German had shot had died, there were a couple of angry cries of 'Jasus wept' and the 'poor hoor' and the talk faded away. Instead they sat there, puffing steadily at their cheap Belgian cigarettes and drinking their whisky with dogged persistence. The Palestinian began to feel uneasy, but told himself that the looks directed towards him every now and again meant nothing. It was just he was not used to working with anyone else; he preferred to operate completely alone.

Just before midnight, the man they called Paddy came back. Tall and spare, his face was pale and cadaverous, hollowed out by hate – and perhaps disease. The Palestinian who had once been a medical student before he had met the chief and become a full-time member of the organisation thought Paddy might be a consumptive. Not only did he have the physique, but also the burning energy of those sick with the wasting disease. In the camps as a boy he had seen enough of them, producing children like rabbits, as if they knew they were going to die young.

'All right,' Paddy snapped, refusing a glass of whisky, 'you can cut out that drinking. There'll be time for that later.'

'Mother o' divine God,' someone protested. 'Yer can't be begrudging old Mick a couple of jars, Captain now. In the old days you went to confession before yer went out on a mission—'

'Knock if off!' Paddy interrupted harshly and coughed. 'These aren't the bloody old days. And look what their drinking got them then! Besides look what kind of a stink this business has kicked up. The whole centre of the city is lousy with police. Goddammit, I wish we'd never got into it!' He looked challengingly at the Palestinian.

The Palestinian knew the tall man had no alternative. Without the money from the KGB, their continental organisation, running in weapons from the CCSR, would fold up within days. The handful of dollars from the armchair patriots in Boston wouldn't keep them going long. As the Russian Resident in Beirut had told him just before he had started on his mission: 'They are hard men, but money is their downfall. When they have too much of it – or too little of it – their organisation goes to pieces. Our advice to you is – don't trust them.'

It had been a piece of advice echoed by his chief, the Doctor. And he should know, after he had been in the *Abwehr*. 'The Russians took over the old *Abwehr* apparat in their country. You can see what kind of people they are. Reared with a pat on the head and now it's too late to give them a kick up the arse.'

The Palestinian had nodded. There were some who said the same of their own Movement. The Egyptians for instance. But it wasn't true. The Doctor was nobody's creature, even the Russians'. His purpose and own line could not be shaken by all the money and bribes in the world. But it didn't do to tell the Russians that. A heavy silence fell on the group crowded in the tight dirty room, lit by a single, fly-blown bulb. Outside a last tram rattled on its way to the depot. The Belgian capital was going to sleep as early as any provincial town. The Palestinian yawned pointedly. 'What's the plan?' he asked after a moment.

The man they called the Captain looked at him venomously. 'Plan – there ain't no bloody plan!'

'What do you mean?'

'I mean, mate that you – we – have blued it. That business this morning screwed up everything. Holy Jesus, can't you see that?'

The Palestinian looked at the circle of heavy, drunken faces and realised that it wouldn't take much to start trouble now. He licked his lips and said carefully. 'But their resident told me you had been paid – and paid well – for this task.'

'Great balls of fire,' sneered the man in the faded blue suit, 'what does that Commie bastard know? Getting his sodding knees brown out there. We're the blokes who get the chop if anything goes wrong.'

The Palestinian slipped his hand to his pocket carefully to feel the comforting weight of his automatic. He would shoot the Captain first. He was sober. Then the little man in the faded blue suit. He would be out of the door before the rest could react. The Captain calmed down. When he spoke again, his voice was reasonable and quiet. 'You see Mr – er – whatever you're called – the British have got Ireland and the approaches pretty well sewn up. Their whole bloody security apparatus is working against us. The SIS,* MI5, Special Branch, Army Intelligence – even those bloody killers of the SAS. And they're not only in the Six Counties, they're in the Republic. Over here too. Whatever those sods in Westminister say, British Intelligence is fighting this one all out. So you see, it's pretty tough.'

The Palestinian tensed.

'They're always just one step behind us,' the Captain continued. 'I hope you can understand that? But we do have one route into your target country which is still not compromised.' The Palestinian began to grow uneasy; the change in attitude had been too sudden. 'Mick, pass me the map, will yer?' The man in the blue suit

*Secret Intelligence Service.

111

passed it over and the Captain spread it over the dirty, glass-ringed table. It was an ordinary Swiss Hallweg map of Europe, the main roads marked in thick red. But the Palestinian noted that the southern autobahn from Stutgart via Aachen to Brussels and onwards was marked in blue ink with numbers at regular intervals. The Captain poked his forefinger at it. 'Look, we've been getting the Czech stuff in via the English east coast. The Royal Navy has got Irish waters tightly tied up. So instead of going in by the front door, we've been doing it by the back.'

'You see, we've got a thing going with a German manufacturer who has a subsidiary in the Six Counties, though,' he allowed himself a careful smile, 'the fat Jerry bastard doesn't know it.

'I see,' said the Palestinian. 'But how does this affect me?'

'Well, we've being using the containers he ships from Stuttgart through Europoort – Rotterdam – to take our stuff in to Hull on the English east coast. They're half asleep there. They never check. Anyway the containers have the TIR seal on them. They've been checked on the other side, as it were. Of course there could be a spot check and then,' he shrugged his thin shoulders, 'and we've had it. We'd have to find a new way in.'

'But how do you get your stuff into the containers?'

'We don't. We have our own containers ready and waiting to do the switch.'

'Switch?'

'Yes, look at this map. Take that big filling station there just above Liège.' He stabbed the spot eagerly. 'And look at that number and initials.'

The Palestinian screwed up his eyes to read the tiny scribbled number. 'S 332 – 456 and – BL. 'A truck number?' he queried. 'And the initials?'

'Berthold Lansch, the bloke who drives that number,' replied the Captain. 'You see truck drivers are creatures of habit. Once they take to some pull-up or other along the road, they always go back to it. You know, Joe Blow serves better or bigger sausages than Harry Arsehole – that sort of thing. So Herr Lansch seems to prefer the Liège pull-up on his way to the coast. When our lads in Stuttgart give us the tip-off that he's running the next shipment we're—'

'Waiting for him with your own shipment?'

'That's right,' the Captain said.

'And on the other side – in Ulster?'

'No sweat, our boys are waiting for the truck in the unloading bays. Our stuff goes one way – theirs the other.'

'And the way-bills, or whatever they call them in English – the details of the shipment?'

The Captain shrugged. 'Things get lost, don't they? Everybody knows those guest workers in German factories don't give a damn, as long as they get their money at the end of the week to send back to Mama and the thirteen kids they ain't got in Turkey. Okay,' his voice rose. 'Now we've got a shipment coming through tonight. Gerhard Baatz, isn't it, Mick?'

The little man in the blue suit confirmed the name. 'That's right. The big feller with the cock-eye. Likes his ball o'malt, old Gerhard does.'

'Good,' he turned to the Palestinian again, 'Friend Baatz usually gets off the E-5 – the motorway – between here and Louvain. He stops in a cafe on the outskirts, where they serve Mutzig Pils. He likes that. Now then, what about it, do you want to chance being Friend Baatz's guest – unknown to him of course – to Hull via Europoort? It won't be comfortable, but it'll be safe in the back of the truck – unless, naturally, there is a spot check.'

The Palestinian's brain raced. The Captain's attitude had changed too quickly. At first he could do nothing. Now he was presenting him with an apparently foolproof method of getting into the target country. The Resident's anxious warning flashed across his brain – 'don't trust them'. He realised they were setting him up.

'Well,' the Captain persisted, 'want to give it a whirl?'

Trying to restrain the sudden trembling that had afflicted his right hand, the Palestinian said: 'Sure, why not. Let's give it a whirl.'

It was about that same time that the Minister, with the rosette of the Resistance Medal replaced now by a miniature of the MBE (military division) in honour of the occasion, made his decision. He was in a bad mood. He had been forced to eat a sandwich like a damned American instead of the lavish four and five course meal he preferred in the evening in one of Brussels' more exclusive restaurants, displaying his young mistress proudly as living proof that he was still the heller he had once been as a young man.

'Goosens,' he called.

The Ministerial Assistant appeared immediately as if he had been listening behind the door. 'Minister?'

'Call off the search.'

The Assistant indicated his surprise only by a slight raising of his trimmed eyebrows. 'Yessir.'

'Wait,' said the Minister. 'You see, Goosens,' he explained, 'I think it would be better if he cleared off. It's obvious that the matter has nothing to do with Belgium. It's obvious too that the Irish are involved. Ulster.' He sniffed disgustedly. 'Can't understand them, fighting each other like that. It's almost medieval. Even the Fl—' He caught himself in time. Goosens was a Fleming from somewhere or other in West Flanders. He might well be a member of the *Volksunie* or something worse for all he knew.

'And the British, sir?'

The Minister had been toying with that possibility all

114

evening – hence the MBE – but he didn't like having to do it. The British wouldn't be too happy with the information he had to give them. They would be polite enough in London. 'How good of you to call . . . now that *is* interesting . . . we are highly indebted to you, Minister . . .' and all the rest of it. But it wouldn't take long before Her Britannic Majesty's ambassador would be making 'a polite but firm protest' about the Minister's conduct. 'Could he not have detained the terrorist in Belgium' etc, etc? 'Such a dangerous man! Surely one should have stopped a man of that kind as soon as possible . . .'

'Yes,' he sighed, dreading what was to come, 'you'd better get me their people in London.'

They took the E-5 out of Brussels. 'They daren't throw a roadblock across the motorway,' the Captain explained. 'They'd have one sod of a ballsup at this time of the night. All those drunks and sugar daddies coming back from the whores in the roadhouses. They'd never stop in time and the bulls know it.' Thus they sped out of the capital eastwards in their ancient Citroen DC-17 until the sign for the Mechelan turn-off loomed up, where they left the motorway. 'We'll backtrack from here toward to Louvain – along the back roads,' the Captain said. 'They won't be expecting us to be trying to get back *into* Brussels.'

'No, I don't suppose so,' the Palestinian said. 'How long will it be until we meet Herr Baatz.'

'Who?' Then the Captain caught himself. 'OH, that boyo!' He shrugged. 'Twenty minutes – thirty at the most. Depends on the road.' He turned in his seat next to the driver and stared out of the window at the white glare of the city centre flashing by.

They left Mechelen behind. The road changed to pavé. Even the Citroen's excellent suspension could not dampen the impact of the wet cobbles. Next to the

115

Palestinian, the little man in the blue suit took out a half bottle of whisky and began to drink out of it with steady regularity.

The Palestinian was worried. He glanced at the green luminous dial of the clock on the dashboard. It was fifteen minutes since they had left the motorway and still there was no sign of the outskirts of Louvain. Although he knew the area around the capital was thickly populated, it seemed to him that everything around was becoming increasingly rural. Lonely farms, shrouded in sleep, the odd windmill, barns, abandoned, ruined houses, silver stretches of snowy fields, bathed in moonlight. Another five minutes past. There was no sound now save the soft purr of the two and half litre motor and the crunch of the tyres on snowy patches in the road. Inside the Citroen the three Irishmen were sunk in gloom, preoccupied with their own thoughts.

The Palestinian closed his eyes as if he were going to take a nap. Through his eyelashes, he caught a vague glimpse of the Captain turning to look at him. He whispered something in a satisfied tone to the driver. It was then that the Palestinian really knew they were going to kill him. He could reason why. He was an embarrassment to them since the shoot-out in Brussels. But they knew their obligation to the source of their funds. The Russians had helped to plan the mission; they would expect their running dogs to help them carry it out. The Irishmen would ensure that he disappeared quietly; then their problems would be solved. They had helped him on his way. How would the German truck driver know whether he had a passenger or not? How could the Russians check up then when the Captain reported he had carried out his part of the mission and not seen the Palestinian since?

The car started to jolt. He opened his eyes a little. They were driving along a rough track through a forest, their lights illuminating the gnarled oaks, their winter-bare branches whipping at the car roof. They were slowing down, the time had come to act. Next to him, the little man was still occupied with his bottle. Cautiously, still allowing his chest to rise and fall steadily, as if he were asleep, the Palestinian felt for the door handle. He eased it slowly downwards. The door gave! The Irishmen had forgotten to lock it. The driver changed down from top. He heard a faint click – the Captain slipping off the safety on his pistol.

The Citroen was slowing down rapidly now. He could hear the branches slapping against the sides of the car. He tensed. 'Hey, you – *wog*!'

The Palestinian jumped. A branch hit him hard against the side. He grunted with pain, then hit the ground. He rolled over automatically as he had been trained to do in the Lebanese commando camps and grabbed for his pistol. A dozen metres away the big black car squealed to a halt and the Palestinian fired. It was a wild unaimed shot, but he was lucky. The nearside window shattered, disappearing in a spider's web of glass, gleaming in the moonlight. Someone cursed angrily and red flame slashed the silver darkness. He dived to the right just in time. A split second later, a burst of slugs hit the ground where he had lain.

The Palestinian's heart was thumping furiously as he crouched in the wet bushes and sized up the situation. On the far side of the car, the rusty doors creaked open. That would be the Captain and the little man sneaking out. In a moment the driver would open up to cover them. They would swing out to the both sides in an attempt to outflank him while the driver kept him occupied. They would expect him to open fire as soon as the driver started again. That would reveal his position and then they could flank him. The Palestinian bit his lip. But he was the professional and they were the amateurs; they had not spent their youths sniping and raiding the Jews, night after night, year after year

117

in a bitter, savage war about which the world knew nothing.

Holding his fire, moving forward every time the moon scudded behind the clouds and blacked out the glade, he crept closer. On his flanks he could hear the other two working their way noisily through the undergrowth. He had almost reached the door. The driver fired again – all he could see was the white hand above the door and the scarlet flame stabbing the darkness. Once he raised himself to rush the door, but the driver would have spotted him and fired quicker than he could have covered the distance between himself and the door. At last he remembered the torch.

He eased it carefully out of his pocket. He took a deep breath, then lobbed it to his left with the light on. The driver reacted at once and pumped a rapid salvo at the sudden white beam. The Palestinian fired in the same instant. The slug slammed right through the door and the Palestinian sprang forward wrenching open the door with a curse. The driver tumbled out, moaning but he kicked him out of the way and dropped into the blood-soaked seat. Frantically he sought and found the ignition key. Outside he heard the cries of the other two.

Desperately he turned the key.

'Joe,' the Captain yelled angrily, 'what in hell's name are you up to, man?'

The Palestinian turned the key again.

'Sweet Jesus, it's not – *it's him*!' the little man screamed.

Slugs streamed from an automatic. The Captain came running out of the bushes, firing from the hip with the sweat lathering his brow, the Palestinian ripped the key to the right frantically. The Irishman was only thirty metres away. The slugs smacked home against the metal.

Suddenly the engine burst into life. The Palestinian rammed home the gear, let out the clutch, and the car sprang forward. For a moment the Captain was outlined in the yellow headlights, arms outflung, as if challenging the car, man against metal. Then he was crushed under the Citroen's front wheels. The car careened wildly from side to side to side, as the Palestinian attempted desperately to keep the bucking Citroen on the rough forest track, leaving the Captain sprawled out behind on the frozen stiff grass in the extravagant posture of the violently done-to-death.

One hour later the Palestinian was speeding past the Atominium, heading towards the coast and England.

DAY FOUR: THURSDAY

'I am distressed to hear from many sides that the pre-
vailing temper of our troops is a half cynical boredom,
as remote as possible from the high crusading fervour
which their situation authorises and requires. They are
not pacifists or disloyal but 'bored stark'. They have
neither the enthusiasm of youth, nor the deliberate purpose of youth, but just acquiescence in an absurd and
unwelcome necessity.'

Bishop Henson, March 1940.

'I think,' the Chief said, 'that you'd better start the ball rolling John.'

The man from the SIS* took his eyes off the sluggish brown flow of the Thames below, stifled the temptation to yawn – he had got up at six to make this 9 a.m. intelligence conference – and glanced at his hastily scribbled notes. 'Mine is in the way of a general briefing to begin,' he explained. 'In recent months, as you all know, the Israelis have been using a revised strategy against the Palestinians – ever since Kiryat Shmonah, Ma'alot and the Palestinians' raid on Nahariyah. The Israelis are no longer confining themselves to attacks on the Palestinian refugee camps and the odd bombing raid. They're taking out individual Palestinian terrorists, not only in the Middle East, but also in Europe. I think you all got the memo we circulated on the killings in Frankfurt's red light district last month and the bomb attack on the offices of the GUPS and GUPA† in Bonn two weeks ago?'

They nodded.

'Well our reading of the situation is that the so-called Palestinian moderates like Arafat and El Fatah, as well as the General Command extremists and George Habash's Popular Front, all agree that their activities should be carried to safer climes than the Middle East. There are several reasons for this. The going is easier – we are not prepared as well for terrorist action as the Israelis are. The fact is that our media give their acts worldwide publicity – and you gentlemen know how the whole

*Secret Intelligence Service, sometimes called MI6.
†General Union of Palestinian Students and General Union of Palestinian Workers.

gang of them there in Beirut lap that up! And in the end the Western Democracies usually cave in when the going gets tough. I don't think I have to remind you of that bad business a few weeks back when the West Germans gave in to their threats, paid them three hundred thousand quid in blackmail and was forced to broadcast anti-Israeli propaganda over the *Deutsche Welle*?'

There was a rumble of hear-hears.

'On that basis, my organisation believes that our man is a product of the new approach, who will be receiving help from left-wingers and similar crackpots throughout his stay in the West. As for his target country, it could be anywhere except France. The Arabs have got a good thing going with the Frogs. It's our guess that the target country is the UK. That's all.'

'Thank you John,' the Chief said, 'that put it in a nutshell.' He turned to the MI5 representative. 'Peter?'

The Counter-Intelligence man, a former army officer like most of MI5, cleared his throat importantly. 'This is the situation as far as we see it at this particular moment in time.'

The chief, who was from the Foreign Office, frowned at the expression. The FO would never have tolerated such a terrible cliché.

'The man in question is receiving active support from the Russkis – that's clear from the info we have received from Cologne. The Belgies have lost him and are now busy passing the buck to ourselves and the DST* in the fond hope that the terrorist is heading for ourselves or the French. Now my department agrees – for once', the MI5 representative nodded in the direction of his rival of the other service, '—with our colleagues of the SIS that the chap is coming our way. But it's only an informed guess, of course.'

'A source of ours in the Belgie *Sûreté* tipped us off,' the SIS man butted in, 'that the Micks were involved in

---

*French Counter-Intelligence.

Brussels. But not the Provos – the Officials. One of their people bought it.'

The MI5 man nodded his thanks. 'We had the same information,' he said. 'Now as you know the Official IRA has not been doing so well these last years, although with their Marxist ideology, they've been receiving support from the Russkis. So we feel that this is a combined operation to put the Officials back in the running and let the Palestinians get some fresh publicity for their cause in safer circumstances in the Middle East. Our terrorist is heading this way – that is certain. The problem is – to do what and where?'

The Chief looked at the Special Branch's representative. 'What do you think Assistant Commissioner?'

The heavy-set professional policeman, who always felt a little out of place in these meetings, sat up straighter in his leather chair. 'Well, sir, if I am reading the gentlemen from SIS and MI5 correctly, they are inclined to believe our suspect is bound for the UK, probably Northern Ireland. There he'll carry out an op with the Officials – let say for the sake of argument – the kidnapping of the present C-in-C of the British Army there.'

'I take it, Assistant Commissioner,' the Chief said, trying to speed things up, 'you don't agree with this theory?'

'No sir.'

'Why not?'

'For several reasons,' answered the man from Special Branch. He ticked them off on his big rugby-player's fingers. 'One, the Officials are simply not in the running in Ulster – all they do is sit on their fat Paddy bottoms in Dublin pubs and talk big. Indeed, it's my guess that the Provos wouldn't allow them into Ulster. Also, the Russians are now supplying the Provos with weapons via the El Fatah. Two – Ulster is not that newsworthy. With the rate of daily incidents there, the media are no longer interested – unless the Provos dropped the Pope on the poor old Europa Hotel. They've dropped everything else on it! Three. Everyone in Ulster is security

conscious and there are enough armed men around anyone and anything of importance to make it very tough
for our Palestinian to get to his target. It's my opinion
that wherever the man's heading for – it's not Ulster.'

It was just then that the morning coffee, laced with
rum for certain key members of the conference, was
served and as the noise of the city's rush hour traffic
started to build up outside, they sat back more comfortably in their chairs to discuss the problem. The Chief
listened in silence, making an occasional note so that if
he had to report to the PM he could give a direct quote.
It was a tiresome business, but better than sticking one's
neck out completely. Idly he wished they would use the
Russian or American system, where everything was recorded on tape – 'farts and all', as the Special Branch
man had once commented indelicately.

An assistant came in with the information that the
special CIA computerised file at Langley with its details
of all known terrorists throughout the world had nothing
to offer, nor the secret US anti-terrorist task force headed
by a former American ambassador. Just then the Israeli
Embassy came on the line with the news that the
Mossad* had no details of the Palestinian terrorist.

'We're really up the creek without a paddle if *they*
don't know,' commented the Special Branch representative.

In the end it was left to the Chief to sum up and make
a decision. Pressing his well-manicured hands together
under his chin, he said: 'Gentlemen, it seems we know
very little – really next to nothing about our man – save
that he is coming our way. My guess is that he is the
usual psychopath these terrorists use. After all he has
two murders to his credit in the space of two days. A
man, therefore, who will stop at nothing because he will
be unable to feel the fears, see the dangers that a normal
person would. A very dangerous man indeed.

*Israeli Intelligence.

'Now I tend to agree with the Assistant Commissioner that his target is not Ulster but England, for the reasons he outlined. The problem, of course, is what he will strike here? So I suppose we'll have to go through the whole wearisome business of sealing the country off once more.' He looked at the Assistant Commissioner. 'The SB will seal off the airports and harbours. You, Peter, will check out our own lunatic fringe – the sort who might be likely to help the Palestinian if and when he arrives here.'

The MI5 men laughed bitterly. 'Lunatic fringe! The whole bloody British population under the age of thirty seems to belong to it these days, sir!'

'Let it be a lesson to you, Peter. Never trust anyone under thirty, if I might coin a phrase. And you'd better put a really good man on to the job, Peter. What about that big chap you once introduced me to in the club. Big tough fellow, who managed to stop the *Stern** publishing the story about the PM's secretary and her unfortunate illegitimate progeny?'

'Oh, yes,' the MI5 representative said bitterly. 'Threatened to chuck one of the Germans in the Thames, together with his typewriter, and kick the pansy photographer feller all the way back to Hamburg personally if he dared take a photo of the woman's kids. The Para, you mean, sir?'

'Well, if that's his name, get him, Peter. If our terrorist is what I suppose him to be, we'll need a chap like that to handle him. Put the – er – Para on to the case at once.'

*West German weekly, published in Hamburg.

2

When he had studied illegal ops under the rector F. D. Ryshenko at the Lenin Institute, the Palestinian's own special subject for the final examination had been illegal port entry and sabotage. Concentrating on the three main Western European ports where the *'illegale'* could anticipate some degree of support from the local party members among the dockers, Rotterdam, Antwerp and Hamburg, he had concluded that the first one would be the easiest to infiltrate. The study had gained him a 'very good' or 'two' and praise from Ryshenko himself, a man not given to easy compliments. But then five years before, the Palestinian had never even considered that he would ever be faced with the real thing: how to smuggle himself on to one of the ships leaving the great sprawling Europoort for England.

But on that icy cold February afternoon, he was in no mood to contemplate life's strange coincidences. He was cold, hungry and angry at the Russians for providing him with the Irish contacts in Brussels. Instead of a smoothly working plan for transporting him across Europe to his target country, they had involved him in one mess after another, almost as if they wanted the damned op to fail.

'Here we are,' said the surly driver of the sand truck, pulling up with a rusty squeak of brakes. 'I go straight ahead to Oostvorne. Over there.' He pointed to the blue and white sign of a ship with the legend *Engeland* beneath. 'That's the way to the North Sea Ferries depot.

'Thank you very much,' the Palestinian said and handed him the twenty mark note he had promised the man to take him out to Europoort so that he wouldn't miss his ship.

The truck driver looked at the note carefully. 'Can't

be too careful with you sailors,' he grumbled. 'Big talkers, big spenders with the whores in town and then no dough to get back to your ships.' He shoved home first gear angrily.

The Palestinian dropped over the side and as the truck drew away heading for the coast, he stared at the black dripping land wrested from the sea by the Dutch over the last three decades, the world's largest port. It looked bleak, bare and as harshly utilitarian as the men who had built it, but it served his purpose. He knew from his study at the Lenin Institute that the North Sea Ferries Depot was empty save for a couple of watchmen for most of the day until late afternoon when the England ferry sailed at six. By that time he had to be aboard and stowed away safely, before anyone started asking him awkward questions. Ducking his face into the shelter of his coat collar, he set off down the dripping cobbled road towards the depot, the wind and the bitter, salty rain lashing in his face.

The North Sea Ferries Depot was a disappointment. It was surrounded by a four-metre-high wire fence, which had not been mentioned in the information supplied to him five years before. And there was only one entrance, guarded by two elderly watchmen who were there, he guessed, not to keep people like himself out, but to prevent any thefts from the long line of containers waiting along the quay for shipment on the evening ferry.

He rubbed the rain from his face and studied the situation. The ferry was already in, its bow raised high in the air, but with no sign of life on board, as if the crew were still sleeping off the previous night in town.

Carefully he checked the whole length of the ship from his hiding place behind an oil tank. There was no guard on deck, as far as he could see. Obviously the captain of the ferry relied on the two elderly Dutch men at the gate to keep off stowaways or otherwise unwelcome guests. So if he could surmount the fence without being spotted, he might have a fair chance of getting on the ship and once the passengers started to arrive, he could mingle with them and take it from there.

He began to trace the whole length of the high wire. On both sides of the cluster of sheds and modern brick buildings which made up the North Sea Ferries Depot, the wire reached right to the water's edge. He quickly stripped off his clothing behind the shelter of a sand dune. The wind was icy on his naked brown body and his teeth started to chatter uncontrollably. With fingers that felt as clumsy as sausages, he bundled his clothes inside his raincoat and gripped the bundle firmly with his left hand. Taking a deep breath, he slipped into the water. Its icy cold struck viciously at his stomach. The rusting bow of the ferry loomed up in front of him. He caught a quick glance of the name, *Norwave*, before he dived. An instant later, he came up again underneath the dripping concrete of the jetty, then with a last effort, he flung his bundle on to the concrete and pulled himself up.

He crawled to the spot alongside the ferry's bows where some piece of kitchen apparatus or the engines were giving out a blessed warmth. For a few moments he luxuriated in the heat. Then drying himself as best he could with his underpants, he drew on his damp clothes again.

While he was thus occupied, the sudden rattle of trucks told him they were about to load the containers above his head. He hurried with his dressing. Five minutes later he was hanging on grimly to the underside of one of the containers as it bumped up and down on the metal ramp that led into the dark bowels of MV *Norwave*, due to sail in exactly two hours time. He was on the last leg of his long journey.

3

In Hull's nineteenth century Station Hotel, the head of the union was beginning the main and last speech of the morning when the steward tipped Joe Harehill on the shoulder and whispered, 'Excuse me, brother, there's another brother outside the hall who would like to speak to you. In the vestibule.'

'Thank you, brother,' Harehill felt foolish as he always did when he was forced to use the word 'brother' at union conferences.

As he reached the door of the big hall, the speaker, thumbs in his navy blue waistcoat, was assuring his audience that 'we will pull out of our economic crisis, just as we did at Dunkirk. Brothers, the only thing that encourages me to believe that we are not heading for doom is that we, the ordinary working folk of this country, have always been able to put our shoulder to the wheel in time of need'. Harehill closed the door behind him, cutting off the loud applause. For an instant he looked around for his visitor. Then he spotted him; it was Myers from the *Pride*.

He walked over to him and drawing him to one side, hissed: 'How the hell did you get here, Myers?'

The little cock-eyed rigman swallowed the rest of his smoked salmon sandwich and said: 'You lot do yersens proud, *brother*, don't yer?'

'Shut up. Now how did you get here?'

'Came in with the regular chopper. Told 'em that my piles are acting up again. Had to see the MO.'

'I see.' Harehill looked around. But none of the fat, white-powdered union wives with their handbags slung over their plump bare arms were paying attention to them. 'And what's the situation?' he asked.

'Bad. They're gonna get that sodding oil. The signs

are getting better by the hour.' He seized another sandwich and thrust it in one piece into his mouth. 'All this morning's tests were positive.'

Harehill's face fell. His only hope of beginning the unionising of the rigs was through the *Pride*. The Americans – hard bastards that they were – would only give in, if all the British rigs were unionised.

'Bugger it!' he cursed. 'Once they strike oil out there, we'll never get them organised. Those rig men can never see further than their wage packets and oil bonuses. As soon as the bonuses start coming in, they'll be as happy as pigs in shit.'

Myers nodded and looked up at the union organiser with his dark eyes. 'I could fix it, *brother*.'

'What do you mean – fix it?'

But before Myers could answer, the doors of the conference hall were thrown open and the delegates started to stream out towards their waiting wives. Waiters began to move forward into the blue-suited throng carrying silver trays of whisky, sherry and gin and tonics. On a platform at the far end of the room, an elderly five-man band launched into 'Take the A-Train' in a poor imitation of the old Glenn Miller band. Here and there a middle-aged 'sister' waggled her silk-clad plump hips in time to the music and made a beckoning gesture to a reluctant husband. Hurriedly Harehill pushed Myers into an empty lounge and whispered: 'All right, now let's have it.'

On the *Pride* they were drilling now through a high-pressure gas zone, thrusting upwards at a pressure of 9,000 pounds a square inch – a tremendous pressure which could destroy everything on the rig if they lost control. But Big Tex was keeping the stuff down with their special mud, a compound of chemicals and other material, which was forced into the drilling hole and kept circulating by the mud pumps. The hydrostatic pressure of this mud column kept the gas below the surface in place, but Big Tex kept his eye on it, checking the mud balance every five minutes or so.

This simple instrument was the safety gauge for the whole operation. It gave the density of the mud being used and if that density was wrong, disaster could follow. Then if the weight of the mud were wrongly calculated, the mud would be unable to hold down the gas. The result usually was a blow-out, that could mean an explosion, fire – the death of the whole platform. Big Tex was just checking the cup, in which the mud density was measured, when Jacko called him to the radio shack. The Colonel was on the radio telephone, as eager for news as ever. Big Tex told him at once about the high pressure gas and even over the crackling phone-link, Big Tex could tell that the Colonel was worried. 'What's new, Colonel?' he asked. 'Problems?'

'Have we ever had anything else but problems with the *Pride*, Tex? No, nothing new. Only time is running out – *fast*. If we don't get the oil out very soon, I'm out on my neck. What's more important, all the little people who placed their savings in Britoil are going to get no return for their trust in me. You understand what I mean, Tex?'

'I understand, Colonel.' For a moment Big Tex's voice, hardened by years of shouting orders against the background of roaring drilling machinery, softened. 'Don't worry, Colonel,' he said, 'We'll get that goddam stuff up if it kills the goddam lot of us. The *Pride* is going to strike oil soon, *over and out.*'

While the radio conversation was taking place in the north, Volker Krause was facing the American Hardman for the first time since the board meeting. For a few minutes they gossiped about the oil business, but Krause knew that Hardman had not flown to Germany to make small talk about Houston and the Gulf.

Dipping the end of his cigar in the glass of Dujardin

cognac and lighting it ceremoniously, Hardman looked at the German and said: 'Krause, you're no fool. You know the score just as well as I do. We both work for the same kind of guys – businessmen, pure and simple, who don't go in for that kind of British crap, tradition and all that malarky. They're the kind of guys who if they put a buck into a business, they wanna earn another buck with it – two if they can.'

'So?'

'Well, Krause, you know as well as I do that we can't go on operating like this. That Britisher – the Colonel – is running the business as if this was 1944 and not 1974. You and me are in it for the dough.' Hardman sighed and puffed at his cigar, which threatened to go out. 'God knows what he's in it for. Now Krause, we've really got to get on the stick. I want your support to call another emergency board meeting in London as soon as possible and at that meeting I want you to back me up when I call for the Colonel's resignation.'

'But what could we achieve, Hardman? You saw what happened at the last one. You wouldn't get a majority.'

'I could offer dough – plenty of it.'

Krause sat up. 'Money?'

'Yeah. My backers in the States are prepared to offer another five million – *pounds sterling*. On one condition.'

'That the Colonel goes?'

'Yeah, naturally, we want him out.'

'And who do you want to put in his place. You?'

Hardman shook his head, his dark eyes sizing up the younger German. 'No, not me. I'm just money and I'm a Yank. The new head would have to be a European. Not me, Krause – *you*,' he poked his cigar at the German aggressively. 'Herr Volker Krause!'

For a moment the German did not react, while Hardman sat back in his chair and regarded him with eyes full of mockery and self-satisfaction. Krause could see

134

the possibilities at once: London and Clarissa, away from the provincial boredom of his present life. All the same he was puzzled. Why were Hardman's backers prepared to pump new money into an operation that had proved itself to be so costly and so far without any financial return?

Hardman took his cigar out of his mouth. 'You're wondering why my backers are prepared to put up more dough, aren't you, Krause? I'll tell you. Not because the *Pride* looks as if it's going to be successful at long last, but because my backers want the *Pride* stopped!'

Krause looked at him, aghast. 'But why, Hardman? Why, for God's sake?'

'Because my backers don't want any more oil to come on the world market at this moment, Krause. Do you know what the world daily oil surplus is now?'

Krause shook his head.

'Two goddam million barrels! All over the world the refineries are full to the brim. Hell, off Tokyo and Osaka, the super tankers are waiting two to three weeks to clear their oil. Now I don't have to tell you what would happen if that oil – all of it – were dumped on the world market, or those goddam A-rabs were scared into something similar by – let's say – a big new oil strike in the North Sea? The price of oil would come tumbling down. And how?!'

'And your backers would be faced with the sort of stock losses to match the staggering stock profits they've made this winter, eh, Hardman?'

'Sure.' Hardman spread out his pudgy hands, palms upwards, as if he had nothing to hide. 'They quadrupled their profits last year. But they bought dear too. Hell, it's understandable they don't want a big new find coming along which might rock the boat and send the prices zapping down. So the answer is that when the *Pride* strikes oil – and it will – the news is kept mum. But if that goddam Colonel is still in charge, he'll tell

135

the whole darn world. "Britoil strikes oil for Britain",'
Hardman's face contorted scornfully. 'You know the sort
of crap he talks? Thats why we've got to act fast—'
  'We?'
  'Sure, Krause. *We*! Hell, you and me are going to be
working together a lot after next Sunday's emergency
board meeting makes you the new chairman of Britoil.'

4

The elegant head of MI5 faced the Para and didn't like what he saw. The big, heavy-set young man with the un-fashionably short hair, old, shabby suit and the tie of the Parachute Regiment looked exactly what he was – an ex-junior officer from an unfashionable regiment, who had little time for the niceties of Counter-Intelli-gence, the 'oblique approach', which the head of MI5 always preached to his subordinates.

Nevertheless, he had to admit that the Para had done excellent work ever since he had come to the Depart-ment from the SAS. He spoke several European lan-guages fluently, plus Arabic, which he had learnt with the SAS. As a new boy he had managed the affair of the defecting Czech Labour Attaché in a very intelligent fashion and had reported personally to the PM on the Czech's contacts to British politicians, as if he were summoned to Number Ten every day of the week. A year later he conducted the delicate investigation into the Russian attempt to blackmail the homosexual member of the cabinet with firmness and discretion.

Still, thought the head of MI5, as he indicated the Para should sit down, the man had something hidden about him, more complex than his heavy-set straight-forward appearance would indicate, something which irritated the senior officer because he could not define it.

'I'd like to talk to you about the terrorist,' said the MI5 Chief, sitting down behind the desk which had reputedly once belonged to Nelson. 'You're in the picture?'

'Yessir – just.'

'I can skip the preliminaries then. You know we've been landed with this particular baby by Joint Intelli-gence. As I see it, our problem is twofold. One – to try

137

to stop him getting into the country. Though these days, with every tinpot amateur sailor and unemployed fishing skipper running in Pakis from Holland and Belgium, I think that is virtually impossible. Two, to try to stop him obtaining his objective.' He sighed. 'Whatever it may be.'

'It is my opinion, sir that the man's objective will be some thing. Since Ulster hotted up, most of our important people here in the UK are too well guarded.'

'What thing do you suggest – the Bank of England perhaps?' the Chief smiled.

There was no answering smile from the Para. He was not a man given to humour. 'No, sir, it won't be a target in London. It'll be something in provinces. Not well guarded but with a great deal of news value.'

'But what, man – that's the problem?'

The Para considered. 'The Concorde, perhaps, an oil rig, a regional TV or radio station – anywhere off the beaten track, as far as security is concerned, but which will get the bastard the headlines he wants.' There was a sudden steely edge to the Para's voice.

The Chief looked at him in surprise. It was the first time the man had betrayed any emotion in his presence. 'I suppose you could be right,' he said thoughtfully. 'All right, you've got the job. What are you going to do?'

The Para answered unhesitatingly, 'I doubt if it's any use trying to nab him at the ports or the airports. I'll leave that to the SB boys. I'll lean on one or two people I know. Then I'll follow my own nose, sir, and see where it leads me.'

Robert Young, the 'Para', had been following his own nose ever since he could remember. His father had been on the bridge at Arnhem with the second Parachute Battalion, one of the handful of surviving officers. After repatriation from the German Offlag in 1945, he had been downgraded and offered a permanent commission in the Pioneer Corps. He had turned down the offer indignantly and become a civilian, doing all sorts of odd jobs in his native Yorkshire until just before Suez, he had been recalled as a reservist. He had been shot by an Egyptian sniper two hours after the official ceasefire. Later the Para realised that his father would have felt himself well dead; he would not have liked to have seen what happened to the country after the Suez debacle.

In that year – 1956 – he had been ten, but he had already known what he had wanted to become – a parachutist like his father. Indeed his obsession about parachuting and everything connected with it had already gained him the nickname of 'the Para' among his school friends long before he volunteered for his father's old battalion at the age of seventeen.

Five years later, commissioned and on his battalion's first tour of duty in Northern Ireland, he had been shaken by the politicos' inability to allow their soldiers do what they had been trained to do – go in and win. At the end of his tour he had applied for a transfer to the SAS serving one of the Trucial State emirs in their usual clandestine role. For the next eighteen months he served in the desert, and under the harsh, burning-white sun, he had discovered a new type of soldiering and a new type of soldier. Loners like himself, who preferred to follow their own star, but who were politically aware and knew that they had been betrayed back home.

The wogs thought naturally that they had bought the handful of SAS officers and NCOs with the gold they paid the Foreign Office for their services. But they were mistaken. The desert operations were just a realistic exercise for the real battle to come. The wogs and their country did not matter; it was England that mattered! Night after night, stretched out in their blankets around the camp fire under the velvet and silver desert sky, they discussed what was wrong and what should be done.

All of them knew now that they had been betrayed of their birthright, born into a fourth-rate country which only a mere quarter of a century before had dominated a third of the world; and all of them knew there were many more young men like themselves throughout the Army who were contemptuous of the new England and disillusioned with the leaders of both parties. But they knew too that they – and the many others – could not afford to make the same mistakes as the disillusioned young men of the French OAS in the fifties. The volatile enthusiasm and senseless violence of the French rebels in North Africa and France were purposeless. The key to the success of any operation designed to change the structure of the country they both loved and hated, was persistent and progressive infiltration into its political, military and intelligence administration. Once established there, they would be in a position to change that structure to their own advantage. Back in England, the Brigadier they had all come to regard as the only man capable of running such an operation had told him that this was a low intensity operation. 'When violence comes, it must be short, sharp and entirely successful,' he was fond of preaching to their group of young officers. 'The time for violence has not come yet. We shall allow the gentlemen in Westminster to play their game for a while longer. But be prepared to act – the day of reckoning is not as far away as many of you might think!'

Encouraged by the Brigadier he had resigned his commission and joined MI5. His work with Counter-Intelligence had been an eye-opener. MPs of all parties bought, blackmailed, bribed by the enemy in the East. Corruption, cynicism, downright crime from the top to the bottom of the political structure in Westminster. Known Soviet agents welcome guests in the houses of ministers, trade union officials, top civil servants; seducing their wives, bribing their children, making a mockery of their loyalty to the state. As Kosak, the tubby little Labour Attaché who had defected from the Czech Embassy, had told him at the beginning of his career with MI5: 'Here is the new Balkans Para.'

140

Kosak had been right. England *was* the new Balkans, occupied by a bewildered, apathetic people, completely betrayed – unknown to them – by their so-called leaders. In the last couple of years with MI5, the Para had learned to operate like a member of those highly successful and highly dangerous secret societies which had run the Balkans in the nineteenth century. The bribe, blackmail, the judicious threat had become his standard operating procedure, one which usually produced swift results among those people in London, who had come to accept such things as part-and-parcel of daily political life.

The Para knew he had all those attributes – and more. But in this particular case it was not a matter of muscle. He might 'lean' on someone, as he had just promised his fool of a chief, a little later. First of all he had to have a start. His face was creased in a frown as he walked slowly along the embankment, apparently unaware of the cold rain, pondering the problem of where to make a start. At last he quickened his pace, found the nearest telephone box and called a number in Bloomsbury not far from London University.

She answered almost at once. 'Hello comrade,' he said, 'how's the glorious revolution making out this wet February afternoon?'

Molly said something unpleasant about his sexual relationship with his long dead mother.

'Listen Molly, I've got a job for you again. What's the situation with you and Aziz Yafi?'

'That creep!' Molly exclaimed in her harsh Ulster accent. 'I get the heaves as soon as he lays his dirty wog paws on me.'

'But does he still fancy you?'

'Does he! Just mention the word "bed" and he's limping as if he's suddenly got a wooden leg.'

The Para laughed. Despite what Molly had gone through for the Service in Ireland and now at the University, where she was supposedly studying sociology, she had not lost her Irish sense of black humour. 'Good. As long as he's still got a hot body for you. Now listen, this is the big picture . . .'

There was an irritated rap on the glass. He turned round quickly. A dirty-overalled truck driver was knocking on it with a coin. The Para held up three fingers to indicate three minutes. The truck driver mouthed a surly retort and turned his back on the Para, who lowered his voice and completed his explanation. 'So you see what I'm up against, Molly. I've got to get a lead somewhere – and quick.'

Molly considered for a moment. The truck driver had turned towards the call-box again and was rapping impatiently on the glass. Swiftly the Para held up one finger – a moment more. The truck driver answered with a swift upward jerk of his two fingers spread out. The Para flushed angrily, but he concentrated on Molly's reply.

'All right. I'll be seeing the brown-skinned bastard at the International Activists Committee meeting at six tonight over at the LSE. I'll give him the come-hither look and let him take it from there.'

'Thanks Holly, I appreciate it,' he said hurriedly. The big truck driver was rattling at the door now.

'The things I do for England,' she said cynically.

5

Myers bent down carefully over the smooth outer casing of the counterweight. He knew exactly what he had to do to fake the mud balance so that it would give an inaccurate reading. Hell, he could even screw up the thing so that it would be like a manufacturing fault if that bastard Big Tex ever came to check up.

Outside it was a fine night for a change. The moon was a silver crescent, bathing the calm sea in its icy-blue light. On the horizon there was a stream of lights indicating the traffic in-and-out of the Humber. On the deck he could see Longbotham quite clearly, sitting by the draw-works console, feeding off the brake by hand. In the harsh yellow light of the arcs, the square steel pipe of the kelly, turning above the rotary table, glinted metallicly, as the drill forced its way deeper and deeper through the high-pressure gas zone. All clear.

Myers sucked at his bad front-teeth and pulled a face at the taste, promising himself as he had done often enough in these last few months that he would get them fixed soon. He looked down at the counterweight of the mud balance, consisting of a graduated bar with a circular cup at one end, a moving rider and, at the other end, a counterweight. It would be so simple. As he had told Harehill, 'I could bugger that thing up so good that you'd have time to unionise even that sod Big Tex himself!'

Still he hesitated. If things went wrong, what then? He'd heard from the other sodding Yanks on the other shifts that high-pressure gas was tricky. Once it got out of control, you couldn't predict what might happen next. In the Gulf, according to Little Tex, they had lost more than one rig through it. Still, he knew that both the firm's Sikorsky choppers were on the rig that night. If things did go wrong and they had to make a quick evacuation of the *Pride*, the choppers could lift them off to Brid. This wouldn't be another 'Sea Gem' – that was for sure.

Still he hesitated. Myers, the 'muscleman', as the rest of the shift nicknamed him contemptuously because of the half a dozen 'male' mags to which he subscribed weekly, was no hero. His motivation for attempting to wreck the *Pride's* hope of ever striking oil was nothing so dramatic. Myers acted because of envy and hate: hatred of those who 'thought themselves better than us' and 'talked pound-notish'. All his life, ever since he had left his miserable nineteenth century secondary modern in the slum area of East Hull, he had hated 'them', that vaguely defined class of people who didn't drive 'old bangers' like the people in the street in which he lived, who weren't always having kids like them, who didn't rely on some anonymous government office to 'tide us over' when the jobs, the money, the food, the clothing ran out, as they invariably did.

Myers was, in short, a product of a post-war England, divided into 'them' and 'us', in which the Myers and the many thousands like him were motivated by one sole socio-political principle: *'the fancy buggers up there never give us nowt; why should we do out for them? Sod 'em!'*

Still undecided, he left the little shed and climbed the ladder to look inside the mud tank. The dun-looking liquid swirled round gently with a soft sucking sound. He looked through the inspection window at the great horizontal plunger-piston, shooting back and forth, driving the mud through the entire system and down into the well hole.

When he was up there with Longbotham, the big bastard would always mock Myers' problem with the girls by singing: 'And the maiden cried: "enough, enough, I'm satisfied", but the prick of steel went on and on.' Then he would break off, point to the gleaming,

144

well-oiled piston and nudge him meaningfully. 'Why don't you get one like that, Myers – then you'd be all right!'

Myers hurried down the ladder back into the shed. For one moment he studied the balance. Then he set about fixing the calibration so that it would give the wrong weight of mud. By the time someone had tumbled to what was wrong, there would be a blow-out or a major breakdown. Then it would be curtains with the *Pride* and he'd be back in Hull, sitting around his mother's grate, toasting his feet on full pay, waiting for Britoil to find him a new job – and if they couldn't, there was always the Exchange. Within a matter of minutes it was all done and he was slinking back to the crew's quarters.

It was Longbotham who spotted the gas first, just as Big Tex was coming up with the new shift. For a moment or two he stood on the wet deck, sniffing the air curiously. There was no smell, but there was a strange boiling sound, as if somewhere someone were heating a kettle of water on an old fashioned gas ring. Then he saw it. A series of huge bubbles exploding on the surface of the silver sea some two hundred yards away, as if a sub were trapped below it and the compressed air were escaping. Suddenly a plume of white water shot twenty or thirty feet into the night air.

'Tex,' he called urgently. 'Come over here!'

The American doubled across the deck clumsily in his gumboots. 'What is?'

'Over there. Them bubbles—'

Big Tex did not give him a chance to finish. 'Oh, sweet shit – *gas*!'

He doubled back the way he had come, grabbing the loud hailer that was attached to the console. 'Hear this,' he yelled, his voice booming metallicly throughout the rig. 'We've got a gas leak about two hundred yards from the *Pride*. God knows how – but we're stuck with it. Now I want all lights reduced to a minimum. You in the galley, put out the ovens. Break out cold rations for anybody who wants chow. And everybody get this – no goddam smoking, understood?'

He dropped the loud-hailer and hurried back to the side of the rig. The silver water was frothing white, as if it were being beaten with a gigantic whisk. Jacko, the radioman, who had come out of his shack as soon as he had heard the warning, ready to transmit any message that the big American might wish to have passed on to the shore station at Bridlington, looked at his grim face.

'What do you think, Tex?'

'Somehow or other gas has started escaping through the cement of the surface pipe.' Tex shrugged. 'Perhaps we didn't give the cement time to set properly. It happens. Now it's found a natural geological fault in the surface sand and opened up a crater.'

Jacko nodded impatiently and looked at the boiling sea. 'I know all that Tex. But that's one hell of an unlit gas jet out there. What happens if it flames?'

The big American looked down at the radio operator's pale anxious face. 'Just pray that it won't, Jacko. We're gonna go on drilling, come what may. Be a good guy now and get on that fancy blower of yours. Tell the Colonel what has happened. And say Jacko, don't make it too dramatic for the old guy, willya? Break it gentle.'

DAY FIVE: FRIDAY

'My experience is that the gentlemen who are the best behaved and the most sleek are those who are doing the mischief. We cannot be too sure of anybody!'

Field Marshal Ironside, Chief of the Imperial General Staff, Summer 1940.

1

'*Guten Morgen, meine Damen und Herren! Es ist sechs uhr dreissig. Das Frühstück wird jetzt in der Cafeteria serviert*', the coarse Dutch female voice recorded in the tape in the purser's office repeated the message in Dutch, French and English. 'It is six thirty. Breakfast is now being served in the cafeteria.'

Obediently the Palestinian allowed himself to be swept inside by the crowd of passengers. Wrinkling his nose at the smell of the forbidden meat, he pushed by the line of servicemen from the BAOR, Dutch businessmen and pale-faced uncombed service wives with their hordes of fat children waiting for bacon and egg, and took a plate of cereal. Hunched over it, hardly aware of what he was eating, he stared out at the heaving green sea, dull and uninviting in the first dirty white light of the false dawn. He had spent the previous evening in the crowded 'snug bar', full of noisy soldiers and civilians, getting drunk on the duty-free gin and Amstel beer. At about ten he had found an empty berth in one of the four-man cabins below on G-deck. When the other occupants had turned in an hour later he had pretended sleep so that he would not have to answer their questions. At five he had risen, stolen a razor from one of his snoring companions and left to complete his toilet in the shower room. Now he was clean-shaven, fresh and relatively well rested, his mind already fully occupied with the pressing problem of how he should get off the *Norwave*.

He knew from talks with his comrades and his own early days as a student in London that the rainy, degenerate island was not an easy place to enter. The British officials wore civilian clothes and were superficially polite, with their eternal 'sir' at the end of every question; yet their eyes were always hard and suspicious, as if they mistrusted anyone who was not fortunate enough to possess one of their own blue and gold passports.

He would have to avoid all official checks until he took the bus from the docks to Hull's Paragon Street Station, a ticket for which he had obtained already from the Purser's Office the previous evening. He guessed that – as was usually the case with provincial ports – the immigration and customs officials would only turn out when a ship docked. If he could get off before the bulk of the passengers started disembarking, he would be through them before they were properly organised. The problem was – how to do just that?

'Them seats free?' a coarse female voice cut into his thoughts.

A pretty but slovenly Englishwoman, made up about the eyes like a Cairo whore, stood there, accompanied by two equally slovenly children, plates of greasy bacon and bread in their dirty hands. He nodded. The Englishwoman took another cigarette from the pack in her hand and lit it from the one already between her scarlet lips, mumbling to the children at the same time, 'All right, yer little bastards, sit down, eat yer grub and keep yer traps shut.' The woman looked out at the rain-soaked horizon and grunted: 'Sodding England! Always raining when we get ter Hull. Bloody miserable place. Don't know why anybody would want to come here.'

The Palestinian nodded. One of the kids was dipping his bacon experimentally in the raspberry jam. 'Stop that, yer little bastard – you're not at home now, yer know,' said the woman without rancour.

The kid continued to dip his bacon in the jam, allowing it to dribble in red lines across the littered table.

'If yer don't stop that lark, Christopher,' the woman said, 'I'll tell the captain there and he'll have yer off and in the sodding nick before yer can say Jacob Rubenstein! . . . Him in the fancy uniform.'

Involuntarily the Palestinian's eyes followed the direction of her gaze. The chief steward was standing at the door, directing the activities of his underlings. As the kid dropped the half eaten piece of bacon in the jam pot and began to cry, the Palestinian knew suddenly that he had it. A uniform – or at least part of it – would get him off the *Norwave*.

He rose and nodded to the woman. 'I know,' she said. 'You don't have to tell me, mate. They make me puke sometimes too.' As he was leaving the other kid was starting to stir his tea with a dirty forefinger, allowing sugar from the sugar container to fall into the liquid like an avalanche of snow.

The Palestinian pushed his way through the throng outside the duty-free store. He opened the door to the outside and clambering up the wet dripping ladder, staggered along the swaying deck till he came to a chain bearing the legend 'Officers Only', which barred all further progress. He looked about. No one, save a fat black cook emptying a case of trash in the face of the attacks of a flight of screaming gulls. Swiftly he swung his leg over the chain and went on.

He peered in at the first porthole. A bearded officer was sitting at a desk, writing something and drinking coffee with his free hand. No go. He went on. The blinds were drawn at the next porthole. He guessed someone was sleeping inside. The third porthole. No one. His dark eyes swept the little cabin. A crucifix. Two centre spreads of naked girls from the *Playboy*. A half empty bottle of Vat 69. Then he spotted what he was looking for – an officer's dark blue merchant navy raincoat and a white officer's cap. He hesitated no longer. A moment later he was back outside again, the coat and cap stuffed beneath his own raincoat. Just in time.

A steward, carrying a pot of slops in his big black hand, was coming down the gangway towards him. With his free hand he pointed to the notice and said, 'You're not supposed to be here.'

151

'No speak English,' the Palestinian mumbled, pushing by him.

'Fucking foreigner,' the black steward said and flung the pot of first class passengers' vomit at the gulls.

Thirty minutes later the *Norwave* was through the lock and entering Hull's King George Dock. The loud-speakers were already beginning to blare out their orders. The duty-free stores were locked and sealed once more. In the toilet, the Palestinian waited tensely, listening to someone still retching violently in the next evil-smelling cubicle. The message started to come through. 'Will all car drivers and their passengers report to the car decks. Foot passengers please remain where they are. There are porters available to take any heavy luggage—'

Emerging from the toilet he flung a last glance at himself in the mirrors. In the raincoat and cap, its golden anchor badge removed, he would pass for a ferry porter, at least to her uninformed eye. He went out and spotted her sitting exactly where she had been twenty minutes earlier: a fat overdressed German woman, mouth full of gold teeth, her thick beringed fingers nervously clutching her case.

He pushed his way through the confusion which he had anticipated and welcomed. 'Can I take your case now, madam?' he asked bending low so that nobody nearby could hear his un-English accent.

'*Wie bitte?*' the fat woman asked, as he relieved her of her heavy overnight bag, bought like her pompous green trouser suit in some local provincial *Kaufhof*.

'*Ihr Gepäck,*' he answered, swiching straight away into German.

'*Ach so – sehr liebenswürdig.*' She gave him the full impact of her gold-toothed smile.

He disappeared into the throng before she had a chance to attach herself to him and pushed his way down to the gloomy, yellow-lit car deck. An officer, directing the unloading, walkie-talkie in gloved hand, threw him

152

an incurious glance, but said nothing. Then he was outside in the raw, bitter northern rain. A couple of white-capped customs men were sheltering in the entrance to the customs shed, smoking, with their cigarettes hidden in cupped palms. He walked towards them confidently.

'Are they coming off, now, Charlie?' one of them asked as he passed.

He nodded and jerked a thumb over his shoulder as the first car started to emerge from the ship's bowels.

The customs men stubbed out their cigarettes on the wet concrete. 'Eyes down, look in, let's shake the bag,' said the bigger of the two.

The other laughed. 'Yer'll never hit the bloody bleeding jackpot in Hull, Tom – that's for sure.'

The Palestinian passed between the two glass boxes which housed the immigration officials already fingering their Intelligence Corps ties, want-lists at the ready. They did not even notice him. He dropped the case with the rest already piled up on one of the long tables, in front of a bespectacled customs man. 'Piss – bursting for a piss,' he gasped, grabbing at his flies to emphasise his need.

The customs man grunted something and the Palestinian hurried on purposefully, as if he knew his way. When he saw the sign 'Gentlemen,' he flung open the door, went into one of the cubicles and bundled the stolen coat and cap up quickly. Stuffing the bundle into the water tank, he drew on his own coat and smoothed his dark hair with his fingers. Moments later he was in the bus taking the foot passengers to Hull station, his face buried in a copy of the previous day's *Hull Daily Mail* which he had found on the seat, his hand holding up his ticket for the conductor. He was through.

'For the sweet Mother of Christ's sake, gimme that sodding coffee,' Molly gasped and seized the coffee cup from the Para's hand. 'What a night. *Wogs*!'

The Para sat down beside her in the scruffy little

coffee bar near the University. The Irish girl's face was pale and there were deep circles under her light blue intelligent eyes. For a while he let her sip her coffee. At the counter the unshaven little Greek homo who ran the place dropped his *Daily Mirror* with its headline 'Million Unemployed Forecast by End of Year', and turned the ancient tape. Once again Melanie wondered what they had done to her song.

'Well?' he asked cautiously.

She put down her cup and looked across at him. 'By the time we got to talking and not screwing, he was beginning to get as pissed as a sodding newt. I wasn't feeling too hot by then myself. You wouldn't have either, I can tell you, with him sticking it into yer – in and out like a sodding fiddler's elbow.' She lit one of the cigarettes and breathed out a stream of perfumed smoke. 'Hot shit, I could go a nice cool beer instead of this warmed-up pee that queer calls coffee!'

'What did you find out Molly?' he persisted.

'Not much really, though I did play the wog bastard along the best I could. That's why I think the thing's big. You know how they usually like to shoot off their mouths and make themselves important. But my wog was well buttoned up this time until he'd had his belly full of nookie and was starting to feel his kali. But this is for sure, it's a big op this time. They've got one of their best operators on his way – a really tough baby, according to my wog – and he's got a big one—'

She laughed at the look on the Para's face. 'Not what you think, you nasty-minded English bastard! A big op, I meant. Why the hell have you got to think so goddam phallic?'

'Pure as driven slush,' he said, telling himself that he would have to go to bed with Molly soon, if she weren't to crack up altogether; she needed the reassurance of being screwed by someone whom she thought liked her. 'Get on with it, you Irish rose.'

'Well, I wanted to get something more specific out of

him naturally. But I didn't dare. I didn't know whether he was really that pissed. So I just did my usual bit – the little question and the big ear – and hoped for the best.'

'Did you get anything on the bloke they're sending?'

She shook her head. 'Nix for negative. My wog didn't even know his name. All he knew was that he was one of the Doctor's intimates – if you'll forgive the expression? A real big wheel in their organisation. He was the guy behind the Nip business and he had something to do with the Munich Olympics affair too. Only he didn't get nabbed. A great hairy-assed hard case, if you could believe my wog.'

'And the target, Molly? Where's the hit to be made?'

She shrugged and her braless breasts moved interestingly beneath her transparent blouse. 'Search me.'

'It would be fun,' the Para said routinely because he knew Molly expected it from him. 'But get on with it, Irish rose. Surely you got something out of him. With all that Irish charm of yours?'

'Just one thing, Para. The *comrades*,' she sneered at the word, 'in the north would be looking after him when he arrived here. Nobody down here in the smoke would be involved in other words.'

The Para nodded. 'My guess was right then, Molly. The hit's going to be made in the provinces then, not in London.' He wrinkled his low brow. 'But where?'

'Don't ask me?'

'No, I won't Molly. I think it's time I did a bit of leaning on your wog.' He reached out a big hand and placed it over hers. 'You're a good girl, Molly.'

She laughed bitterly. 'That's the best joke of the sodding year!'

2

As the helicoptor touched down on the swaying platform, the Colonel could see the gas escaping; the sea was boiling angrily, as if a vast whale were sending up its jets just below the surface. As the pilot switched off his motors, Big Tex hurried towards the Sikorski, head bent against the wind that tore at his yellow oilskins. 'Welcome aboard, Colonel.' He affected surprise, 'Say – where's the Derby hat? I thought all you London gents had Derby hats, went to bed in them in fact?'

The Colonel grinned. 'Good to see you again, Tex,' he said, as they hurried away from the whirling blades. 'Good to see you're not letting it get you down.' He made a vague gesture towards the boiling water.

'It only hurts when I laugh,' returned the American.

Together they went towards the side of the rig facing the escaping gas. 'My God, Tex,' exclaimed the Colonel, 'have you been operating all night with that witch's cauldron bubbling away out there?'

'Yeah.'

'But if that stuff ign—'

'Ignites? I know. Colonel. That's what everybody and his goddam brother has been telling me for the last twelve hours. Listen, Colonel, I've done this one time before – in the Gulf. The trick is to keep every light to a minimum. No smoking below or above decks even if the Joes squawk till the pips start popping. Galley out. Cold chow only. Only the recognition and working arcs on above the deck. Constant checks on the electrical gear by the electricians. It can be done if you're lucky—'

A hundred yards away, the escaping gas belched obscenely and vomited a thick jet of water into the grey morning sky.

The Colonel licked suddenly dry lips. 'That was close.'

'They tell me you can drown in a puddle of water in Brid's main street if you're unlucky,' Tex said drily.

'Have you checked the mud balance? We have our leak, I know. But we don't want to compound the damage by drilling off.'

'Yeah, I checked it, Colonel. Funny thing, it was off.' The American shrugged carelessly. 'Can't understand it. I had my best guy on it – Harrison. He's been around since Rockefeller struck kerosene in 1859. He couldn't have slipped up.'

'A technical slip?'

'Perhaps.' Big Tex was guarded. 'Remember the lemon we've got on board, Colonel?'

'But you can't mean it?' he asked appalled.

'In the oil game, Colonel, anything goes. But I can tell you this, if I catch the goddam lemon – he'll be swimming back to Brid, with lead weights fixed to his crappy feet.'

The escaping gas belched once more and Big Tex swung round to look at it. 'Okay, Colonel, this is the deal, I'm going to go on operating for a while longer – as long as those jets don't get any worse. If they do, then I'll kill the gas.'

'You mean pump in gel?' The Colonel knew the process from his own early days in the field. A slanting hole would be drilled into the upper porous horizon and gel, bentonite, a grey powder, would be used to make heavy mud, which, with luck, might kill the gas hole.

Big Tex nodded. 'But you know what that means?'

'The end of our own drilling for oil?'

'Right in one, Colonel.' He looked significantly at the Englishman. 'And if we do that, well, I guess the strike you've been waiting for will be out – and everything that goes with it.'

The Colonel stroked his trim grey moustache carefully. 'I'm afraid that one must take that possibility into account,' he said, as they turned and started to walk back

157

to the office. 'But then the men's safety comes first, doesn't it, Tex?'

The big American paused and shook his head in bewilderment. '*The men's safety comes first!*' he echoed. 'Jesus H, Colonel, I'll never figure you limeys out, if I get to live to be a goddam hundred years old! Come on, let me get you a warm Coke.'

Myers chewed the stale bread and cheese sandwich with distaste and stared at Longbotham across the littered mess table. 'Bloody awful rotten nosh, Longie,' he ventured.

'Eh?' Longbotham raised his eyes from the air-dried dyed pubic hair – he referred to it as 'public 'air' – of one of the *Mayfair* nudes.

'I said, awful rotten nosh,' Myers repeated patiently.

'Ay. But yon galley is out,' Longbotham explained. 'On account of the gas.'

'I sodding well know that, Longie! But I mean how can a bloke do a proper day's work on grub like this?'

'You and a proper day's work,' sneered a driller at the other end of the table. 'All you need yer nosh for is going into the shitehouse and paying the one-armed widow a bloody visit.' He gave an explicit demonstration of what he imagined the cock-eyed Myers did in the latrine.

Myers flushed. 'It ain't like that at all, Bernie, you dirty-minded sod,' he protested. 'It's me bleeding piles. I've got to treat them every two hours regular with the ointment the MO gave me.'

'Ay,' said the driller, winking at the others. 'I'm daft as a brush, tha' can tell me out. I didn't even know that lasses was different from lads till I got me periods when I was seven.'

The rest of Myers' shift laughed dutifully at the old jokes.

'Go on, laugh yer sodding heads off,' Myers retorted angrily. 'But you bastards'll be laughing on the other side of your faces when this bugger really goes up.'

Longbotham withdrew his gaze from the naked blonde who was admiring the precious thing she had between her white legs in a gilt mirror. 'What was that, mate?'

'You heard! Or have yer got wax in yer lugs?'

'You'll have a thick fist in your lug, Myers, if you give me that kind of lip,' Longbotham said.

'Well, it stands to reason,' Myers answered, pulling himself together. He knew Longbotham's temper. 'It only takes some stupid bastard to light a fag in the bogs or one of them pansy cooks to make himself a fly cup of char and then we'd all be up the creek without a paddle.' He brought his hand down on the littered table hard. 'It'd be the big chop.'

Longbotham's mouth dropped open, 'Go on, Muscleman. Big Tex wouldn't let that happen. You're pulling my pisser, arent yer?'

Myers sensed abruptly that he had caught their interest, 'Pulling yer pissers!' he stared round at the rest of them significantly. 'Why should I, mates? I'm one of you lot. But Big Tex' – he shrugged – 'he's a boss-man, ain't he? He's not gonna tell us nothing what's gonna affect his bonus, is he? We can stick our sodding necks out all right so that he can fill his pockets at our expense. I mean, it stands to reason, don't it? What do we mean to him? We're English. He's a Yank. If somat goes wrong, who's gonna hold him responsible? Remember that Yank who screwed them fourteen-year-old twins in Great Yarmouth? The bosses got him out of the country right smartish, didn't they. Social Security's paying for the little bastards now.'

'All right, four-eyes,' the driller interrupted. 'Don't give us a sodding lecture. What yer trying to get at?'

Myers turned on him. 'You want it short, sharp and not very sweet, mate? Okay, I'll tell yer. We've got one chopper on the *Pride* at the moment. If owt happens, who do you think is gonna to be in them two extra seats there is in the chopper? Not me and you – that's

159

for sure. It'd be the General, old tashie, and the Big Tex. And what about us lot?' He looked along the length of the mess table. 'Them of us what survived the flame-out would be starting on a long bloody swim to Hull. Think of that, mates.'

The others stared at each other in shocked silence. There was no sound now save the creak of the drill and the soft insistent plop-plop of the escaping gas.

'And what exactly do you think we should do, four-eyes?'

'Do?' Myers shrugged easily. 'What the shitting hell can we do, lads – we can make the sods stop operating *now*! ...'

3

The Para was puzzled. The nig-nog op was too well advertised, it seemed. As he drove his Mini to the pre-luncheon appointment with his boss, he attempted to interpret the situation. The terrorist had blazed a trail through Western Europe a mile wide ever since he had landed at Frankfurt-Main. Now even the LSE's parlour-pinks and their English middle-class hangers-on knew he was on his way – if he hadn't arrived already? What was the deal? Why was a professional like that – if Molly was right – carrying out the op in such a damn amateur-ish way? What were the Russians up to – and it was certain that they were behind the whole business?

He parked by the Chief's ancient silver-painted Rolls, a give-way to every Eastern intelligence service in London, and went through the usual absurd control procedure (hell, even the ancient defectors of poor old stuttering Philby's day had known about it) before he was escorted in to his office.

'Sir,' he said, without preamble, 'you can see what's going on.'

'*Can I?*' the Chief gave him the full broadside of Eton, Balliol, the Life Guards, White's, the SOE, the George Cross and all the rest of the crap.

'Yes sir,' he answered, his Yorkshire accent more noticeable than usual. 'The wogs are playing their little game and the Russians are playing theirs.'

'What are the two games?'

'You remember the ploy in Sweden a couple of months ago which really screwed them up?'

The Chief frowned. The Para was always pulling nasty tricks like that. How the hell was one expected to read everything? 'I'm afraid I don't.'

'Well after the Czech Major Robek defected to the

Swedes in Stockholm, the Russians leaked a nice old story about IB* agents carrying out ops for the Israelis and South Vietnam. The left-wing weekly *Folket i Bild-Kulturfront* picked the story up and published. The SAPO† nicked the authors and the balloon went up. The Swedish commies in their parliament demanded and got an inquiry. The result? A reorganisation of the Swedish service which means their intelligence has been effectively 'Finlandised'‡ and no one even had time to bother about old Robek. That's the way they operate – the Russians. They are trying to make us believe that they are out to achieve objective A. In fact they are trying for objective B. It's the way their minds work.'

'Oh for Christ's sake, Para, come off it. Don't you start pretending to be the great interpreter of the Russian soul. If you knew how many of that kind I've had in this office in these last six years!'

'All right, this is the way I see it. They're out to discredit the Doctor's organisation to which our man belongs. That for a start.'

'But surely they wouldn't go to all that trouble to discredit the Doctor's organisation?' the Chief protested.

'No, I agree there, sir,' the Para answered earnestly, still bewildered himself. 'That's only part of it. But what the rest is I don't know. One thing is for sure, our man is meant to be caught, the trail he's left behind him shows that, don't you think sir?'

The Chief nodded. 'So?'

'So, our man is a fall guy.'

'A what?' the Chief asked, although he knew full well what the Americanism meant.

'A fall guy? A victim, sir. Our man is meant to be a victim.'

The Para picked Aziz up as he came out of his four

*Counter-Intelligence.
†Swedish National Security Police.
‡Placed under Russian control.

o'clock lecture. It was easy. The bitter winter rain was falling again and the crowd of students hurrying for their buses back to their digs had no time to notice the short-haired burly young man who grabbed Aziz's arm and said something which made the swarthy Palestinian's face pale suddenly. A minute later when the other two, who always watched Aziz, came out, briefcases heavy with books, notes and Walther Police Specials, the London representative of the Doctor's organisation had vanished.

The Para didn't waste words. All that CIA interrogation-crap, drawn up by the Yid professors of psychology from Harvard and Georgetown, was not for him. He preferred the standard British Army approach, at least as it was practised by the Paras. A good belting straight off until the suspect started to wet his knickers; then the questions.

He worked with a will on the student, punching him back and forth across the dark cellar, ignoring the Arab's screams of pain, telling himself every time his big fist jarred into the other man's guts or smashed into his big hooked nose, that he was doing it partly for Molly. Then he'd had enough, and let the bruised and bleeding Aziz sink to the dirty flags for a moment.

Wiping the blood off his bruised knuckles on the student's shoulder, he grabbed him by the hair and jerked his head up brutally. 'All right, you greasy nig-nog,' he barked, 'I'm going to ask you a simple question and I want a simple answer – where's your tame killer heading for when he comes here.'

'Please, I don't know what—'

The Para slashed his free hand across the other man's face, still holding him by his dark long hair.

The Para contained his breathing. 'I told you I wanted an answer. If I don't get it, you'll be leaving this cellar feet first, believe you me.' He hit him again – lightly – to emphasise his point. 'All right,' he jerked the other man's hair, 'Let's be having it, smartish!'

163

The Para did not like brutality. He knew of course that the British had no special claim on decency, but most of them had been brought up to abhor physical brutality. It was something that they would have to learn, if they were going to survive what was to happen to them in the next few years. As the Brigadier was fond of saying after he had allowed himself a couple more whiskies than was his norm and he took to philosophizing: 'We are standing, chaps, in the dusk of our long history and there is no place here for a conscience.' And of course, brutality worked. It always did, in spite of what the books he had read as a boy said about heroism under torture. Everyone had his breaking point as long as sufficient brutality was applied.

Aziz hesitated. The Para doubled his big fist threateningly. Aziz Yafi started to sing like a sweet little bird. It wasn't much, but it was enough. Their man would not be run by the Russians or any of the other Eastern Embassies during his time in the UK. The Doctor's own organisation would take care of him, using their student groups spread all over the country. The Para nodded as the words poured from the student's split lips. It made sense. When the op was blown, as the Russians obviously intended it should, they would not be linked with it. The wogs would carry the can back all on their own little lonesomes.

'But which group is going to hide him when he arrives?' he asked.

The student shook his head, which was an unfortunate thing to do as the Para was still gripping his hair. 'I don't . . . don't know,' he cried through gritted teeth.

'Come on, don't give me that shit,' the Para urged. 'Where – in the north perhaps?'

'Yes, yes, the north.'

'And what part – what university town? Leeds, Hull, York, Bradford?'

The student looked up at him desperately. 'Honest, I don't know . . . I don't!'

The Para thought for a moment. Then he released his grip on the other man's hair. 'All right, I'll believe you. Get up on your feet – and wipe that muck off your face.'

The student rose and began cleaning his face with his handkerchief, while the Para watched him cautiously. 'All right, you're beautiful enough now,' he snapped after a couple of minutes. 'Now listen, I'm going to take you outside to my car. It's parked behind here. I want you to walk with me to it and not make any fuss.'

'But where are you taking me?'

'You'll find out in due course. But don't cream yer knickers. Nothing'll happen to you there,' the Para answered and thought that the only person who would cream his knickers would be the Chief when he was faced with the legal problem of having Aziz locked up without any valid reason. 'All I want you to do is to walk next to me, nice and quiet, as if you are a real human being and not something that has just come down from the trees. Get it?' The Para unlocked the door of the cellar and beckoned to the student. 'All right, Ali Baba, let's go.'

But Aziz still had a little fight left in him. As the Para fumbled with the lock of his Mini, blocked by the freezing rain, he suddenly turned and tried to make a run for it. The Para cast a quick look up the back street. It was black and empty with the rain. He didn't waste another second. Bursting into that spectacular gallop which had made him the pride of the Para Brigade's rugby eleven, he overtook the student. His big fist fell on Aziz's shoulder. In the same instant, he whirled him round and rammed his knee into the student's crotch. The Palestinian screamed and went down on his knees, the vomit bursting from between his clenched teeth, his hands groping blindly for his injured genitals. The Para grabbed him and hauling him to his feet, dragged the moaning student towards the little car, telling himself that the wog wouldn't be sticking it into Molly or any other woman for a goodly while to come.

165

For the first time in the last five days, the Palestinian relaxed. As the bells rang from the big church which overshadowed their dingy flat, he gazed around their eager faces, staring at him in expectant admiration, and felt happy to be with his own people once again. After the failures and betrayals of the last five days, it was good not to have to be on one's guard. With them he was safe.

In the fashion of the camps in which they had all been brought up, rich and poor alike, before they had joined the Doctor's movement, they chatted easily about mutual acquaintances, the girls they knew in common, the bewilderment their fathers felt at the way things were going among the young.

The Palestinian waited till the bells from the ancient grey church, now disappearing in the wet February dusk, had ended, then he said: 'Comrades, I won't waste any more time. Let me explain why the Doctor has sent me here.'

They settled more comfortably in the rickety chairs of the hired student flat.

'As you know the Jews are becoming an almost unbearable burden to the West. Since we have finally discovered the power our oil gives us, every one of their criminal acts makes them more and more of a nuisance to the bourgeois western societies. It is the Doctor's opinion that every western government regrets the day Israel was born and that its days are truly numbered. Even that Israeli agent Kissinger cannot hide that fact. Now it is only a matter of time before the West agrees to end the life of that bastard state and gives us our homeland back once more. But for the sake of those fathers of ours and all like them, we must hurry that process along. We must force the public here, in particular, the Anglo-American one, to be aware constantly of our presence, our cause, our rights. We must always be in their headlines – day after day – until we can finally return to Palestine. Then they shall hear no more of us and we can turn to other things.' His hard dark eyes swept their faces to check whether they had understood the importance of the Doctor's preoccupation with the headlines. Their gleaming eyes told him they had.

'But like any other publicity campaign we must always find new means to bring our cause to their attention – an international sports meeting, the kidnapping or assassination of one of their important men, an attack on a major airport. That is why the Doctor has chosen our new objective with such great care and forethought.' He lowered his voice deliberately. 'What hope has this old decadent nation – the British – of getting out of the mess it finds itself in? None really, but its leaders have led them to believe there is still hope for them. With their usual cynical manipulation of public opinion, they have held out the belief in a fresh Dunkirk to their people – a fresh escape. And what is that escape? North Sea oil – the cure for all their economic ills.'

Outside, an ancient newspaper seller was crying the headlines of the local paper as he passed towards his pitch. 'All out tonight at power stations . . . Unions call out railways in sympathy . . . Others might follow . . . Read it all in the Press . . . Read it all in the Press . . .' His voice died away as he turned the corner. The Palestinian nodded at the long-haired student they called George and he rose to draw the threadbare flowered curtains. But when he clicked down the light switch, nothing happened.

'What's the matter?' the Palestinian asked puzzled.

George grinned and took a candle stuck in a beer bottle from the sideboard. Placing it in the centre of the table, he lit it, saying. 'Nothing new here. Just another strike. Happens all the time.' He shrugged. 'The English disease.'

'I see. Well, as I was saying – North Sea is to be the answer to everything, so the Doctor reasons we must take even that hope from them. We must strike at it and make it quite clear to the British that this new treasure

167

situated right on their own doorstep is just as vulnerable to our commandos as any Israeli frontier settlement.'

'You mean a rig?' George said quickly.

'Yes, a rig. The Russians just want a token blow made against one of them. They reason that such an action would show the American imperialists that the Kremlin is all-powerful. It would also exhibit to certain possessors of oil that they – the Russians – are prepared to give them support, if the North Sea stuff ever threatens to become a danger to the new power they now have. That is the Russians' intention – a token blow.' He paused and took a sip at the tea they had prepared for him. He wrinkled his nose in disgust; it was ice-cold.

'But that is not the Doctor's intention. Our cause is too close to success to waste time with token blows. A bomb scare, a token occupation of a rig – a one day sensation. *No*. Such things happen every minute these days all over the world where people are fighting for their freedom and their homelands. That is not what the Doctor wants. We want to achieve a blow that will destroy the hopes of this nation and reveal to them that there is no future for them – that they are finished, *passé, kaputt*.' He wet his lips and looked around their tense faces, hollowed out and hardened by the flickering light of the candle. 'The Doctor has ordered the destruction of the key rig, the one that they have really pinned their hopes on. It is our mission, comrades, to destroy *England's Pride*.'

4

'The bitch is blowing another crater, Tex!' Longbotham yelled and pointed at a spot some three hundred yards from the original gas-leak where the sea was frothing a dirty yellow. The Colonel and Big Tex turned, startled, holding on to their white hard hats against the bitter North Sea wind.

'Shit,' cursed Big Tex. 'Look at that, willya?'

The Colonel nodded grimly, his eyes narrowed against the wind. A jet was rising high into the air, spume flying off it like snow.

Longbotham cupped his big hands around his mouth and shouted: 'That's the second crater, Tex.'

'I'm not goddam blind,' the American answered angrily, not taking his eyes off the new eruption.

'And not stupid either,' the Colonel told himself. Even the ex-Yorkshire fishermen and dock workers who made up the *Pride*'s crew knew what this meant, although they were new to the industry. Sitting as they were on top of an oil field, they could expect another crater to blow right underneath at any moment; then the 20,000 ton structure could disappear as if it were some kid's meccano construction. They would be swimming for their lives in the North Sea even before the radio operator had time to flash the 'mayday' signal.

Harrison, one of Big Tex's best men, dropped a wrench. It echoed hollowly on the wet, mud-stained deck. Somehow it seemed to act as a signal. Another man dropped a piece of equipment. And another. At the console, Longbotham cut the engine.

Big Tex spun round and stared at them, his red-face wet with sea water. 'What the hell's going on? What did you kill that engine for, Longbotham, you big dummy?'

Longbotham did not answer but dropped his gaze like a schoolboy.

'So that's it,' Big Tex yelled. 'Now hear this, I've seen a gas hole blow before – plenty of them – and I'm still here to tell the story, so you don't have to cream yer skivvies like that.' Behind him the sea belched again and a column of thick yellow water shot into the air. Big Tex pretended not to notice. 'Do you know what happens when a gas hole blows? It caves – do you lugs hear – *it caves*! And what happens then? The crater kills itself and we're in the big time. We hit pay dirt and we're drilling for oil!'

Myers standing next to Longbotham spat scornfully. 'Who you trying to kid, mate? One of them craters could spew up right under our sodding arses and what then? We'd be right up the creek without a paddle!' He looked challengingly at the silent Colonel. 'The front office buggers'd be all right, of course. They've got the chopper to evacuate them. But what about the likes of us? Us poor buggers'd be left to give the sodding fish a free dinner.'

Myers wasn't liked by the rest of the crew. But since his outburst on the mess deck that morning, they had come to regard him as their spokesman; for he was stating openly what all of them felt and feared. There was a self-conscious murmur from them.

Big Tex opened his mouth to say something, then thought better of it. It was up to the Colonel; after all he was the boss. But Colonel Hammond's face reflected only his own hesitancy and bewilderment. It was not the face of the man who had hired Big Tex three long years before. Big Tex realised that the Colonel was thoroughly worn-out, exhausted, washed-up like those company commanders he remembered seeing coming out of the green hell of the Hurtgen blubbering like hysterical kids. Yet he knew that this was the Colonel's pigeon; he had to be given the chance of dealing with it.

'What exactly do you think the management should

do Mr – er, I'm afraid I don't know your name . . .' the Colonel said apologetically.

'Yeah, and how should your lot know my sodding name!' Myers snapped, sensing weakness and seizing on it like a hungry dog on a bone. 'Well, it's Myers – Alf Myers – for your information. And what do we want? I'll tell you that as well. We want off, don't we mates?' he turned eagerly to the others for their approval.

'Ay, that's it – we want off,' they responded in their flat East Yorkshire accents.

'Before the sod goes up under us and we're swimming back to Brid!'

'But Mr Myers, the Colonel said aghast, 'that would mean closing down the rig!'

Myers looked at him triumphantly. 'So – what do yer want me to do – cry?'

'But we're so close to success,' the Colonel stuttered. 'And a lot depends on the *Pride* striking oil. We're—'

'Yeah,' Myers interrupted him brutally, playing to the gallery now, 'I bet a lot depends on it. So that you lot up there in London with yer cut-glass accents and yer fancy women can rake in more fat dividends while poor buggers like us out here are sitting on a shitting time-bomb! That's what it's about, ain't it?'

'Not at all, Myers,' the Colonel retorted hotly.

Myers looked at him curiously. A thin flurry of sudden rain swept the swaying deck. The rest ducked instinctively. Not the Colonel. He stood there erect and silent, the raindrops trickling down his pale cheeks like cold tears.

'Well, come on.' Myers urged, 'out with it, man?'

Big Tex knew it was time he acted. 'All right, fellers,' he roared above the obscene noise of the second crater, 'I know you're scared that another gas hole might blow underneath the rig. Hell, I'm a bit scared myself. But it'll never happen, take it from me and I've been thirty years in this business. Still me and the Colonel here understand your point of view. We discussed the eventuality as soon as he came aboard and worked out a deal. In the case of a second crater opening up, we decided that we should offer the crew an extra fifty English pounds – regardless of trade or skill – per day if they would work till the end of the shift. Didn't we, Colonel?' He looked appealingly at the Britisher.

The Colonel nodded, his eyes dead, as if he were not part of what was happening all around him.

'There you are, guys. You heard it – *fifty pounds per day*! And that ain't hay, but the fellers in the head shed appreciate your feelings, so they're prepared to pay it.'

'Don't listen to the Yank bastard,' Myers shouted angrily. 'What's the money worth if yer in Brown's garden, looking at the daisies from underneath? What good then?'

But the promise of a bonus was having its effect. Big Tex threw Myers a look – he knew now who the lemon was – and said: 'So what if that gas out there gives a couple of wet farts – they can't scare a bunch of hairy-assed oilmen like you, can they? Besides we're gonna hit pay-dirt this tour. I can feel it in my bones. And if we do,' he leaned forward a little and dreamed up the figure recklessly, not caring now, concerned solely with getting them back to work, 'then it means an additional bonus of two hundred pounds per man. With that kind of green and the danger money on top of it, you guys could get laid and stoned the whole of your down-time.'

'Two hundred quid!' breathed Longbotham at the console. 'Did you hear that lads – two hundred nicker!'

They had. As Longbotham fumbled with the start switch, Myers aimed a vicious kick at a metal pail and sent it rattling across the wet deck; he knew he was beaten. The men were picking up their tools and starting work again.

As the engines began to roar once more, Big Tex took the Colonel's arm and said, 'Better come on into the office, Colonel. I'll get one of the hash-slingers to bring up a cup of Joe.'

Surprisingly enough it was the Chief himself who gave the Para his next lead. The Para had just finished undressing the beautiful bronzed *Madrileña*, whose fond father had sent her to London to study English in the safety of conservative England, when the bedside phone rang. The Para cursed, took one hand off her delightful left breast, and picked up the phone.

'Are you alone?' the Chief asked, with barely concealed excitement.

'I will be in a moment.' He took his hand away and Mercedes sighed. 'Just keep your motor running, darling. I've got to telephone next door. But we'll have you up to top gear as soon as I get back.'

'Pig!' she said.

'All right, sir,' he said, 'You can talk now.'

'You were right, Para,' the Chief answered.

'Was I? How?'

'In your estimate that our man's target would be in the provinces and that he's – what was that Americanism you used? – a fall guy. He's that too.'

'I see.' Next door the bed squeaked as Mercedes rolled over. The Para said a quick, silent prayer that she was not attempting to drive the motor without his aid.

'Yes, Para, I've just got back from one of those boring Livery dinners and do you know who was my neighbour at the table?'

'Who sir?'

'*Their* second secretary,' announced the Chief triumphantly.

The Para forgot Mercedes. '*Him!*'

'Yes,' the Chief chuckled, 'I thought that would surprise you, Para.'

In the little intimate intelligence world of the capital, where his own organisation and the SB kept permanent tails on every single member down to the maids of every Eastern embassy, it was common knowledge that the second secretary was the head of the KGB, in other words, the espionage resident and, therefore, in charge of Comecon intelligence in Britain.

'Of course, it wasn't a coincidence. Later I checked with Beeston and he said the second secretary had specifically asked to be seated next to me. Said we had a lot more in common than the rest of the guests. After the usual chit-chat – you know the Russkis with their oblique approach – he said completely out of the blue, "One could imagine that your rigs in the North Sea are very vulnerable to attack". No more, no less. I tried to tackle him again on the subject after the loyal toast, but all I could get out of him was a flash of those stainless steel teeth of his.'

The Para pondered. Next door the springs were squeaking urgently. Among other things, he would have to get them oiled soon, he told himself. 'So we're a little closer, sir.'

'I think so. The chap in question has been set up by the Russkis for some damn purpose of their own – whatever it may be. Now, I've already alerted the Admiralty, but naturally they can do little these days with that pathetic handful of ships they call the Royal Navy. After all there must be quite a number of rigs about.'

'There are twenty-nine operating in North Sea at the moment within the Aberdeen police's security area.'

'I see. Well, I'll alert the Aberdeen Chief-of-Police as well, though God knows what his bobbies could do in the case of an attack on a rig. I've also contacted the security chaps of the big oil firms here in the City, as far as I could get hold of them at this time of the night. But naturally the rig crews are not trained to deal with such things.' He paused, and then said, almost as if he were speaking to himself. 'In the final analysis, those damned rigs are wide-open once our man gets into the UK and starts operating.'

'Not if we stop him at his base, sir,' said the Para firmly. 'The trick is, not to let him get on to the rig he picks. Once he's got that far, he's got us by the short

and curlies. You know their usual blackmail tactics –
hostages and all that bit?'

The Chief of MI5 sighed. 'All right, Para, it's up to
you to outguess the bugger. I've done my bit.'

'*Venga,*' Mercedes said at the door, her bronzed breasts
heaving excitedly. '*Tengo prisa!*'

The Para put down the phone hastily, hoping the
Chief had not heard. 'All right, Mercedes, don't race
your motor. The driver's coming.'

Much later, when Mercedes had gone, the Para crouched
over his cold cup of coffee, trying to carry out his Chief's
instruction: to outguess the bugger.

From only a casual study of the problem of the defence of the rigs, he knew it was almost hopeless. Although both the IRA and the Wogs had good reasons
for trying to hit them – the Wogs did not want to lose
the power their new oil weapon gave them – the British
Government simply did not have the power to protect
them. By 1980 there would be one hundred giant production platforms operating in the North Sea alone and
thirty to fifty remotely situated bases such as Nigg. In
order to protect them, not only would the Navy have to
be equipped with fast new patrol boats and the Air
Force with new planes, troops would have to be found to
defend the shore installations. And where would they
come from, without stripping NATO or Ulster? Con-
scription was the only answer, but none of the dummies
and crooks playing politics in Westminster would ever
have the courage to re-introduce that measure, the Para
knew that. In essence the rigs were and probably would
remain wide open to attack. It was essential then that
somehow or other this first one should be foiled, or
plenty others would follow. Once the Beirut boys
thought they had a new game which would bring them
plenty of publicity, they would play it up to the hilt.

The Para took a sip of the cold coffee and frowned.
The Brigadier had told them often enough at his brief-

ings just how important North Sea oil was. In his preliminary economic plan for the country, he had already included oil in the industries which must come under direct state control.

The Para stared at the large-scale map of the North Sea he had laid out in front of him with the position of the rigs operating between the Argyll Hamilton field in the south right up to the Thistle Signal in the far north. One of them was the terrorist's target. But which? Was it the Forties BP field or the Montrose Gas Council – Amoco? Both were expected to come into operation soon with tremendous daily yields – they'd make good publicity and they had both been photographed by the Soviet spy ship. But they were both pretty far out and somehow he felt the Wogs would pick a target closer to the shore.

He tugged at the end of his big nose and tried a new tack. How would the man – and those who would be helping him once he got into the UK – tackle the op? By plane? He could see from the map that there were plenty of RAF fields still in the North of England, but since Ulster they were pretty well guarded by the RAF Regiment. There were several private fields all along the coast. Perhaps the Wogs could nab a plane there and attempt to hit the rig with a home-made bomb. Like those nuts in Ireland with their milk churn. But the possibility of an amateur hitting a relatively small target like a rig in the middle of the North Sea was pretty remote. The Para shook his head. No, it wouldn't be a plane. It had to be a boat. But from where?

He looked at the map once more. Hull was out. Security there was too good – and besides the type of boat a handful of men could handle would not be present in the great port. The Wogs would have to operate from one of the small harbours along the Yorkshire coast. But which?

He ran his eye along the line of small harbours on the coast. It wouldn't be Withernsea. There was no harbour

176

there and hence no boat which could manage the trip out into the North Sea in winter. Bridlington? He remembered the harbour from his holidays there as a kid. A handful of fishing boats stranded in a sea of mud at low tide. Still, he mused, a possibility. He looked further along the coastline. Scarborough seemed a better possibility, or Whitby. Bigger harbours with both the fishing trade and tourists represented. At this time of the year there would be plenty of boats in both ports which could make it out to the North Sea rigs all right. 'Bugger it,' he cursed and took another sip at the cold coffee. 'Where are you, you bastard?'

For a while the Para's mind went blank. Then he tried a third tack. Obviously the unknown terrorist would not be working alone. Aziz had already confessed that he would be looked after by a group of his own people in the north once he had smuggled himself into the UK. It followed, therefore, that their man would use those same people to help him man the boat and carry out the op. It was unlikely that the Micks, strategically placed all over the North of England, would want to get themselves involved in a mission which would finally bring the law down on them like a ton of bricks. No, this particular op would be pure Wog from here on in. Both the Russians and the IRA would not want to be involved once the chop came down. So where might he find the kind of Wog concentration, the unknown terrorist would need? The Para had an idea. He picked up the phone and dialled a number.

The Brigadier was not even surprised to be called at this unearthly hour. 'Yes,' he snapped, as soon as Para had apologised, 'give me details, please?'

The Brigadier listened without interruption though the Para could somehow sense the older man's brain already beginning to race, working out plans, solutions, suggestions. Finally he said when the Para was finished, 'Your interpretation seems correct on the whole, Para. This is what I suggest. As soon as you're off the line, I'll

177

get on to our people in Strensall, Catterick, Hull and Leeds. We're pretty thin on the ground in the last two places, but we've got enough there to get the info you need. They'll check out the Palestinian student population at all the universities and what do you call those new things—?'

'Polytechnics?' ventured the Para.

'Yes, polys. Well, they'll check the Palestinians out and have the details for you by – at the latest – zero nine hundred hours tomorrow morning. In the meantime you get yourself up to Yorkshire – let's say York as a fairly central location – and we'll take it from there.'

'There's a train strike, sir.'

'Then you'll just have to drive Para.'

'Sir.'

'Phone me at zero nine and by then we'll have found them. And Para, don't do anything foolish. We'll have need of you in the years to come.'

The Para was moved. 'Don't worry, sir. I won't take any chances.'

'Fine. But don't let the buggers get that oil.'

DAY SIX: SATURDAY

'It was no picnic despite what anyone might say later . . .
Most of us were pretty scared all the bloody time; you
only felt happy when the battle was over and you were
on your way home. Then you were safe for a bit, anyway.'

Colin Gray, Battle of Britain pilot.
Winter 1940.

1

It was bitterly cold, a February night like an old-fashioned Christmas card, with everything white and glittering with frost. There was no sound in the old walled city. The cobbled narrow street, usually full of tourists babbling in half a dozen languages and snapping everything in sight, was still and empty. George waved from the shadow cast by the ancient half-timbered house.

'Okay, let's go,' commanded the Palestinian in a hoarse whisper.

Silently they glided from their cover and across the road. They came parallel with the sports shop.

'Wait here,' George said.

They crouched in the shadows. Somewhere a clock started to strike two. The Palestinian's gaze was caught by the dummy wearing the jock strap, with the male bulge unnecessarily emphasised. He could just make out the wording on the sign beneath it. 'The Jock Sock – for the guy who doesn't want to feel up-tight.' He was repelled, yet somehow fascinated.

A moment later George came back, sucking his knuckles as if he had grazed them. 'Third window at the back.' He grinned, his excellent teeth gleaming whitely. 'Easy as falling off a log, as the English say.'

The Palestinian returned the handsome boy's happy grin. He was obviously so proud of himself. 'You lead, George. I'll bring up the rear. And remember – once we're inside, no unnecessary lights and no unnecessary talking. You all know from the briefing what we're looking for. Okay?'

They doubled swiftly down the little lane at the back of the sports shop, past a line of overflowing ashcans and heaps of boxes. A cat, disturbed in some nocturnal hunt, skipped spitting from beneath their feet. 'Shit!' the one they now called Tony, exclaimed in surprise.

'Knock if off,' ordered the Palestinian.

'That's it,' George said pointing to the window he had just forced.

'In you go then. You follow Tony. Then you Peter. All right – *move!*' While they hauled themselves up and inside with the light ease of youth, he checked the opening to the street. But still nothing disturbed the heavy winter silence. The city was dead. He turned and followed.

The Palestinian flashed on his little torch. The thin white pencil of light illuminated gotesque figures everywhere: sugar-sweet girls in white tennis dress, rackets raised in a permanent back-hand; distinguished plus-foured gents about to tee off; half-naked hearties sitting in skulls, arms rippling with heavy, waxen-yellow muscles. Then the white beam came to rest on what they had come to find: a tall dummy, dressed in a black frogman's suit, armed with the latest Champion harpoon, and laden with twin air cylinders. 'Over there,' he said. 'Get to it.'

While they occupied themselves finding the right-sized wet suits, the Palestinian checked out the twin oxygen cylinders. As Tony had ascertained earlier in the day when he had enquired at the sports shop, the cylinders were already charged: 1,000 litres of free air, compressed at two hundred atmospheres. He did a rapid calculation. That would give them two hours supply if necessary. He nodded to himself thoughtfully. Three times as much as they would actually need on the morrow.

PC 147 was something of a romantic, in spite of his no-nonsense policeman's look and his six-foot-three, eighteen-stone frame. As he plodded dutifully down the silent street, his face gleaming red with cold, his breath escaping in regular white clouds, he turned down the incessant chatter of his walkie-talkie so that it wouldn't disturb his fantasies. He allowed his policeman's imagination full rein, as he always did on these lonely night beats in winter, peopling the ancient thoroughfare with elegant gents in white-powdered wigs, hearty types pushing their way through the eighteenth century with their sedan chairs, proceeded by ragged, bare-foot boys bearing flaming torches aloft, rouged fine ladies with beauty spots, clad in great hoop skirts. He paused to check a door. It was locked. They always were. He plodded on. He'd read somewhere that even the fine ladies had not worn knickers underneath their elegant silken gowns. For a moment he allowed his imagination to dwell somewhat unromantically on that exciting possibility and though of Agnes, his wife of some thirty years, who always wore woollen bloomers at this time of the year. He sighed rather sadly and stopped at Smallpiece, the Jeweller. He checked the door of the only shop in the street that would really attract a villain's attention. Predictably it was locked. He flashed his torch on the alarm system. It was in operation too. He flicked off the beam and went on with his slow masterful, size eleven tread. Nothing to worry about now after 'shortcocks', as the lads on the force nicknamed the jeweller's. He would pause at the corner where the XII Roman Legion had once had its HQ back in the second century, have a little clandestine spit-and-a-draw and enjoyed the sensation of being a masterful centurion and not a humble bobby with thirty-seven years' service behind him and still on the beat.

But the big, red-faced policeman was never fated to have that cigarette. Just as he came parallel with the sports shop, he heard them. He stopped immediately. The eighteenth century vanished. He cocked his head to one side and strained. There was no doubt about it – there was somebody inside the dark sports shop. He crept closer. Muffled voices. There was more than one

183

of them, that was for sure. PC 147 might have been a romantic, but he was no coward. He didn't hesitate.

Disdaining the help his walkie-talkie would have brought him, he drew his truncheon, marked where he had used it to crack some hazelnuts one Christmas. He tried the door. It was locked. The intruders had used some other means of entry. Moving very silently for such a big man, he went down the dark alley, gently touching the windows. The third window gave. It was open. The sound of voices grew a little louder. But he could not make out what the speakers were saying. He gripped the truncheon in his teeth by means of the leather strap and hauled himself inside with some difficulty, but silently. Crouching instinctively, he crept forward down the box-lined, stale-smelling corridor that led into the display room.

Three dark young men were kneeling on the floor bundling up what appeared to be frogmen's suits. From the back they looked like Pakkis and he knew from his pals on the Leeds force that they sometimes carried knives, more for show than use. But still knives. He would have to avoid frightening them into a show of force. Nice and easy – that was the trick.

PC 147 cleared his throat loudly and switched on his torch in the same instant. 'Now then,' he said in his broad Yorkshire accent, 'what do you lads think you're up to?'

The three turned, startled, their dark eyes full of fear.

PC 147 raised his truncheon significantly, the knuckles white against his hamlike red fist. 'Well, come on now, let's be having it,' he said easily, knowing already he was in full control of the situation. He had caught them with their knickers down and they were scared.

Behind him the Palestinian, the new Champion harpoon gun in his hand, surveyed the other three and realised that the British policeman had completely cowed them. Although they were three to one, he had the psychological advantage over them. For a moment he considered what he should do. Should he overpower the cop with his bare hands – he couldn't risk any noise? But what would he do with the big man once he had overpowered him? Besides there were George, Peter and Tony. They would have to learn what violent death was like. It would prepare them for what was to come on the morrow. Coldly, clinically, he decided that the policeman should die.

'All right, on your feet,' PC 147 was saying, as the Palestinian slipped off the safety catch of the harpoon gun. 'You lot of likely lads is coming with me to the station – and I don't want no messing. Or you get a taste of—'

The Palestinian fired and at that range he couldn't miss. The rubber thongs whammed down the barrel. The three foot barbed harpoon hissed forward, snaking its nylon line after it.

The big policeman's order broke off in an agonized scream of pain as the barb penetrated his body. His truncheon clattered to the floor hollowly. While three young men stared up at him in frozen horror, his big hands shot to his chest attempting to grab the harpoon. Blood poured over the clawing hands. His knees started to buckle. His helmet slipped across his face. PC 147 was dead before he hit the floor.

The Para looked at his watch. Still five minutes to go. When the Brigadier said call at nine, he meant nine; not five minutes before, nor five minutes after.

The Para stamped his feet on the icy platform and wished he could have just an hour's sleep. It had been a nightmarish journey up to York on a frozen, icy A-1. He lit yet another cigarette and stared at the grey-faced people hunched over the tea in the waiting room, waiting for trains that wouldn't come. They didn't look very good. Next to him an elderly railwayman in a big peaked

185

cap that made him look like an elderly refugee from the *Afrika Korps* was cheerfully chalking up a list of trains that had already been cancelled because of the strike, slapping a noisy full stop at the end of each name, as if the job gave him great pleasure.

'Happy at your work?' the Para queried.

'Only doing my duty, mate,' said the refugee from the *Afrika Korps* without stopping. 'Informing the public, you know.' With relish he hit the slate at the end of another cancellation and straightened up. 'Think the silly buggers'd go home,' he commented, indicating the crowd. 'They should know there'll be no trains. The lads won't give up so easily this time, believe me, mate.'

But the Para had already stopped listening. It was time to call the Brigadier. He slipped inside the box and dialled the Aldershot number. The Brigadier answered at once. 'You're in York then?'

'Yessir. But only just. The roads were like glass.'

'Good, well this is the situation. Our chaps in the north have checked up. Bradford and Leeds are out for Palestinians. Too many Jewish militants there. They would make life too uncomfortable for the Palestinians. So if your analysis of the situation is correct – namely that the Palestinians are going to launch their attack on whatever rig they've picked from the Yorkshire coast – these two places come into question. Hull and York. Hull has a few of them as students, but according to our chaps, York has over twenty of them and most of 'em are activists. York could be the base for their operations. Start your enquiries where you are. If nothing turns up, off you go to Hull. And by the way if you need any help, contact Major Robinson at Strensall Camp. Infantry type. Good man. I knew him in Ulster.' The Para noted the Major's duty phone number. 'Any questions?'

'No sir.'

'Good. Then get to it. Report back as soon as you get on to something.'

'Will do, sir.'

As the Para stepped out of the kiosk the elderly refugee from the *Afrika Korps* was chalking on his slate the words: 'All trains cancelled!' With a triumphant flourish he underlined the word 'all' twice.

'That's right, dad,' the Para said as he brushed by, 'really sock it to them. Enjoy yourself.'

The railway worker looked at the Para's broad back sourly. 'Ay, go and laugh, but tha'll be bloody laughing on t'other side of yer face one o' these fine days,' he said, but not loudly.

The gleaming white university situated on the outskirts of the ancient city was a disappointment. The dark, aquiline faces he had come to know and hate during these last couple of years were conspiciously absent from the university. A girl came towards him with a bundle of books under her arm, dressed in the usual faded jeans and high boots, her tiny breasts trussed up beneath her pointed chin, as if she were presenting them to him on a platter.

'Excuse me, miss,' he said stopping in the middle of the path. 'I'm looking for the Palestinian student group. Any idea where I might find them?'

She looked up at him. 'Fuzz?' she asked, he voice was cool and insolent.

He nodded slowly. 'Sort of.'

'How sort of? Looking for the speed freaks?' Her skinny shoulder did a sort of fan dance. 'You can make with the feet, if you are.'

'The Palestinians?' he urged, edging back.

'They're not here today. None of them. Karin — she's in hall with me — is going about with one of them. More fool her. A bunch of them usually pick her up in York in the morning with that old bomb of a Volkswagen they have, then the whole bunch of 'em have coffee in the Union before splitting up for lectures. None of them

187

turned up this morning and when Karin went over to the Union to check, they weren't there either.'

'Any idea why?'

She shrugged. 'God knows! They're a funny bunch altogether. Not my scene.'

'Do you know where they have their digs?'

'Yes, the lot of them have taken over a big house in the suburbs.' She gave him the address and told him how to get there.

'What have they done?' she asked.

'Nothing to write home about.'

The house was in a suburban street not far from the railway line, taken over completely by students. Once it had belonged to a prosperous middle class family. Now it was run-down, the windows curtainless, dirty milk bottles standing on bare, disorderly tables. The Para stepped over a pile of fresh dog faeces past the fading yellow arrow pointing to the basement with the legend 'AID RAID SHELTER' painted above it, and looked at the long list of names scrawled roughly above the bells. Husseins, Yussafs – the whole house seemed to be firmly in Palestinian hands, save the top flat which belonged to 'Graham W. Seeton (Landlord)'. The Para sucked his teeth thoughtfully. The tall narrow five-storey house was completely silent. No smoke curled from its cracked, cowled chimneys. He stumbled through the dozen or so dirty milk bottles and pressed the bell labelled 'Graham W. Seeton' – once, twice. Nothing. He waited and then pressed again. High above him a window was flung open and an angry voice cried: 'What yer trying to do – wake the sodding dead?'

'Mr Seeton?'

'Ay.'

'Could I speak to you for a moment, Mr Seeton?'

The face looked down at him suspiciously. 'I've got no flats free. Besides I only take students, and you ain't no student.'

I bet you do, the Para thought, and pack them in four to a room at three quid a head. 'No I'm not a student and I'm not looking for a place. I just want a word with you – in private, Mr Seeton.'

The landlord hesitated. 'All right, come on up. But you'd better make it smartish. I'm just going to have me dinner.'

The landlord was a big slovenly man, with his long bushy side-chats dyed a poor brown and his toupé set at an angle so that the Para could see the netting under the artifical hair. 'What do you want?' he asked, removing the cigar from the tight hole he called a mouth and putting it back almost immediately.

'Where are your Palestinian students?' the Para asked. 'This place seems deserted and they're not at the University.'

'Gone,' the landlord answered, doing the quick transfer act with his cheap cigar.

The Para fought to keep his temper. 'Gone where?'

'How the hell should I know? As long as they pay their rent regular, they can go to the sodding moon, as far as I'm concerned. Bloody wogs! None of my business.'

'Then make it your business, 'the Para snapped. 'If you've got a spare key to their places, let me have it.'

'Don't you get tough with me, Jack,' said the landlord, taking out the cigar from its hole and keeping it out this time.

The Para sneered. 'What you gonna do – frighten me by taking off your toupé, *Jack*?'

For the first time the landlord saw the look in the Para's eyes. He shrugged. 'Do what you like, yer mother's drunk.' He pointed the spittle-wet end of his cigar at the key board. 'Take the sodding lot, if you want.'

The Para picked up the keyboard. He was grinning. 'Don't hit me,' he said, 'I'm not insured.'

The first room he entered was heavy with male sweat

and stale cigarette smoke. The Para wrinkled his nose in disgust. His Army training had made him fastidious and this place was really in what the boys in the Parachute Regiment had once called 'shit order'. He kicked a used sock out of his way and forced himself to touch the mess on the table – bits of clothing, dirty half-full cups of tea, empty coke bottles. Whatever had happened, they had left in a hurry. He strolled into the next room, not knowing really what he was looking for. Idly he picked up a few books from the battered, scuffed dresser. They were the usual radical student stuff. The sociology of this, the theory of that. 'Isms and ics', he said aloud, 'the crap of the intellectual revolution—'

He broke off suddenly. At the base of the pile of books, there was one which was strangely out of place – *Jane's Fighting Ships*. He picked up the weighy, illustrated catalogue of the world's naval vessels and stared at it in bewilderment. What the hell would a bunch of radical Palestinian students want with Jane's? Besides the thing was damned expensive. Frowning he began to leaf through the book. Stark black silhouettes, displacements, armaments. But not a hint of why the unknown students might have purchased the book. He closed it again and checked whether any particular page had been turned down at the corner. Again he drew a blank.

Then it struck him. The waste-paper basket or wherever they threw their trash. He walked from the bedroom into the scruffy kitchen. The place stank of stale food and the spices they had used to season their meals. In the corner there was a paper sack filled to overflowing with garbage. He gritted his teeth and fighting back his revlusion, forced himself to examine its contents.

Wee cigarette ends, sloppy tea bags, limp brown lettuce leaves, a used condom. The Para gagged, but stuck at it. Paper, screwed up and thrown away in a hurry. With his dirty stained hands, he unfolded the paper. A bill – paid. And then he had it, stained with the liquid from one of the teabags, and torn at the corner but clearly recognisable: a picture of a rig, torn from one of the glossy Sunday supplements, with a list of details and the rig's name below. The Para did not need to look at the name, he knew it already. It was *England's Pride*.

2

The wind had changed during the morning. Now it was whipping up cross-seas, which attacked the swaying, heaving platform, first from one side then from the other. The waves crashed against the spuds, drenching the deck with icy spray, while further out the escaping gas bubbled and pulsated, soiling the sea's surface with its yellow froth.

But despite the worsening weather and ever-present danger of a gas explosion, the terrible race to find oil went on. As the drill bit deeper into the hard rock hidden below the tossing surface of the sea, the whole rig seemed to tremble, as if it were a living thing in pain. On the deck the brake of the drilling drum screeched persistently. At the console, a grim, resolute Longbotham, still clad in only his shirt-sleeves, forced the drill down and down, while the long column of special mud fought its own silent battle with the escaping gas 9,000 feet below his feet.

Big Tex was driving the men with all his energy now, not even pausing for a cup of hot coffee. Early that morning he had had canvas screens rigged up around the drill. Twice they were torn away with a savage crack by the howling wind, and in the end he had given into the wind.

The floormen were working in impossible conditions, the spray streaming down their yellow oilskins, their brick-red faces frozen and soaked but Big Tex, driving them on relentlessly, did not seem to notice their condition. The slightest check set him off now in a stream of obscenities of a kind he had not used since the green hell of the Hurtgen Forest thirty years earlier. Yet the men did not appear to mind either the miserable conditions, the terrible pace or Tex's savage tongue. For the first time in the long history of the *Pride*, they were caught up by the adventure of it all. Dripping with icy sea-water, their oilskins stained with mud up to the thighs, their chests heaving with the strain, they staggered back and forth, emptying the rack of high-grade pipe joints needed for the drill. All that mattered now was to find oil.

Once a gasping Myers staggered up to Longbotham at the console and whispered hoarsely: 'Longie, this is crazy . . . They should kill that hole down there.' He gasped and wiped the spray off his pinched face with an oil-stained hand that trembled violently. 'Drill a slanting hole into the gas zone . . . and pump in gel. That'd kill it. If that buggering Yank doesn't, we'll all be for the chop.'

The big Hull man did not even raise his eyes from the console. 'Sod off, muscleman!' was all he said.

Above the workers, the arc lights swung crazily back and forth in the mounting wind. The derrick moaned. The wind braces sung. The green and yellow heaving sea prepared itself to attack *England's Pride* one last time. But the drilling did not stop.

A chain being used to haul up a kelly snapped. With a report like a field gun being fired, it zig-zagged madly through the air. Big Tex, standing next to the Colonel, watching the operation, lunged forward. With all his strength he threw himself against a roustabout standing in the path of the broken cable. Together they sprawled in a heap on the wet deck as the chain hissed viciously through the air only inches above their heads.

'You all right, Nolan?' Tex asked the man, rising to his feet, his white overall trousers grey with mud and grease.

'Sure,' Nolan answered. 'Missed me by miles.'

Big Tex turned to the Colonel, his brick-red face full of admiration and new enthusiasm. 'Hot shit, Colonel, did you just see that? That Nolan didn't even blink an eyelid. Twenty-four hours ago, I'd would have had a goddam mutiny if a thing like that had happened. They would have downed tools just like that!' He snapped his fingers together. 'And for that matter, Colonel, they wouldn't have worked like this twenty-four hours ago, going at it like bats outa hell!' He stared at the blue-lipped Colonel, his eyes ablaze. 'Don't you see, I've got them! For the first time since I came on to the *Pride*, they're behind me every man-jack of them.'

It was just then that Jacko called the Colonel to the radio shack. There was a call for him. Feeling vaguely sick, yet at the same time fired with new hope by Big Tex's heady enthusiasm, he picked up the radio phone. It was Pat, his secretary.

'Colonel,' she gasped, 'I've just heard from one of the girls in the office that they've called an emergency meeting for Sunday at nine sharp. Krause's coming from Germany. So you can see what they're up to—' She broke off abruptly, her breath hectic with emotion and outrage, as if she expected an outburst of anger from him.

'I see,' the Colonel said stiffly.

'But don't you understand, Colonel? An emergency board meeting – and they don't even have the common decency to notify you. The girl at the office says that Hardman is giving out the story that you don't want to come to London. The way he's telling it is that you want to stick it out on the rig in a last desperate attempt to strike oil before it's too late. According to him, if you find oil, you think it will "save your hide" – as he puts it.'

'We'll find oil,' the Colonel said. 'The signs are getting better by the minute and the men are working flat out. I shall stay here.'

He clicked back the radio phone.

As the radio phone went dead in the hotel's little phone box, Pat began to cry, staring uncomprehendingly at the stuffed bird in its glass cage which trembled violently with each fresh draught, as if it were trying to escape, and the tears streamed down her face unheeded.

'What did she say?' Big Tex roared above the howl of the wind, as the Colonel opened the door of the radio shack.

As the Colonel explained, Big Tex cursed violently, the sea-water dripping from his suddenly angry face. 'Oh that ape-shit Hardman! He's been trying to give this operation the purple shaft right from the start, the bastard.' He looked curiously at the Colonel's pale face. 'You okay?'

The Colonel nodded numbly.

'Well, we'll beat the crummy bastard yet, don't worry, Colonel. If we get that oil – *and we will* – we'll have him by the short and curlies. As soon as we strike pay-dirt, Colonel, that bastard Hardman can run off at the lip as much as he likes, but all his talk won't be worth a wooden nickel.' He cupped his hands round his mouth and yelled '*Jacko*! Jacko, I want you to button down. Total radio silence. From here on in, we're neither sending nor receiving. Understand?'

Jacko looked at him aghast. 'But you can't do that! Tex, that's illegal.' He appealed to the Colonel. 'We're not allowed to do that, sir. Regulations, you know. In the case there's an emergency—'

He broke off fearfully. Big Tex was doubling his mighty right fist. 'You looking for a knuckle-sandwich, Jacko?' he asked softly. 'Or are you gonna turn that darn radio off. Because if I have to do it myself – brother, you'd better believe it – somebody's gonna get hurt and it won't be me.'

'Okay, Tex,' he stammered, backing into his shack. 'Keep yer hair on . . . I'll do it as long as you take the responsibility.'

The wind whipped viciously at their clothes as Big

Tex and the Colonel walked back to the drilling platform, where the operation was now reaching its peak.

In the shack, a reluctant Jacko started the job of closing down his station. Five minutes later *England's Pride* was sealed off from the outside world, riding the green-tossing North Sea like a monstrous ghost ship, on its own at last.

3

'But my God, this is the first time one of our men has been killed on duty within living memory! Things like that simply don't happen in a place like York,' said the fat sweating Superintendent brokenly. 'I simply can't believe it happened – even now.'

The Para nodded his head sympathetically. He knew the provincial police officer was in a state of shock. He would have liked to order the man to belt up, yell at him that things like this were happening in Ulster every day that dawned. But he knew that would be going too far.

'But what exactly happened, sir?' he asked.

'Happened?' the Superintendent said bitterly. 'The pigs killed him with a harpoon! Went right through him – transfixed him.'

'A harpoon, sir?'

'Yes. It seemed an ordinary little bit of a crime. Break-in at a sports shop in the centre of the city. But when he tackled them, one of the bastards let fly at him with one of those harpoons they used for underwater fishing. You know, you've seen them in the TV documentaries – Cousteau or whatever he's called?'

'What did they take?'

'*Take*, nothing worth killing a man for, I can tell you. A couple of bloody wet suits – the things the frogmen wear. Perhaps three hundred quids' worth of gear at the most, according to the owner. And for that, poor old Charlie had to go and buy it – and him going through the Desert without a scratch. Normandy, too . . .'

The Superintendent's incredulous voice faded into the background, as did the constant ringing of the phones in the outer office. The picture of the rig he had found in the Palestinians' digs, the theft of the wet suits: slowly but surely the pieces were beginning to fit into place. He shook himself out of his reverie. 'Have you any clues, sir?'

'Not a bloody sausage,' the police officer answered bitterly. 'But I can promise you one thing, we'll get the bastards who did this to poor old Charlie. You can bet your bottom dollar on that.' He put his big hand to his eyes. 'He wasn't one of the brightest, but he was a damn good lad. He was always good for a laugh at a smoker—'

'I think I can help you, sir,' interrupted the Para, and filled him in with what he knew. 'As far as I can see it at the moment, they're preparing for an attack on the *Pride*. Hence the wet suits. How exactly they're going to do it sir, I haven't a clue. But they've got a plan of attack, that's for sure, and the man who drew up that plan is the professional. The man I told you about – the terrorist – is already in the UK. In fact, he could well have been in York last night. Now, he and the rest of them are heading for the coast – somewhere between Spurn Point and Whitby is my guess.'

'What are we going to do?'

'Well, the first thing is to alert the *Pride*. Once they're on the rig, we're sunk. They'll blackmail us till the pips begin to squeak as soon as they've got the crew in their hands, that's for sure.'

The Superintendent picked up the phone. 'Get me the radio room,' he barked, 'and bloody quick! Listen Tom, this is top priority. I want you to raise a rig in the North Sea – No, I don't know how you do it. You're the expert – it's your baby. As soon as you get her, warn the skipper or whoever is in charge to expect a terrorist attack. Yes, you heard me right, Tom. How it's going to be carried out, we don't know. But it is.' He slammed down the phone and looked at the Para. 'Now what?'

'Contact the nearest RAF base, sir. See if we can't get them to patrol the coast in the area I mentioned. Navy too, if they've got any small craft in this area.'

'Good idea. I'll contact Northern Command HQ

straight away.' He picked up the phone again. 'Get me Northern Command HQ right off.'

Then the Para remembered the conversation with the student, the girl with the dangerous breasts. 'And by the way, one group of the Wogs drives a beatup Volkswagen. It was missing from outside their digs. So we can assume that they're using it for the journey to the coast.'

'Good, that's a great help,' the policeman exclaimed and picked up his other phone. 'Put out a general call to the North Riding and Humberside to keep a look-out for an old Volkswagen driven by Palestinians. Should have a York number.'

Five minutes later the bad news started to come in. The unknown Tom in the radio room rang through to inform them that he could not raise the rig. He had tried every possible means, but the *Pride* simply did not answer. She was off the air. The Superintendent looked across at the Para after he had relayed Tom's message. 'What do you make of that?'

The Para shrugged glumly. 'God knows. All I know, sir, is that it's not bloody good.'

Ten minutes later Humberside police came on the line with the news that they had found the Volkswagen and the Palestinians. The Superintendent's sudden smile died when he learnt where. The driver had hit an icy patch on the second-class coastal road that led from Hornsea to Withernsea. He had lost control of the vehicle and it had gone careening through a fence, across a narrow field and over one of the mud cliffs peculiar to that stretch of the coast. The cliff hadn't been very high, but high enough. All four occupants had been killed instantly.

Forgetting all official procedure, the Superintendent yelled over the phone: 'Serve the black bastards right! It's just what they deserved for killing poor old Charlie.'

The Para cut in icily: 'Would you ask them if they'd found any wet suits or similar stuff in the crashed car, sir?'

199

The Superintendent shook his head. 'Negative. No wet suits or any other kind of swimming gear in the crashed car.'

'Bugger it,' the Para exploded angrily. 'They've bloody well got away with it!'

The Para lay stretched out on the couch in the station rest room, shoes off, tie pulled loose, sipping the warm lager out of the can like they had done in the desert, and staring blankly at the high ornamental Victorian room. It was sheer hell to keep his eyes open. The all-night journey north without sleep was beginning to tell. It was obvious that the dead men in the Volkswagen had been intended as a feint. The Palestinians had had plenty of time to go to ground before the dead policeman had been discovered. Why then was the Volkswagen still driving around hours after his body had been found? The answer was clear. The terrorist – the professional – who was planning the whole op had deliberately sent them off on the drive which ended in their deaths.

It was clear now that the group which would launch the attack on the rig was already in position somewhere along that lonely Yorkshire coastline. The Volkswagen being found on the Hornsea-Withernsea road seemed to indicate that his initial guess about their probable base of operations was correct and that his warning to all local harbour masters – passed on by the fat Superintendent – to check all craft leaving their harbours was justified. So how were the Palestinians going to do it?

He forced his eyes open again. 'Where are the buggers going to find a boat?' he asked aloud, looking up at the fat-arsed cherubs dancing across the ceiling, tossing grapes about in plaster prodigality. Of course there would be small craft outside the harbours. They'd be easy enough to nab. But they'd find nothing in the shallow water capable of taking them far out into the North Sea in the middle of winter.

He finished the warm beer and let the can drop to the

200

floor. In essence, the coast was sealed off. It could only be a matter of hours before the local Humberside police picked them up at their hiding place. After all the swarthy-skinned Palestinians stood out like a sore thumb among the local Yorkshire population.

He closed his eyes and sighed. All he had to do now was to wait. Yet there was still nagging doubt at the back of his mind. Why was the *Pride* on radio silence, cut off completely from the outer world until the C-in-C Northern Command finally gave his permission for the RAF to be used? And then there was the business of the stolen wet suits. What the devil did they want those for? Even the Palestinian hotheads couldn't be that stupid – they couldn't swim out to the rig! Impossible, the wet suits. As he drifted off into an uneasy sleep, peopled with fat sweating policemen, harpoons stuck through their dark-blue chests and girls whose breasts were polished metal sharpened to points, the words descended into the whirling vortex of his mind. *Wet suits . . . wet suits . . . wet . . .*

The Para awoke with a start, the solution clear in his head. The op was still on. The Russians hadn't gone to all that trouble to set up the op just to have it fail because a few elderly harbour masters would be checking on the craft leaving their waters. The terrorists would get their boat. How, he didn't know. But they'd get it. By the time the C-in-C Northern Command had made up his mind to release the RAF, it would be too late. Even if he managed to get the Brigadier to talk to him, it would still be too late. The professional terrorist must know he couldn't keep his group hidden much longer. He must launch the attack within a matter of hours, and he, the Para, had to act now if he were going to stop the Palestinians.

He recalled the Brigadier's conversation of that morning. If he needed help, he was to contact the infantry major at Strensall Camp. What was his name again? He clicked his fingers excitedly. Robinson – Major Robinson! He tugged on his shoes and straightened his tie. Moments later he was in the York Station's radio room. He flashed his ID at the big grey-haired sergeant in charge. Tom Perkins had never seen a Counter-Intelligence card before, but he recognised it for what it was and acted with commendable speed.

'Get me Strensall Camp. It must be around York somewhere—'

'Seven miles north of here, sir.'

'Good, well get me it on the phone and find me a Major Robinson of the Infantry. My guess is that he's on the permanent staff. But get him for me at the double.'

Tom Perkins, ex-Coldstream Guardsman, grinned at the old familiar military expression.

Three minutes later a cool Sandhurst voice said: 'Robinson here. Who's this?'

The Para explained quickly who he was and added, 'the Brigadier said I should contact you if I need help. And I need help now. I need a chopper – and I need it quick.'

Major Dick Robinson gave a short laugh. 'A chopper – is that all you need?'

The Coleman lantern hissed viciously, throwing a blinding white light into the interior of the hot caravan. Outside now in the deserted caravan park there was no sound save that of the crash and thunder of the North Sea, a hundred yards or so away. The heat was suffocating from the stove. But they dared not open a window in case the light gave away their presence in the caravan; they knew from the police wave-length on their radio to which they had listened most of the evening that the Humberside force was still looking for them. Somehow or other the British had tumbled to the fact that the dead comrades in the crashed Volkswagen were not the ones who had broken into the York's sports shop and

202

killed the policeman. Their feint to throw the British off the scent had not worked.

The Palestinian brushed the two empty cans of sardines, which had been their evening meal, off the table on to the cigarette-littered floor and began to spread out the big map of the Bay. The others, sprawled sweating in their coloured underwear on the bunks, watched him curiously. He anchored the two top ends with the overflowing ash trays and glanced at George, at the bulge of his loin and the line of his hard muscular thigh. Then he tore his gaze away.

'Please pay attention now, will you?' he began. 'It is very important that we make no mistakes. We made one this morning with the policeman. It must be our first – and last.'

Tony and Peter lowered their eyes, as if they were ashamed. But George kept his gaze fixed on the Palestinian's face. The Palestinian felt his blood begin to race. He controlled himself with difficulty, feeling the sweat trickle down the small of his back. There would be time for George and *that* later.

He stabbed a finger at the Bay. 'Here is what is called the Smithic Sands, some one hundred metres from the harbour. Can you see?'

They craned their necks forward to look at the map and nodded.

'They are dangerous. Most craft – even the local fishing boats – have to slow down there. Our boat will also have to. In fact, our Russian friends tell me that it is standing operating procedure for the dawn patrol to make its slowest speed there. For about five minutes it moves across the edge of the sandbank at about five knots – not too fast for us to catch up with it in the flippers. But there will be no need for us to catch up with it. We will be there half an hour before the patrol boat leaves the harbour.' He looked at George's hard chest and easy-breathing diaphragm, outlined against the cotton material of his undershirt. 'The water will be cold at this time of the year, but you are all hard and in the wet suits you'll be protected against the worst of it.'

'Now we'll operate in twos. George and me. Tony and Peter together. The two of you will bring up the rear with the explosives and the automatics. They will be heavy, but the insulated bags will help with buoyancy.'

Peter and Tony nodded. 'Don't worry,' said Tony proudly, his eyes gleaming boldly, 'We'll make it.'

'Good,' the Palestinian acknowledged his confidence. 'I'm sure you will. That is why the Doctor picked the two of you for this mission and not someone else from the York group.' He turned to George. 'You and I will tackle the boat itself. According to Jane's, it carries a crew of at least five, but it has no armament and our Russian friends state that the crew members carry no weapons. All the same the boat has both radio and Very flares. We cannot afford the slightest mistake or they'll have signalled the shore before we're aboard and then everything will have been for nothing. The drill is to come in from both sides, George. You take the captain up across the bows and into the little cabin I showed you in Jane's. Thrust the pistol into his back and say – stop engines. That's all. No word of explanation. Just – stop engines. As soon as you see the wake die away, Tony and Peter, come on after us like hell. I'm only going to give you a matter of two minutes. We don't want to give any busybody on shore an opportunity to discover something is wrong.'

'And you?' Tony asked.

'I shall tackle the radio operator.' He brought down his hard hand in a karate chop. All of them knew of his reputation for being able to kill silently and efficiently.

'Once he's dealt with, I doubt we'll have much trouble with the rest. Within a matter of five minutes, the boat should be in our hands. Then it's full speed ahead. I calculated we should be at the rig one hour and a half later.' He paused. 'Any questions?'

Peter, the youngest of the group, a smooth-faced eighteen year old, said hesitantly: 'What if they've got a look-out? It's possible, isn't it, especially if those sands are dangerous, as you say they are. What then?'

The older man pointed to the Champion harpoon lying across his bunk. It was the one with which he had killed the policeman that morning. 'I shall use that. It's completely noiseless, as you know. And let me add one more word. None of you must have any pity. The motto is kill or be killed. This morning I killed a British policeman. You can imagine what his comrades must feel about us now. They will shoot first and ask questions later.' He looked around their faces, hollowed out by the glaring white light of the hissing Coleman. 'In their eyes we are already dead men. We must ensure that they die first, you understand?'

They nodded.

He looked at his watch. 'Now comrades, I suggest we should get some sleep. It is late.' Without waiting for their reaction, he reached out his hand and shook Tony's. 'Good luck, comrade.' He repeated the words and gesture with Peter. Then George. Despite his hard masculine body, George's hand felt soft and warm, like a woman's. The Palestinian felt his blood begin to race. 'Good luck, George for tomorrow,' he said, suddenly hoarse.

'Good luck, comrade,' George answered and from the tone of his voice, the older man knew that George had guessed.

'All right,' he rapped harshly, 'into your bunks! I'm going to put the lantern out now. We wake up precisely at zero three hours. It that clear?'

Like well-trained soldiers, they rolled into their bunks. He caught one last exciting glimpse of that bulge, then he snapped the Coleman off. There was a last harsh hiss and the glaring white light went out suddenly. For a moment he was blinded as he groped his way to his rumpled bunk.

Within five minutes they were all fast asleep. But

despite his weariness his mind was still racing frantically, obsessed by the memory of that terrible yet fascinating bulge. He thrust his hard fist into his mouth to prevent himself moaning out aloud. Above him, within the reach of his hand, George slept on, unaware of his needs, and his shame. He fought himself to prevent himself from reaching up to touch the other man. If the others ever found out, he could not live.

Finally he conquered himself, while outside the wind from the sea tore at the caravan, making it shake with the impact. Trembling with relief, he drew the rough woollen blankets up about his head and lay with his knees drawn tightly against his body. His heart ceased to beat so wildly. The sweat dried away. The Palestinian lay in a dark and secret place and all was well again.

DAY SEVEN: SUNDAY

'The first generation of ruins, cleaned up, shored up, began to weather – in the daylight, they took their places as the norm of the scene . . . Reverses, losses, deadlocks, now almost unnoticed, bred one another; every day the news hammered one more nail into a consciousness which no longer resounded. Everywhere hung the heaviness of even worse, you could not be told and could not desire to hear. This was the lightless middle of the tunnel.

Elizabeth Bowen, The Heat of the Day.
c 1942.

1

'Char, Flight?' the Erk asked, holding up the half gallon thermos of tea, legs braced apart against the swaying of the deck.

'No, not just yet, son,' answered the Chief Tech steering the launch, not taking his eyes off the faint green light of the rows of dials in front of him. 'I'll take her through these sodding sands first. But you can do me a favour. Go and check the bow, will you lad and sing out smartish if it's getting too shallow!'

'*Roger*, Flight,' said the Erk and doubled away on the heaving deck of the thirty-foot rescue launch.

The wind was fresh from the north-east, mixed with sporadic sweeps of rain hissing across the dark choppy sea and it was hard to judge depths under such conditions. The Chief Tech throttled back even more so that he could listen to the run of the waves against the blue-painted bows of the launch and 'hear' the depth. Behind him the automatic foghorn of the little harbour they had just left started to sound like the bleat of a lost sheep. Automatically the Chief Tech told himself there'd be fog further out to sea. He reduced speed even further. The Smithic Sands were bad enough at any time – they had shifted fifty feet or more since the last Navy survey the previous year – without a sea rook coming in to make things even worse. Gingerly he began to steer the boat into the sands. Next month he was being posted to the Rock and he couldn't afford to risk that three year tour of sun and duty-free booze by a moment's carelessness on this icy February dawn.

Minutes passed by. All was silent on the little bridge as the grey-haired NCO concentrated on his task: a silence seemingly intensified by the whirl of the radarscope. To the east the watery, luminous moon was making its last struggle with the grubby white of the dawn. In thirty minutes or so, it would be properly light and they would be heading for the open sea at forty knots, joyfully released from this agonizingly slow crawl across the sands.

The Palestinian touched George's arm as they floated together in the icy shallow water. 'There,' he said behind the goggles, though he knew the younger man could not hear.

George nodded his head very deliberately. He'd seen it. The Palestinian gripped his harpoon more firmly in his frozen hand. The blurred silhouette was less than a hundred metres away now. Together they started to swim silently towards it, neither legs nor flippered feet breaking the surface of the water.

The launch came closer. It could not have been doing more than five knots at the most. There was just a hint of white foam at its sharp bow. The Palestinian touched the other man's arm and indicated he should stop swimming. The boat was less than twenty metres away now. The Palestinian could see the vague shape of a man standing on the deck, staring at the water. The Palestinian indicated that George should stay where he was. He kicked out with his flippers and shot to the rear of the launch. He circled it, carefully avoiding the churning propellers. He broke the surface again. George and the others would be in position now. The boat was moving terribly slowly. It would be easy. But there was still that damned look-out on the deck. In their clumsy gear they couldn't swing themselves aboard without being seen by the man.

He upped the safety catch of the harpoon. The look-out was less than seven metres away now – well within the Champion's range. He raised it out of the water and thrust up his goggles so that he could see his target more clearly. There was no sound now save the lapping of the waves over the sands and the steady purr of the launch's engines. He caught hold of the low gunwale and felt the drag on his left arm, as he was towed with the boat. He fired and without waiting to see the accuracy of his aim, pulled himself on board.

The Erk screamed, shrilly like a woman. He lolled grotesquely over the rail, hoarse bubbling sounds coming from his pierced lungs. The Palestinian frantically pulled off his flippers. George's black helmeted head appeared on the other side of the boat. Good! He dropped the second flipper on the deck. The deck was ice-cold on his naked feet as he doubled swiftly for the hatch. He caught a last glimpse of George stepping hastily over the dying look-out, then he disappeared down below.

The crucifying torture of his terrible wound broke through the Erk's insensibility. Instinctively he knew what was happening. From somewhere down below he could hear the sound of breaking glass and shouts. Through the red haze in front of his eyes, he could see a monstrous figure, clad in dripping black, standing next to the Flight, pistol in hand. The launch was being hijacked.

He breathed out hard and pink bubbles formed on his lips. For a moment he thought he would choke on the blood coming from his pierced lungs. Then he spat a great gob of red blood on to the deck and he could breathe once again. Slowly he raised his head and stared at the klaxon. It was ten feet away. If he could only reach it and sound the alarm, it would be heard back in Brid. There was always someone on duty at the harbour-master's office. If he could sound it between the regular every three-second bleat of the automatic fog-horn on the harbour wall, they would hear all right.

The Erk began to crawl agonisingly towards the klaxon. Placing his hands beneath his shoulders, he levered himself upwards and forwards. Three feet. It might well have been three miles. He collapsed on the deck and shrieked inwardly with the pain, but he let no sound escape his bleeding lips. For what seemed an eternity he lay there and tried to blot out the pain.

As a kid, the Erk had been a fan of the old wartime flying movies on the TV – *Reach for the Stars, the Dambusters, 12 O'Clock High* and the like. In a way they had inspired him to join the RAF. Then those careless young pilots, with their trim moustaches, cool air, outdated 'wizard prangs' and all the rest of that romantic legend, had been his boyhood idols. But in the modern RAF, one needed a good grammar school education and 'A' levels, not romantic notions. Thus he had ended up, not as pilot, but as simple aircraftman in Air-Sea Rescue – an Erk. As he lay there dying on the icy blood-stained deck, he knew instinctively that his idols – those dated young men of more than three decades before – would not have given up. They would have still gone in for a final hit on the target, brought the crippled Wellington back to base, mixed it with the Messerschmitts, even if the Spit were outnumbered six to one. He forced open his eyes and saw the klaxon once again, swaying wildly through the red mist in front of his eyes. 'Bandits at twelve o'clock high,' the old, old voice came crackling across the intercom of that other age.

He levered himself up and started to crawl once more. Five feet now. It was almost within reach. The Erk could no longer raise himself the full stretch of his thin arms. He was advancing only a few pitiful inches at a time. The crackle of the Spit's eight cannon filled his ears now. He collapsed, lapsed into momentary insensibility, came to and crawled on once more. His hands blundered into something. The snarl and roar of the dog-fight was rising to a crescendo. He peered through the red mist at the object that barred his way. For a moment he could not make it out. A Messerschmitt was falling out of the sky like a broken black leaf, white glycol streaming out of its engine in a thick deadly cloud.

The object was the klaxon. Gasping with the relief,

the blood filling his lungs where the Jerry slug had struck him, the Erk hauled himself to his feet. He broke into a paroxysm of blood-filled choking coughing, but his hand continued to search for the button. He knew he was dying. He must have taken a whole burst from the Messerschmitt in the chest as he had come out of the tight roll. Behind him at the bow, two black figures were throwing bundles on board. They did not see him. They were too busy concentrating on their task.

The button! There it was. Before he crashed, he'd take one more of the Jerry bastards with him. The Messerschmitt was roaring towards him at 400 mph now, growing even bigger in the harsh circle of his sights. An evil blackbird coming in to crow over its victim.

'Take that!' he croaked and pressed the button.

At the controls, George wheeled round and fired instinctively. The salvo of 9mm slugs ripped into the swaying figure at the klaxon.

'What the hell—'

The Palestinian's angry yell died as two dazzling white beams, one from each side of the harbour entrance, stabbed blindingly through the grey dawn sky. The Palestinian fired a wild, enraged burst. But the lights were too far away. He pulled himself together. 'Get the bastard to move, George;' he yelled at the younger man, standing next to the grey-haired launch's skipper. 'We're spotted!'

George dug his automatic into the man's side. 'Quick – move; he yelled. 'Full power!'

'But the Smithic—'

George hit him in the small of the back with the muzzle. The Chief Tech groaned. His kidneys felt as if they had been holed. 'All right, you bastard,' he gasped. 'All right!'

He cut in all six cylinders and opened the throttle wide. The surging roar of the big Diesel cut out every other sound. The boat shot forward and its sharp bow lifted high out of the water as the engine crescendoed to

213

its clamorous maximum power. The Palestinian grabbed for support. As the launch started hitting the waves as if they were solid, he crawled forward up the steep slope of the heaving deck towards the bridge.

'Give him the course, George,' he yelled, cupping his free hand over his mouth. 'And full power now – all out!'

As the greying skipper pulled the heeling craft sharply round to starboard, the deeply dipped stern leaving a long furiously seething ribbon of brilliant white behind it, the Palestinian bit his bottom lip and stared at the rapidly disappearing twin beams of the little fishing harbour. The next hour, he told himself, would be crucial. If the English did not intercept them within the coming sixty minutes, nothing would be able to stop them carrying out their mission. Once they were aboard the rig, they had all the aces.

The dun-coloured Army Air Corps Bell helicopter came in low across the heavy dark green sea, its metallic clatter growing louder every second.

'Enemy plane!' Tony, who was acting as look-out, yelled urgently. 'To the west!'

At the controls, the RAF NCO instinctively took his hand off the throttle. Savagely George dug his pistol into the man's ribs. 'Keep up the speed, you English pig!'

The Palestinian, rocket launcher held at the ready, countermanded the order. The chopper might only be on routine patrol. 'Stop engines,' he cried. 'There's a chance it might not see us. The wake is a dead give-away.'

The NCO cut the engine and the frenetic shaking ceased as the boat started to wallow in the swell.

The chopper entered a bank of cloud. Its clatter was deadened for an instant. Then it swelled up again and Tony yelled: 'There it is! It's coming lower too!'

The Palestinian licked his salt-dry lips and braced himself against the heaving deck. The chopper pilot had

214

seen them all right. He was not on a routine patrol; he was looking for them. 'Stand by everybody,' he cried.

Tony and Peter clicked the safety off their Russian automatic rifles. He did the same with the rocket launcher. Grimly they waited as the chopper drew closer and closer. He could just make out the white lettered ARMY on its side now; but the deadly twin-barrelled rocket guns on both sides of the cockpit were all too visible. American-made air-to-ground missiles, the kind they had developed for Vietnam, and then kindly handed to the Jews to massacre peaceful peasants in Syria, Lebanon and the other border territories, hunting them through their stony fields, as if they were on some kind of monstrous duck shoot.

With an ear splitting roar the chopper clattered over their heads at 100 feet, dragging its black shadow across the water behind it. They ducked instinctively, deafened momentarily by the roar, while the launch rocked in the sudden turbulence. The chopper pilot, a white-helmeted blur in the glittering cockpit, did a long, lazy turn under cloud level, as if he needed time to make up his mind whether they really were his quarry. Suddenly the plane seemed to stop in mid-air. It danced there, the wind from the whirling blades churning the water a mere twenty metres below into crazy, white-tipped frenzies. The pilot started to come in again; he had recognised them.

'This is it,' the Palestinian yelled and sighted the slim launcher on the oncoming plane. 'Get ready to fire! You,' he ordered the RAF NCO, 'start up when I shout! If you don't, you're a dead man! All right, George?'

The roar grew louder and louder. The Palestinian, braced against the bridge, legs straddled, rocket-launcher held across his shoulder, could make out two other men with the white-helmeted pilot. One of them was in civilian clothes. A policeman perhaps. His finger began to curl around the big trigger. But the plane was still out of range. He needed another fifty metres before he could hope to fire with any degree of accuracy. In spite of the icy cold, he felt himself beginning to sweat.

Suddenly the chopper stopped and commenced dancing over the water again, just out of range. The Palestinian relaxed the pressure of his finger on the trigger. A huge metallic voice drowned the clatter of the prop. 'Now listen to this down there. You haven't a hope in hell. We can blast you out of the water within thirty seconds. So this is what you have to do. Start up your engines and turn round. Make a course for Bridlington. We shall follow you – and don't make a false move. All right,' the metallic voice thundered with a note of finality, 'let's be getting underway. NOW!'

Tony swallowed. He looked across at the older man, his swarthy face very pale. 'I don't want to drown. Those rockets of theirs—'

'Shut up!' the Palestinian interrupted brutally, lowering the rocket launcher as it came to him. 'We have nothing to fear. You.' he shouted above the roar at the NCO, 'start your engines and carry on the original course.'

'What do – do you intend to do?' stuttered Tony in alarm.

'Carry on to the rig,' the Palestinian yelled triumphantly as the six cylinder engine burst into frantic life once more. 'Don't you see? If they attempt to sink us, they sink them too – their own comrades.' He sneered suddenly. 'And the lily-livered English don't have the courage to do anything like that!'

'There was a little man
    And he had a little gun
    And the bullets were made of lead, lead, lead,' the big Major, with the long scar from Belfast running down his left cheek, sang monotonously as they hovered there. waiting for the Wogs to react.
    'He saw a little duck
    That was sitting in the brook,

216

And he shot it right through the head, head, head.'

'Oh, shut up,' snapped the Para irritably from his uncomfortable perch behind the sergeant pilot from the Army Air Corps and the Major sitting in the observer's seat. 'Can't you give it a rest? – You've been singing – if you can call it that – ever since we started out.'

Major Robinson paused and smiled at him, unoffended. 'My dear Para, one can tell that you never enjoyed the advantages of a good regiment – a happy regiment.'

He broke off suddenly. The white helmeted pilot was gesturing downwards urgently. The Major and the Para craned their necks. The stolen RAF launch had started its engines again. The Para caught his breath anxiously. The launch's bow rose steeply into the air, but the boat did not turn. 'Christ Almighty,' he yelled angrily, 'they're sticking to their original course!'

'What now, Para?'

'Try the loud hailer again.'

Robinson nodded. As the sergeant pilot kept the chopper level with the speeding boat below, he repeated the original message. For a moment there was no reaction on the launch. Then one of the terrorists, rifle in his hand, appeared from below pushing a scared figure in blue uniform on to the deck. He shouted something and the two of them stared upwards at the chopper, their hair ruffled wildly in the chopper's wind.

The Para slumped back into his canvas seat angrily. 'You get it, Robinson, don't you?'

The Major stroked the livid scar that ran the length of his cheek – gained when arresting an IRA battalion commander and his bodyguard single-handed in the Falls Road – and nodded thoughtfully. 'I think I do,' he said. 'If we attack the RAF launch, the crew buys it as well as those naughty boys down there?'

'Right in one.'

'What are we going to do then?'

The Para looked at him and then down at the launch

ploughing on steadily eastwards towards the rig. 'I think you know, Robinson, don't you?'

Major Robinson was not given to emotionalism; Sandhurst and his years with the infantry had eliminated such indulgences. But he could not quite hide his shock. 'But—'

'There are no buts, Robinson. There are perhaps five or six RAF men down there who will die. It's a shame. But they are the professionals. When they joined up, they accepted that risk.'

'But to be killed by their own people, Para;' Robinson protested. 'Not to be killed by their own people!' but his words had no energy.

As they watched anxiously, the chopper suddenly veered to the left and began to clatter to the west. Tony breathed a sigh of relief and lowered his automatic rifle. 'You were right,' he said to the Palestinian. 'They are too lily-livered to fire on their own people.'

The Palestinian did not take his eyes off the chopper, nor relax his hold on the rocket-launcher. 'We will see,' he said.

The chopper flew steadily westwards and then it levelled out. For a moment it hung there, dancing two hundred feet above the swaying green water, then it swung round and dropped a quick hundred feet. The Palestinian recognised the pilot's intention at once. He was going to buzz the launch full on the beam. 'Stand by,' he yelled. 'You,' he bellowed at the RAF NCO, 'When I shout now – break off to port, damn quick!'

The chopper started to move in, the rocket guns glinting menacingly in the watery light. The clatter of the prop grew ever louder. The Palestinian licked his lips. Three hundred metres – two hundred and fifty – two hundred. The chopper must fire soon.

Suddenly the Bell seemed to stop in mid-air. *'NOW!'* he screamed. A burning violet flame shot out from the chopper. A series of rockets hissed viciously towards them, filling the air with the stink of burning explosive. As the NCO threw the launch into a frantic turn to port, the Palestinian felt the searing heat on his face, dragging the air from his lungs.

'Zig-zag — *for God's sake, zig zag,* man!' The Palestinian screamed as the chopper turned and started to come in at an angle to widen its target.

The NCO threw the lithe thirty-foot launch from side to side so that they had to hang on with all their strength, as its sharp bow hit the waves as if they were solid walls. But the Palestinian knew that the gunner in the chopper would have some 'fixing' device. All he needed was to home in on the launch and all the twisting and turning in the world would not prevent him from blowing it out of the water.

Desperately he wedged himself between two stanchions, his thigh muscles screaming out against the strain. In the launcher's ring sight, the chopper was looming larger, as it came in for the kill! Trying to control his breathing, forcing himself to remain steady, the Palestinian started slowly to squeeze the trigger.

A vicious punch, he staggered back. The super-heated air seared angrily through his throat and lungs. For a moment he thought he must suffocate, his breath coming in great, whooping gulps. A gout of flame sprang from the launcher's muzzle. A ball of bright red flame, followed by a zig-zag line of dull white smoke hissed towards the chopper. It exploded with an angry crack. For a moment the Palestinian thought he had hit it. The chopper dropped a sheer one hundred metres. But the cry of triumph died on his lips. The white-helmeted pilot, struggling wildly for control before the Bell struck the angry waves below, righted it just in time. The engine noise rose to a crescendo as he took the Bell up to its original attack height.

Peter and Tony loosed off a desperate burst of fire at the chopper, but the slugs were way off their target, and the pilot did not even seem to notice. The Palestinian, useless launcher held in a slack hand, felt his eardrums must burst at any moment as the chopper whirled in for the last time. And then everything was blotted out by a thick grey mist, and the chopper had gone. The Palestinian stared increduously at the other two, squatting on the rolling deck, surrounded by the bright-gleaming empty cartridge cases. '*Fog*,' he croaked thickly. 'We hit the fog bank!' 'We've . . . we've done it . . .' With its speed reduced to twenty knots, the RAF launch ploughed its way steadily towards the unsuspecting rig.

2

When the news arrived at the Britoil offices in the capital, Hardman was making his final all-out bid for control of the company.

The money men in Houston had waited long enough and Hardman knew they would give him the old heave-ho as quickly as they might any $600 a month assistant bookeeper. Life would be misery without the company-paid suites at the New York Hilton, the London Dorchester, Hamburg's Hotel Atlantik; the silver-grey Rolls Corniche meeting him at the airport; the massive expense account – and the delicious nubile young playthings all these things would buy, whenever he managed to escape from his wife. This time he had to swing it and gain control of Britoil through the German whiz kid Krause.

'Gentlemen,' he said, 'this morning I'm not gonna pull any punches. We're broke – flat broke – and our chairman is fooling around a couple of hundred miles north of here instead of facing up to the harsh reality of our situation.' He glared around him aggressively.

Krause, the chairman-to-be, pretended to stare at the papers in front of him.

'Now,' Hardman continued, 'there's only one possible way we can borrow the dough we need to get us out of the mess we're in – and all of you know it. It is dependent on getting rid of Colonel Hammonds, our chairman.'

'But you can't do that without him here,' Hardacre protested.

Hardman ignored the northern solicitor. 'You have my proposal tabled in front of you. Hammonds goes and Herr Krause here takes his place as chairman. Now I'm not gonna waste any more of your time – or mine. I'd like a show of hands.' He licked his fat lips. This was it. 'All those in favour?'

Six of them raised their hands.

Hardman nodded satisfied. 'With my casting vote,' he announced, 'that makes—'

The door burst open. A pale secretary, all jiggling braless breasts and beads, gasped: 'Sir, sir, we've just had a call from the Ministry of Defence—'

'I don't give a damn if you've just had a call from Jesus Christ himself,' snapped Hardman angrily, cheated of his moment of victory, 'What the Sam Hill do you mean – bursting in like this?'

'But sir,' the secretary protested, 'Palestinian terrorists have taken over the *Pride*. And they've got the Colonel . . .'

While the Britoil meeting broke up in disorder with nothing decided the Joint Intelligence Committee still attempted to find some solution to the new problem. But in spite of the fact that the Foreign Office representative who chaired the meeting knew he would have to report to the PM himself at midday, the discussion dragged on without any practical result.

Half way through the news was brought in that Moscow was demanding some sort of international control of all North Sea oil rigs – a military force of all parties with any kind of interest in the North Sea, which would naturally include herself – so that 'this kind of outrage', as the *Pravda* called it, could not take place again.

As the message from HM's Embassy in Moscow was read out to the Intelligence men, the Para's Chief told himself that this was what the surly young operative had meant. The whole operation had been set up by the KGB in order that Russia might get a hold on Western Europe's sole major source of independent energy.

The man from the FO dropped the message wearily on to the polished desk in front of him and took a sip of his Vichy. 'I don't know gentlemen, but I think we've come to some sort of impasse. What can we do? The Navy and RAF cannot tackle them. The terrorists have threatened to sink the damned rig if any attempt of that kind is made.' He laughed bitterly. 'As if the Navy or the RAF were in any position to carry out an offensive op of that nature. To use a somewhat crude phrase of my misspent youth, they have caught us with our knickers down and we'll just have to stand there in that somewhat absurd position and let our stupid bare bottoms be kicked . . .'

At Leconfield RAF Station, just west of Hull, Robinson and the Para sat gloomily in a corner of the half-deserted bar of the Officers' Mess and stared at each other in silence, half listening to the excited chatter of the young Phantom pilots discussing the hijacking. Major Robinson took a sip of his pint and looked across at the tall windows. The morning frost had clawed at the panes and had left long ragged lines, lines bent in torment, lines at war with each other so that he could hardly see the ugly jets warming up on the hard stands outside.

The Para followed the direction of his gaze and shook his head slowly. 'No, Robinson, those dummies in Whitehall won't use them – they daren't and they know it. They're just making threatening noises for the newspapers' sake – and the great stupid British public.'

'I suppose you're right, Para.'

'What do you think they'll do?' Robinson asked after a while.

'Get the max publicity for their cause,' the Para answered. 'Then one of two things, blow the rig and themselves to kingdom-come, or blow up the rig after using the hostages to get them a safe conduct back to the bloody place they came from.'

Robinson put down his pint mug. 'You really think they'll take out the rig?'

'Of course,' said the Para. 'Think of the publicity they'll get and how it'll enhance their standing with the oil sheiks! They'll be quids in the Middle East, once they're safely back in Beirut or whereever they originally came from. They are the movement which can blow up a European rig right in the middle of Europe's backyard. Imagine what that'll do for their status?'

'You don't have to draw me a picture,' Robinson said gloomily, finishing his beer. 'How long do you think they'll stick it out on the *Pride*?'

The Para shrugged. 'Twenty-four hours at the most – that's my guess. Enough time for them to receive the publicity from the media that they want and not too much time to make the commies more angry than they already are. After all the Russians wanted them captured in the act before they ever got near the rig and they still need the Russians to supply them with weapons.'

'Twenty-four hours,' Robinson mused. 'Twenty-four hours.' He put down the empty pewter mug and began tonelessly to hum his little song about the little man with his little gun, his tall brow creased in thought, while the Para stared blankly at the overalled pilots with their blue-and-white check scarves. He broke off suddenly. 'Para, if you're prepared to take a risk – a *bloody big risk* – I've got an idea.'

3

But if the violent take-over of the rig had shocked Whitehall into complete apathy, it had shaken the Colonel out of his strange lethargy. Now the old light gleamed once more in his faded eyes, as he faced Big Tex across the littered mess table in the crew's mess where the terrorists had herded them after the hi-jack.

'What's it feel like Tex?' he asked, nodding at the thick blood-stained bandage which swathed the American's hand. The terrorists' leader had shot Big Tex when he had tried to go for the man with a wrench.

'As if some cruel bastard is bouncing a twenty-pound hammer off'n the end of each individual finger. But I've been hit worse in my time, Colonel.'

'Do you want the orderly to have a look at it?'

'No, let him stay with Myers,' he indicated the dying man stretched out on the floor next to the blanket-covered body of Longbotham. Both of them had been shot in the first minute of the take-over as the terrorists had come swarming up the ladders on Spud Two, firing indiscriminately at the men working on the platform. 'When Myers turns up his toes, the medic can have another look at it. But I could go a butt, Colonel.'

The Colonel took out the slim worn cigarette-case, decorated with the East Yorks' regiment badge, which had been presented to him by the 'officers and other ranks' when he had left his battalion in 1945, and lit a cigarette for Tex.

'Thanks. That's swell. What do you think those greasers up there are gonna do with us?'

'Nothing good, Tex. You can rest assured of that. The usual blackmail, of course. We're hostages at their disposal to do with as they wish. If they get their way – the authorities give into them – we might be lucky. If the authorities don't surrender to their wishes, whatever they might be, well then—'

'Curtains?'

The Colonel nodded. 'Once people like those have you in their power, your future is decidedly uncertain.'

'That's my guess too, Colonel. But what the hell can we do?'

'For a start we don't sit on our bottoms and let them make the decisions. That would be fatal. Somehow or other we must regain the initiative. After all there are only four of them.'

The Colonel rose to his feet. Unconsciously he placed his hands behind his back in a manner he had not used these last thirty years; it was the pose he had once adopted to address the Battalion. 'Would you pay attention for a moment please,' he said in low but firm voice.

Slowly, reluctantly, the mud-stained unshaven crew turned his way and stared at him. On the floor Myers gasped for air.

'I don't want to alarm you men, but we are in a mess – a very nasty mess. The *Pride* has been hijacked by terrorists and you can see yourselves from what they did to those two poor chaps that they are completely unpredictable and without mercy. Whether we escape with our lives or not—' he shrugged. 'I'll leave you to draw your own conclusions.' His voice rose. 'Now are we going to accept this take-over lying down? I think not. There are over twenty of us and only four of them. I've been listening to the sounds outside. My guess is that they've only got one chap guarding us. Twenty to one, even if the man's armed. Not bad odds. So we must attract that man's attention – and dispose of him.'

'Well, I don't know how you'd go about attracting the Wog's attention,' a burly driller said politely. 'But even if we did manage to nobble the bugger, he still might get off a few shots with that automatic of his – and we saw what them bullets did to those poor sods in the corner.' He looked around at the others. 'And I don't think I'd make a very handsome corpse.'

'I'm afraid that is just one of the risks we will have to take. Now come on, chaps, what do you say? Are we going to have a bash?' The old Battalion rallying cry came back to him. 'Come on, East Yorkshire, let's be having you,' he exclaimed, not caring if the guard outside heard him or not.

But there was no response from the sons of those same men he had led into battle over thirty years before. The fear remained in their eyes as they stared down at the deck in stubborn silence.

'Sorry Colonel,' Big Tex said softly, as the other man sat down again. 'I'd give it a whirl myself. But what good would I be to you with the clapped-out mitt of mine?'

The Colonel looked across the table at him, eyes full of determination. In the mess there was a heavy silence now, as the men slumped at the tables, each one preoccupied with his own fate. 'Don't worry, Tex. If they won't help me, I'll got it alone. Perhaps they'll join in then. Nothing could stop the old East Yorks in the war. I don't see why their sons should be any different. All they need is a lead – an inspiration,' he added confidently. 'I'm going to give them that lead.'

'I hope you're right,' Big Tex sighed. 'I just hope you're right.'

'Wakey, wakey, sir,' said the electronic sergeant, one of the three specialists aboard the black-painted Nimrod, and shook the Para's shoulder. The Para stirred, groaned and fought his way back up from the depths of an exhausted sleep. He wriggled in the aircraft's metal-framed, bucket seat and opened his eyes. They felt as if they were filled with harsh grains of sand. Next to him, Major Robinson was doing the same. The young specialist, standing in the gangway of the spy-and-search plane, crowded from roof to deck with the most advanced electronic detecting equipment, grinned down at them. 'The skipper says we've got a fix on the rig. It's pretty accurate – we think,' he added modestly.

The Para wiped his dry lips. 'Pretty accurate! They tell me with all that gear you've got in here, you can hear a pin dropped in the Kremlin.' The Para dug Robinson in the ribs. 'Come on, open those pretty blue eyes, Cinderella. Your Prince Charming has arrived. We're about there. Let's go and see the skipper.'

Together they stood in the green-lit cockpit behind the two pilots, staring out at the thick cotton-wool wall of fog, listening to the skipper, a flight-lieutenant who affected a great Flying Officer Prune moustache in the fond belief that it made him look older than his twenty-three years. 'According to equipment we have on board, which I'm afraid I can't tell you about, gentlemen, the rig is some three miles away to our west.

'With this fog the sound of our engines should be pretty well muted – at least until we come within – say – half a mile of the rig. So we could get you that far. Then in accordance with Major Robinson's original plan we'll cut out the engines and glide in perhaps another quarter of a mile, coming down to about four hundred feet.' He looked up at them. 'Is that a good height for jumping?'

'The minimum normally accepted in the Para Brigade is five hundred,' Robinson explained. 'But we're in for a soft landing, aren't we? So we can reduce it by another hundred feet.'

'Soft landing!' the co-pilot sniffed, without taking his eyes of the green glowing controls. 'You can say that again, Major.'

The pilot tugged at his moustache. 'And that's about all we can do for you. A quarter of a mile from the rig. We'll glide on for about another half a mile before switching on the engines again. We won't be able to wait much longer than that, I'm afraid, we'll be down in the drink ourselves. I hope you appreciate that?'

'Of course,' answered the Para. 'You're taking a risk as it is.'

'Not much as you are, gentlemen.' The young Nimrod pilot looked at them directly. 'You realise what will happen if our gear is off – you'll be down in the North Sea—'

'And it's a hell of a long cold swim to Holland, gents,' butted in the co-pilot irreverently.

'In short, we'll be put up the proverbial creek without the necessary means of propulsion,' Major Robinson said airily. 'But still there's always a gong in it for us.'

The pilot shook his head. 'Not even that, Major. This mission is strictly off the record. Something you and the CO cooked up between you. If it ever comes out, the lot of us will be for the big chop. Okay, gentlemen, I think it's about time we cut the engines.'

There was no sound now save the hush of the plane and the hiss of the icy wind. The Para peered out of the emergency escape hatch. Nothing, but grey billowing clouds of fog, although the sea was only four hundred feet below them. Standing next to them, the specialist glanced up the length of the fuselage to where the skipper was eyeing the altimeter and the rest of the controls. Imitating the Flight-Lieutenant's gesture, he started to raise his free hand, clinging on grimly with the other.

'Get ready gentlemen, we're going in now!' he cried above the wind. The two men in the frogmen's suits pulled down their goggles obediently. The Para tapped his chute. It was over three years since he had last jumped. Through the slightly clouded glass, he stared up at the specialist. Next to him, Robinson, as imperturbable as ever, sang to himself:

'There was a little man
And he had a little gun
And the bullets were made of lead, lead lead . . .'

The specialist was bringing his hand down very slowly. Robinson took a deep breath. Next to him the

229

Para hunched his shoulders, hands firmly pressed against the sides of the hatch. He would be first to go.

'NOW!'

The Para launched himself into the fog. The icy wind struck him in the face and flung him round. His black rubber-clad head smacked against something hard and for a brief instant he blacked out. When he came to, the black silent silhouette of the Nimrod had vanished and he was alone, floating down rapidly through the wet grey clouds of fog. He tugged at his shroud lines to right himself. He was only a hundred feet off the water. He felt a knife of fear slide into his guts. If the pilot was off in his calculations, he was dropping into a miserable death by drowning. His big hand flashed down to the release toggle. He must release the chute as soon as he hit the water or be dragged under. The waves raced up to meet him. He pulled up his knees to cover his belly instinctively although it was water he was going to land on, not hard earth.

He hit the crest of a wave and slapped his fist against the release toggle. The wind tore the chute away from his body. Then he went under and all was a green streaming light in front of his goggles. He kicked out with his flippers and came back to the surface. Where was Robinson? God, don't let him be alone in this crazily swaying empty waste.

A dark shape came into view, ploughing its way powerfully through the waves. He breathed out a sigh of relief. Springing out of the water, he raised himself to his full height momentarily before falling back again. It sufficed. Robinson spotted him. He changed direction and swam towards him with his powerful crawl. A second or two later he was at the Para's side, holding up his thumb to indicate success while he trod water. Swiftly the Para attached the thirty foot-long nylon line to the Major's waist, threading it through the metal ring on his belt. In this manner they would be able to keep together while they searched the fog for the rig. Then the Para surveyed the area. But the sea was too high – swaying back and forth in great green swells – for him to see more than a few yards. They would have to find the rig with the aid of the bearing the pilot had given him.

Taking a quick look at his wrist compass, he punched the Major's arm to indicate that he was going. With a steady stroke, his black-clad head half buried in water, he set off in the direction indicated by the compass bearing. Their desperate last minute attempt to outsmart the terrorists was under way, but even as the Para began the search, a small, panic-stricken voice within him was crying out: 'Remember, you've only got air for two hours . . . After that, you're dead . . .'

In the little radio shack, the Palestinian laboured over the message he wanted the English radio operator to send at sixteen hundred hours precisely, while George lounged on the table, munching an apple, rifle slung over his shoulder. The Doctor had given him some tips before he had set out on the mission, but he had left the final formulation of the message to him. The Palestinian grinned – a rare gesture for him. Perhaps the Doctor hadn't really believed he would pull it off. But he had. Alone he had defied the British Lion – mangy, dying animal that it was – and with three men captured the source of their most precious treasure.

'Why do you grin?' George asked, showing his excellent white teeth as he paused in mid-bite.

'Nothing.' The Palestinian put down his pencil. 'Listen, this is the message. How does it sound to you?' He cleared his throat. 'To the British Government. We are in full control of the rig *England's Pride* with twenty-two members of the crew as our prisoners. In the return for the safety of those men, we make the following demands. One, a ransom of one million pounds sterling, a safe conduct by boat to the shore and a flight to Beirut from the nearest British field. Two, a declara-

231

tion by the British Government to be broadcast by the BBC and published in the *Times*, *Guardian* and *Daily Telegraph* that it deplores the creation of the Jewish state of Israeli and demands the return of the Palesttinians to their homeland. 'He looked up and got the expected look of admiration.

'Phew,' George whistled. 'That's really magnificent! A declaration by the British Government! Even though England no longer counts much in the world, a declaration of that sort would really set the cat among the pigeons.'

The Palestinian nodded gravely. 'That is the Doctor's intention.'

'But will they do it?'

'Of course, they will. They will have to, now the election's coming up this autumn. The government knows it cannot survive if it has the stigma attached to it of being responsible for the destruction of the *Pride* and the twenty-two man crew. The Israeli government wouldn't care – they wouldn't give in to our blackmail. But the British politicos,' he shrugged contemptuously. 'Everybody knows what they are like – little men, concerned solely with their positions, money and prestige.'

'And what happens to the rig when they give in?' George asked. 'Can't you guess?' the Palestinian put away his pencil. 'Our charges will be set to go off as soon as we are evacuated from it.' He thrust his thumb downwards. *'England's Pride'* will disappear that way within five minutes of our leaving it.'

George could not restrain his admiration. 'My God, what a plan!' He pressed the Palestinian's hand fervently. 'Our poor people owe you everything!'

The Palestinian's blood pounded. His heart beat like a trip-hammer. For a moment he could not speak, a choking sensation smothering his throat. Then he pulled himself together. Thrusting aside George's soft hand, he commanded: 'Now bring the radio operator to me. I want to talk to him before I send the message.'

232

The Palestinian stared down at the paper, still not free from the heady sensation of George's hand on his. There was a faint twitching in his left cheek and his lips were suddenly very dry. Nervously he bit his thumbnail. He was wondering if he dared approach George when this was all over, when his train of thought was brutally interrupted by a burst of automatic fire. He sprang to his feet. It was coming from the direction of the crew's quarters. Pulling out his pistol, he flung open the shack's door.

'What is it?' he yelled at George and Tony, standing there, automatic rifles at the ready, the cowed figure of the radio operator trembling at their side.

'One of them got out!' George yelled back. 'Tony here—'

'He rushed me,' interrupted Tony. 'Believe me, I was on my guard. But I didn't expect him to make a break for it like that.' He broke off miserably.

'All right, all right, Tony,' snapped the Palestinian irritably. 'Don't go on about it! Get the radio operator over here – that's important. After all,' he added, 'where can he go?' His arms swept the arc of fog-bound water around the rig, 'And he's not armed. There's not another weapon aboard. Let him play games, if he wants. We've got more important things to do.' He pushed Jacko roughly through the door of the shack. 'All right, you, now listen to what I want you to do . . .'

The platform loomed out of the fog like a flying arrowhead, splendid, grandiose in the relentless, never-ending movement of the sea. As the Para trod water, he breathed out a deep sigh of relief – listening to the soft hiss of the air escaping from the mask. They had made it. Next to him, the Major grinned happily through the round yellow glass of his mask. His relief, too, was obvious.

For a couple of minutes the two of them trod water and surveyed the metal monster rising out of the heaving sea, the clangs, squeaks and heavy churnings coming from it like a chorus of high-pitched, steel flutes, muted by the noise of the waves. The thing was as high as a ten-storey office block, rising far, far above them on its three stilt-like legs. The Para craned his neck and tried to see what was going on on the platform. All he could see was the sparkling row of red warning lights, glowing far above him. Still he consoled himself – if he couldn't see what was going on on the platform, whatever look-outs the terrorists had on duty would not be able to spot any activity in the sea so far below. Their air was running out. They couldn't remain in the sea much longer. He nudged Robinson and indicated he should follow him. An instant later they were swimming underwater to-wards the rig.

Within five minutes they were facing the problem of clambering up the foot of the great steel spud, as the sea pounded against it in white fury, receded, and pounded it once again. Twice the Para allowed himself to be swept forward by the raging sea and when he had reached the spud, grabbed desperately for a hold on the slimy, dripping metal. But all he got for his pains was a painful blow in the ribs and the sensation of having his finger-nails ripped off by redhot pincers. In the end it was Robinson who pulled it off. Untying the line, he swam underwater for a couple of dozen yards emerging directly below the rig. Here the waves were less violent, their force already broken somewhat by the great spud. The Major waited in the trough. A wave swept in, broke against the spud, hissed beneath the rig and started to move back. Swiftly the Major dived into it. As the back-wash recoiled against the spud, dragging him with it, plunging and corkscrewing violently. he leapt upwards. For a moment the Major hung there at the length of his arms, unable to move, gritting his teeth together with the pain, as the water swept about him. The spud swayed backwards. The Major pawed for a fresh handhole as it did so, his body supported by his knees. He found it. As another giant white comber smashed against the spud,

234

he heaved himself upwards. For a moment he disappeared beneath its angry fury. But when the water fell back, the Para could see he was still there and moving upwards. The wave had not dislodged him. Catlike the Major worked himself up the slippery, swaying spud. To the watching Para, it seemed he would never make it, as the water beat against his black-clad body, trying to wrench him from his perch, hitting him time and time again with a sickening, rending crash.

But ten minutes later Major Robinson was hauling him upwards by means of the nylon line, whistling his silly song about the little man and his gun through his clenched teeth as he did so. They were on the *Pride* and they hadn't yet been spotted.

Kneeling so that the terrorists couldn't see him, the Colonel carefully turned the key in the lock of the explosives magazine. The lock clicked home in well-oiled silence. The Colonel allowed himself a couple of moments to recover, fighting to control his trembling hands. Then he hauled the empty *Vat 69* bottle out of his jacket and breathed a prayer to British liberal rig regulations. Unlike the American rigs, booze was allowed aboard. Hence a hurried scared search of the abandoned galley – with the steady crunch of the terrorist guard's boots on the deck only a matter of yards away – had turned up the bottle he needed in a couple of seconds. It was a pity it was empty. At this particular moment, he would have given his beloved Bentley for a stiff drink. But no matter, at least he was armed and could fight back.

Cautiously he crawled across the floor towards the petrol stacked in the red jerricans. With a grunt he heaved one down and flipped open the cap. There was a soft hiss, as the fumes escaped. He knew what he was doing was dangerous with the gelatine dynamite cartridges neatly piled in the sawdust-filled bins only feet

235

away, but he had not other alternative unless he wanted to chance discovery and sudden death.

Poised on his knees, trying to avoid spilling any, he started to pour the petrol into the narrow neck of the whisky bottle. When it was three quarters full, he stopped and closed both the jerrican and bottle. He wiped the bottle on the leg of his once elegant trousers, now sorely stained and flecked with mud, and crawled back to the sawdust-filled bins. Outside there was no sound save that of the wind howling like metal bagpipes through the *Pride*'s rigging.

He buried his free hand into the sawdust until he found a cartridge. Sitting down again and wedging the bottle securely between his shoes, he forced the cartridge open and gingerly took out some of the gelatine dynamite. It was a messy business, but after a few minutes he had managed to force some of the stuff into the bottle. He closed the cap again and held the squat bottle up to the light, smiling at it as he did so. It was over thirty odd years since he had learned the technique, when the Battalion had come back from Dunkirk with nothing in the way of equipment save their rifles and revolvers. The bereted veteran of the Spanish Civil War – a communist if he'd ever seen one – had sworn that the device was deadly in close-quarter fighting. But the Battalion had never had an opportunity to try it out. The Germans had not come and within a couple of months new, more conventional weapons had started to arrive at the Battalion. But the Colonel had never forgotten the technique. He ripped off his tie and tore off the end. It would serve as his fuse when the time came. As an afterthought he put what was left of the treasured East Yorks tie into his pocket; then he re-opened the door. The howl of the wind rose. He did not hear it. All he heard was the steady pace of the unseen look-out, somewhere ahead in the fog-bound confusion of girders and machinery. Taking a deep breath, he slipped out into the open, the Molotov cocktail gripped firmly in his right hand.

The climb up the spud's dripping iron ladder was a nightmare. A brutal gasping agony, with the wind and bitter squalls cruelly whipping their faces and bodies, threatening to rip them from their precarious perch at any moment. Under normal circumstances no one in his right mind, even a professional climber, would have tackled such a climb in that kind of weather. Somehow, the Para and Robinson, climbing below, found hidden reserves, resources they had not known they possessed, which enabled them to go on.

Now the Para was able to make out the platform itself. It loomed up, wet and dripping with sea water, some hundred feet above his head. But he knew he dared not look up at it long. He must concentrate on the next rung. Fifty feet. Thirty. Once Robinson slipped. The wind whipped the scream of fear from his mouth. The Para did not hear it. When he looked down, Robinson was hauling himself back on to the wet rung from which he had slipped. Twenty feet. Fifteen. Down below the sea, cheated of its prey, rose and fell menacingly.

Suddenly the Para's nostrils was assailed by the stink of diesel. It smelt better than the perfume of any woman he had ever bedded. They were almost there, the deck was just above them. The next instant the two of them had hauled themselves over the side into the confusion of drill pipes, oildrums, stacked crates, mud, sludge, oil puddles – and fallen flat on their faces, bodies spent, the breath rasping into their starved lungs.

'Can see you've got soft since you left the Army, Para,' Robinson said finally, sitting up slowly and rubbing the mud off his wet suit with hands that trembled.

Wearily Para joined him. 'You don't look so hot yourself.' He unzipped the front of his suit. His hands felt thick and numb. He could hardly manage to keep hold of the silenced automatic he had within the wet suit.

'What's the drill now, Para?' he asked thickly.

'A recce first. We don't want to risk the lives of the crew unnecessarily. Let's pin-point the Wogs first. Then we can decide what to do. Okay?'

'Okay.' Robinson slipped off the safety catch of his own pistol.

Like black wolves, their feet bare on the icy, muddy, thickly cluttered deck, they slipped forward, pistols at the ready.

The Colonel, crouched behind a heap of piping, snapped the lighter. Shielding it with his hand, he raised the flame carefully to the cigarette clenched between his teeth. A couple of hasty puffs and the cigarette began to glow. Putting the lighter in his pocket, he unscrewed the cap on the whisky bottle and inserted the strip of tie in the hole he had made in it. He pulled the strip through so that it would be immersed into the explosive mixture once he had screwed the cap back on.

The terrorist leader and another of the hijackers were in the radio shack into which they had dragged a terrified Jacko – obviously they were going to make him send a message for them. He could guess what it would be. Blackmail and more blackmail, with the imprisoned crew as the bait. But they would never send that message if he had his way. His plan was simple. The Molotov cocktail launched at the radio shack's wooden door. If the cabin didn't catch alight, at least the burning door would trap them sufficiently for him to dash to the crew's quarters and release them. The men would be able to arm themselves somehow or other – shovels, wrenches, pick-handles. Once they were free and under confident leadership, he was convinced they would be able to tackle the other two terrorists who were busy on the drilling platform below, fixing what looked like explosive charges.

The Colonel took another puff at the cigarette and began to crawl forward towards the radio shack, thanking God for the howling wind which drowned any noise he made on the wet metal deck.

'*Je-sus Christ!*' the Para cursed bitterly sotto voce. 'Robinson, look at this.'

The Major ran swiftly towards him, pistol at the ready. 'What's the matter?'

Mutely the Para pointed to the five bodies in RAF uniform sprawled behind the huge concrete mixer. They were already stiff, their faces waxen.

'The crew of the RAF launch?'

The Para nodded. 'The bastards – they didn't need to kill them, did they? A lot of clapped-out RAF types who couldn't fight their way out of a paper bag. Why the hell did they have to butcher them for?'

Robinson pressed his arm. 'It's the ruddy time in which we live, Para,' he said. 'That's all.'

The Para shook himself and gripped the pistol more firmly. 'You're right, Robinson.' He licked his lips. 'Okay, let's start playing butcher ourselves and give the murderous bastards a taste of their own medicine.' He indicated the two terrorists kneeling at the far end of the deck, obviously fixing explosives charges. 'That pair of sods for openers.'

'Spot on!'

'You come in from over there. I'll make it this way. I'll take the lanky bastard on the left. You can have his pal.'

When he was twenty yards away from the lanky terrorist setting the charges, the Para crouched, legs set apart against the roll of the deck, both hands holding the silenced pistol as he had learned to do in the SAS, and took a deep breath. Then he snapped. 'Put down that rifle and turn round!' Even as he said the words, he knew in his heart that the boy would not obey and he was glad he wouldn't; it would give him the opportunity of killing him.

Peter stiffened. The Para could see the hunching of his

239

shoulder muscles quite clearly. For what seemed a long time nothing happened. Suddenly the boy spun round, rifle still on his shoulder. But in his hand he clasped a small pistol.

The Para fired first. A soft plop. The pistol kicked upwards. But his aim was true.

'Bastard!' the Para cursed softly. 'Take this!' He fired again, aiming deliberately for the boy's dark, agony-contorted face.

In that instant, Robinson challenged Tony. Tony's reaction caught the Major off guard. He dropped to the deck. The Major fired instinctively. But the slug whined off a girder harmlessly. Tony fumbled frantically with his rifle. The Major fired again. The bullet hit the terrorist in the shoulder. Tony freed the rifle. He was lathered in sweat now – the sweat of fear. He loosed a wild burst at the Englishman. The slugs scythed through the air, careening and ricocheting off the metal. He pressed the trigger again, but this time nothing happened. Frantic with fear, he pressed it again. Nothing.

Major Robinson knew instinctively what had happened. Pistol clenched firmly in his hand, he started to advance on the boy spread-eagled on the deck, still fumbling with the useless rifle. In despair, the boy dropped the rifle and raised his good hand in the token of surrender. But his assailant did not lower his pistol, nor did he stop his barefoot advance.

Tony swallowed with difficulty. The other man was almost on top of him now. 'I surrender,' he said, his voice thick with fear. 'I surrender.' The Major raised his pistol and took aim. To the wounded boy lying on the bloody deck, he appeared to be singing. 'No, please,' he croaked, looking up at the white-faced Englishman, 'please . . . I surrender . . . No – *NO*—' Major Robinson fired. A soft plop. The slug, striking the terrorist at a range of no more than four feet, took the back of his head off, and at that moment, George crouched above him on the derrick opened fire. His aim was deadly. The Major took the first burst in his chest.

'Fuck,' he gasped, as the pain ripped through him, 'that's torn it!'

George fired again.

'Die, you English bastard – *die*!' George pressed the trigger hard and kept his finger there until the magazine was empty. Gratefully Major Robinson crumpled to the deck, his big body ripped to bloody pieces.

The Para shot George in the pit of the stomach as he tried to fit another magazine. He crashed heavily to the deck and lay gasping there, spread-eagled, like a stranded fish. As the Para doubled to the Major, he shot George twice. George screamed. The Para bent down urgently by the Major but he was too late. Major Robinson was dead.

The Palestinian crouched panting between two pipe racks, his back covered by the thirty-foot lengths of steel. He stared down at George's rain-lashed, bleeding mask of a face and felt an impossible desire to rush to him and cradle his lifeless body in his arms, stroke his wet hair, press a kiss to his bloody lips. Then he fought his desire, and became again the cold calculating killer he had always been.

He calculated his chances clinically. The crew was still locked away. For the time being they presented no problem. Somewhere one of them was wandering around, but he was unarmed. In essence he was opposed by one man only – the bastard who had killed George! That man he would kill in due course, and then he would make the terrified little runt of a radio operator send the vital message to the British Government. He threw a glance at the charges. They were still in place. The unknown Englishman had had no time to remove them, once he had fired at him. He had been too busy saving his skin, flinging himself behind the cover of a great packing case and disappearing into the industrial mess of the deck.

Even though he was alone again, he was confident he could still bring the operation off successfully. The British Government would submit to his terms and he would destroy the rig in one last act of revenge. Its destruction would be a fitting tribute to George and the other two – their sacrifice would not have been in vain. With renewed confidence he set about the task of stalking the Para.

'Hey, mate, I've got the bastard – over here!'

It was an old trick, but it worked. Even as the Para rose from his cover, he knew he had been tricked: the voice from nowhere did not belong to a Yorkshireman. But then it was too late. The slug from the Palestinian's automatic tore into his chest. It struck the sternum and exploded.

The light faded suddenly. The deck came up and smacked him in the face. The loss of feeling swept up from his legs. He felt the salty hot taste of blood in his mouth. The last thing he saw was the man who had shot him rising from between some pipe racks, and behind him an elderly man in a muddy, once elegant suit with what looked like a whisky bottle raised in his hand. Then all was dark. As the terrorist leader hesitated, wondering whether it was safe to go in and finish off the man he had just wounded, the Colonel applied the glowing end of his cigarette to the petrol-soaked rag-fuse. It spluttered and caught at once. He watched it carefully as the tiny red glow grew. There was a tiny pop and the rag caught alight.

At that moment the Palestinian straightened to his full height and prepared to finish off the wounded Para, the bottle crashed against his arm, spilling petrol over his left side, tumbled to the deck and burst into flame. In a flash the Palestinian was transformed into a living torch. Panic-stricken and screaming with fear, he beat his hands against the burning cloth. His hands caught fire. Blinded by the mounting flames, he blundered forward, his groping outstretched arms ablaze. He stumbled and fell heavily over Peter's body. Writhing and tossing, he tried to fight the greedy flames. But his struggles became weaker and weaker. A couple of times his red, burning body twitched convulsively. Then the Palestinian lay still, his black head silhouetted in a puddle of fitfully flickering blue flame.

Yet in that moment of his death, the Palestinian came close to achieving the objective for which he had travelled so far, blazing a trail of murder and mayhem right across Western Europe.

Just before the fire died out altogether, leaving his charred, blackened body reduced to the size of some crouched Central African pygmy, a red tongue of flame reached out for the charges which Tony had set. The heat did its work. Far below, half-way up spud two, there was a dull menacing rumble and a second later a great crash. *England's Pride* lurched to one side and inside the crew compartment, personal gear and tools showered from the racks. A table skidded the length of the room. Tin mugs showered to the deck. The lights flickered and went out.

Big Tex caught himself from falling just in time. 'All right,' he shouted above the panic-stricken bedlam of the sudden darkness. 'Hold ya goddam water, willya! It's okay!'

'We're sinking! screamed a hysterical voice next to him. 'They're leaving us here to die.'

Big Tex hit him. 'Knock it off!' he bellowed in a red rage. 'And for Chrissake, let me through – I'm gonna bust open the lousy door – gun or no gun!'

He pushed his way through the struggling, panic-stricken crowd of workmen, knowing that if he didn't get them into the open soon, they'd be trampling each other to death in their unreasoning fear. With all his force he launched himself at the door. Under normal circumstances he would never have opened it, even with his brute strength. But an unreasoning fear lent power to his attack. Suddenly the door gave and he staggered blindly out into the open. 'Follow me – quick,' he ordered, his wide-eyed gaze taking in the bloody scene of death and destruction on the debris-littered deck, sloping now at a thirty degree angle. 'The bastards have gone and blown up the—'

He broke off, mouth dropping open with astonishment. A thin yellow-black rain was dropping on the dead men sprawled out on the deck, turning their clothes the same colour. He peered over the side of the rig. Two hundred feet away just at the edge of the fog bank, the sea was boiling crazily, its surface becoming blacker and blacker by the second, as the stuff blew wild from over 9,000 feet below. He turned to them, his lips opening and closing soundlessly. Then he found his tongue: 'Jesus wept – we've struck it! The *Pride*'s done it at last! Can't you see, you bunch of dummies?' he yelled, as the black rain drenched him. *'Oil – we've struck oil . . .'*

'We are the unwilling
Doing the unpleasant
For the ungrateful.'

*Doggerel circulating
British Army Barracks
in Ulster. Summer 1974.*

Krause, Britoil's new chairman, had wanted to give an informal 'cocktail', as he called it in his German fashion, to celebrate the completion of the *Pride*'s refit and the influx of fresh US capital, in the Britoil Building. Clarissa had objected. Still in mourning – black leather trousers, transparent black silk blouse, through which her nipples were plainly visible – she had insisted it be held in her big new flat overlooking the pond in Battersea Park. And as usual with Krause, ever since her husband's death of a heart attack on the *Pride* in that moment of triumph, she had had her own arrogant careless way.

Now – although some said that Battersea was still on the unfashionable side of the capital – the place was filled with the chic people she was teaching a hesitant, somewhat bewildered Krause to associate with, talking loudly, drinking greedily, gesturing a lot, flashing too perfect smiles at each other.

The Para, still very pale and shaky, leaned in the corner nursing a lager, watching them, his contempt barely concealed. Farmer Giles muttonchop whiskers, buckskin shirts, deerslayer boots; US combat jackets, from some Army & Navy stores, jeans and polo-necked sweaters; transparent white, embroidered peasant blouses, revealing skinny braless breasts, long skirts made of flowered curtain lengths, jingling love beads hanging low to the belly, bare-feet; Berthold Brecht caps, cord trousers, baggy at the knees, Army surplus ammunition boots and all the rest of the proletarian look. Only the sweating waiters forcing their way through the loud throng were dressed in white shirts and black ties. To the Para, it looked as if the place had been suddenly taken over by the mob from Ford's old film, *The Informer*. But the long line of Porsches and Jensens outside in the shabby street gave the lie to that impression. This was London's jeunesse dorée, which these days, he told himself cynically, could mean anyone under sixty-five, doing 'their thing'. The hostess drifted by in a haze of glamour and expensive clothes, escorted by a hairy young man in combat boots and US jacket, who looked like Fidel Castro just coming down out of the mountains.

'Hello, Para,' a thin voice said.

He turned round. It was Pat, the Colonel's secretary. She had visited him a couple of times in Scarborough General and he had told her how the Colonel had saved his life and sacrificed his own by doing so. On her last visit she had cried a lot and sobbed that she had loved the dead man. That had been two months ago.

'Why hello, Pat,' he said, happy to see someone he knew, 'what are you doing with the nobs?'

She smiled wanly. She was a lot thinner than when he had last seen her. Automatically he noted she was old-fashioned enough to wear black and he could guess why she had lost weight. She shrugged. 'The chairman asked me to come along and help out. But what could I do with that lot?'

She indicated an immensely tall elegant young woman, swathed in a Regency coachman's cape, who was shouting at the Union leader Harehill in his shirt-sleeves: 'Of course, during the day I only wear what's most practical. Simple things like this cape. But let's not talk about me. Tell me about yourself, Mr Harehill. You must lead a fascinating life.'

Harehill, the man who had unionised the *Pride* and was well on his way to unionising all the North Sea rigs, flashed her the 'open, frank' smile he had acquired ever since he had begun to appear on the TV discussion

248

shows after the media had taken him up. 'Oh, I wouldn't say that, Countess,' he said with his newly acquired modesty – 'the modesty of a really big man', as one of the BBC talk-show moderators had expressed it recently. 'But it can be tough—'

The Para grinned down at her. 'I know what you mean, Pat. God knows what I'm doing here myself. But my chief passed on Krause's invitation to me. I thought at least I might get a free beer out of them.'

She reached out and pressed his hand. 'You deserve it,' she said. 'If it hadn't been for you—'

He laughed down at her a little bitterly. 'And what did it all matter? Robinson, your Colonel – they both bought it for nothing. Look at the *Pride*.'

'Yes, the rumour in the office is that it won't be producing for another twelve months at the earliest. I don't know whether it's accurate, but Big Tex – you remember him from the Scarborough General?'

He nodded.

'Well, if it's an indication, he handed in his resignation last week. He's moving on – to the Amoco field.'

He took an angry swallow of his beer. 'See what I mean. All for bloody nothing! Besides, control of the *Pride* has passed out of British hands. If and when it ever starts producing, the oil will—'

He never finished the sentence. His words were drowned by the sound of a cowbell – stolen from some Swiss Alpine meadow or other – being rung. There was a buzz of laughter from the crowd. The talk dropped away, but not altogether, until Clarissa, thrusting her elegant breasts through the expensive black silk, said: 'Oh belt up, will you! Voelker' – she made a hopeless mess of his name – 'would like to say something.'

The new trendy Krause, freed temporarily from the provincial restraints of Ludwigshafen, smiled a little warily at the expensively drab crowd. 'Well, boys and girls,' he began.

Next to Pat, the Para groaned softly.

'I don't want to spoil your jolly mood, but I hope you'll allow me just a few moments to express the company's pleasure at the successful refitting of the *Pride*. Undoubtedly some of you are now waiting impatiently for the rig to start producing. But as they say in the oil business,' Krause beamed at them. 'God put the stuff there 150 million years ago so it'll keep a few more days no doubt. Yet however long it takes *England's Pride* to strike pay-dirt, you can rest assured that this country will get its fair share of its natural heritage when that time comes and that . . .'

'Listen, Pat,' the Para said urgently, 'shall we get out of here? This lot puts years on me.'

She nodded and grabbed his arm. 'Yes, let's! We're outsiders here after all.'

They walked silently, hand-in-hand towards the Underground. An old woman in a tattered man's tweed coat barred the pavement as she poked around in an overflowing ashcan. Her bare legs were swollen to twice the normal size and mottled green and brown like some lush tropical plant. 'Excuse me, missus,' said the Para.

'Fuck off,' the old woman said without looking up. 'Sodding nig-nogs everywhere!' She pulled some piece of obscene rubbish out of the can and stuck it into her pocket.

They walked out of the thin watery spring sunshine. A young blond American in sandals with a flowered band around his forehead was strumming idly at a guitar, an empty cap spread out in front of him on the floor which stank of cat urine.

The Para stopped and pulled her towards him. Clumsily they kissed, blindly groping for each other. Their mouths clung together. Behind them on wall the rough, dripping-edged spray-can message announced: '*Let's give the dump back to the Ancient Britons – and start all over again!*'

Gently she released herself and looked up at him, her eyes full of sudden tears. 'I must talk to you, Para.'

His face was as hard as a chisel. 'Remember,' he said. 'I can't promise anything. There are other things to be done now. You realise that?'

She nodded mutely.

'Come on then.' He grabbed her arm with rough tenderness. 'Let's be getting on with it, Pat . . . Time's bloody well running out.'

THE SEVEN UPS
RICHARD POSNER

A novel of New York's police elite, the dirty-tricks squad that frightens even the regular cops.

Now filmed by Phil D'Antoni who made BULLITT and THE FRENCH CONNECTION.

THE SEVEN UPS

are a special squad of New York City detectives working undercover to ferret out the hoods whose crimes will net them seven years or more in gaol. They don't look like policemen and they don't behave like them.

Buddy is the man who leads the squad in a nerve shattering manhunt to uncover the kidnappers who are extorting money from the city's loan sharks. One problem is that the hoods are masquerading as policemen.

Although written as a novel, **The Seven Ups** dramatises events that actually took place, gathered from New York City's police files by detective Sonny Grosso, who also collaborated on **The French Connection.**

ESCAPE FROM THE RISING SUN
IAN SKIDMORE

'The oily dust fell everywhere, on hungry
stragglers searching for their units, on armed
deserters who roamed the streets searching for
loot, on . . . fear-crazed men fighting their way
at the point of a gun or bayonet, pushing women
and children aside . . . The dead lay in the
streets . . . but no one collected the corpses now.

Singapore had fallen. The British Army, retreating
in disorder before the onslaught of the Japanese
shock-troops, had been told to surrender. One
man was convinced he could escape.

Geoffrey Rowley-Conwy seized a junk and sailed
for Padang. There he joined a group of fellow
officers for a desperate escape-bid in a dilapidated
sailing boat across the Indian Ocean to Ceylon.
1,500 miles of open sea swept by the fury of the
monsoon and patrolled by Japanese fighter planes
on the lookout for British survivors.

'One of the best and liveliest escape stories of
the Second World War . . . enthralling.'
Times Literary Supplement

WHEN THE MOON RISES

TONY DAVIES

A trainload of British prisoners of war steams slowly through the Italian mountains. Suddenly there is a screeching of brakes and the sound of shots from the guards. Two British officers have made the leap for freedom . . .

Tony Davies's first escape bid ends in recapture and transfer to a new camp in the north. When he escapes again he and his companions are faced with a 700 mile walk along the spine of the Appenines to the Allied beach-head at Salerno. The journey begins as a schoolboy adventure: it ends as a terrifying and deadly game of hide-and-seek where the Germans hunt down the fugitives like animals and courageous Italian peasants risk their own lives to save them.